"A passionate and graphic tale of hunger, prostitution and survival.... Dzovig and Vecihe have travelled far and carry the reader along with them on a journey, which will be of interest to those familiar with Armenian history and will stimulate others to find out more about this fascinating part of the world." *Winnipeg Free Press*

"De Vasconcelos's novels offer a bounty of sensory details—food, colours, fabrics, smells [and] have an alluring receptivity to life outside Canada." *Quill & Quire*

"De Vasconcelos describes war and the crimes of Communism with a stunning combination of ferocity and intimacy, and she builds believable, nurturing relationships among her characters.... *Between the Stillness and the Grove* is an ardent, idiosyncratic book." *The Edmonton Journal*

"Full of heartbreak and romance." *Flare*

"The novel deals with the Armenian genocide of 1915 by setting it on a vast, Renaissance-size canvas of many generations and multiple characters. The expansive narrative darts wildly through layers of time, lifting bitter dust as it searches for the genesis of modern Armenia's woes." *Hour Magazine*

"De Vasconcelos has a gift for beautiful language and for describing the significant detail, some small thing that tells the reader so much about the matter at hand. Her writing is lyrical and even tender, creating a striking contrast with the brutal events described. The author demonstrates that sometimes out of hatred can come love." *Uptown Magazine*

Between the Stillness and the Grove

A novel

Erika de Vasconcelos

VINTAGE CANADA

A Division of Random House of Canada Limited

VINTAGE CANADA EDITION, 2001

Copyright © 2001 by Erika de Vasconcelos

National Library of Canada Cataloguing in Publication Data

De Vasconcelos, Erika
  Between the stillness and the grove

ISBN 0-676-97328-0

I. Title.

PS8557.E8437B47 2001   C813'.54   C2001-901549-6
PR9199.3.D48B47 2001

Pages 358–360 constitute a continuation of the copyright page.

www.randomhouse.ca

Printed and bound in the United States of America

10 9 8 7 6 5 4 3 2 1

For Sarah
For Virginia
and
For Nino

meus amores

A NOTE FROM THE AUTHOR

This is a work of fiction. While some parts of this story were inspired by actual events of history, certain liberties have been taken with time and place. All of the characters, with the exception of Fernando Pessoa, are creations of the author's imagination and not based on any actual persons, living or dead.

Fernando Pessoa was a Portuguese writer who lived from 1888 to 1935. I have made him a character in my story, and any dialogue that I have taken directly from his works is in quotation marks in my text. The rest is my own invention, though heavily inspired by Pessoa's poetry and prose, and in particular by *The Book of Disquiet*. The editions of Pessoa's writings that I have used are listed in the acknowledgments.

The region known as Mountainous Karabagh is a territory on the border between Armenia and Azerbaijan that was acquired by Russia in 1813. In 1923, the Soviet government established it as an autonomous province of the Azerbaijan S.S.R., even though its population was 94 per cent Armenian. In the late 1980s, Armenians within the province began to agitate for the administrative unification of their territory with the Soviet Republic of Armenia, a demand that was strongly opposed by the Azerbaijanis and the Soviet government. The ethnic fighting that ensued escalated into a full war in 1992–93.

PART ONE

After the first death there is no other.
Dylan Thomas

Prologue

DZOVIG

There is the sea. Dzovig is staring at it. She does this often in the early hours of the morning, makes her way to the wall at the edge of the beach, determined, like an addict seeking out her drug. And the sea is never very far in this country: Portugal, a thin strip of land stretching along the Atlantic, on the edge of the Continent. The people here also stare at the sea; they stare at it so often that reflections of light bouncing off the water pass across their eyes even after they have gone home, at night, even as they sleep. They carry the smell of the sea with them in the wool of their coats, in the breath they exhale, after bread and wine. But they don't think of the sea, as Dzovig does. They dismiss it as husbands and wives of decades dismiss each other, or as peoples of the mountains dismiss geography, though it has shaped all that they are. But Dzovig is from another country, and therefore different. She stores up the sea like a beggar at a feast.

In her favourite painting of Pessoa, his shape is also standing at the edge of the water, a thin black line before a huge expanse of grey, in this country where the sea is rarely grey, or white.

In every painting of him that she has seen, he always wears a hat, a black fedora which sits on his head like an extension of his body. Even a picture of his room that depicts little else but squares of sunlight on the floor and half a chest of drawers contains his hat, left on a chair. She likes this about him, a carapace. She likes the hat, the round glasses, the cropped moustache and bow tie. Such a prim dresser, for a modernist. She likes the empty bronze chair that stands beside him, part of that sculpture in front of the *Brasileira* café, as if in wait for someone. She had gladly occupied that chair. She could think of him now as an old lover, as real as any man whose body she has ever slept beside, though she won't. Pessoa has been dead for more than fifty years.

Best of all she likes his name: Pessoa, meaning, literally, person. Anyone, or everyone.

The sea is particularly blue today, or perhaps only seems so because of the intensity with which Dzovig is watching, wondering if she will ever come back here, to this stone wall, to this adopted country. She had thought for a time that she would never leave Portugal, like Pessoa. That any other place would be a poor substitute for the black and white mosaics of pavements, all leading to the water. But tomorrow she will cross the Atlantic in a plane full of Portuguese who, given steaming towelettes, will wipe the surface of their dinner trays rather than their own hands. She will land in Toronto, a city without sea, where, her friend tells her, there are flowers like blue planets. Where, Vecihe tells her, everything is new. Come and visit, her friend says. But Dzovig knows that there are no visits. She knows now, deep in her stomach, that each arrival is a return.

I

TOMAS

The steady grinding of wheels comes to a stop. She is still sleeping; not even the shuffle of bodies leaving the train wakes her. It is the man sitting across the aisle who pulls at her arm, saying "Menina. Lisboa." On the platform dozens of people are walking in semi-darkness, a network of black beams high overhead, under a glass roof that has grown opaque. Daylight seeps through it as if through layers of green water.

Dzovig's hair is cropped short and falls haphazardly into place when she shakes it out. She is wearing a shapeless sweater and a green skirt, a skirt she has held onto since Armenia. In a bag she carries the rest of her clothes, a hair comb, a few pens.

It is early morning in the streets of Lisbon. Outside the station, by the doors, two women are selling flowers, each with her own buckets of roses set out at her feet. The women are dressed in black wool. They could belong anywhere, Dzovig thinks: the widows of Europe. They throw words at each other across the passing people, oblivious, apparently, to the loss their clothes are commemorating. Maybe this is all it takes to get through it, she thinks, to dress in black wool and sell flowers.

She hasn't eaten for hours and she is very hungry, her last meal a sandwich with the French student, Jean, who had offered to follow her across Europe, thinking, perhaps, that she was one of those students with giant backpacks that gathered outside the train stations of European cities. "Non merci," Dzovig had said. She might have slept with him if she'd thought that he had any money, but she knew by then that only older men would pay. She had enough, in any case, to last her for a while.

She approaches one of the widows, and asks in French for a place to buy food. The woman consults her companion. She speaks only Portuguese but points with thick fingers in one direction. "A Menina quer a baixa," she says.

"Menina, baixa?" Dzovig repeats. She doesn't understand. The women laugh and confer again. They point to Dzovig. "Menina," they say. Finally they add, almost in unison, "Centre, centre."

She walks down a long, wide avenue, past squares where the fountains are running, past a statue of a man on horseback in a sea of pigeons. She has grown accustomed to it now, the beauty of non-Soviet cities. In the beginning it had struck her with a kind of perverse pleasure, like vengeance. *Look at us*, Tomas used to say, *packaged into neat little Soviet boxes*.... He liked to say that Yerevan, the capital of Armenia, wasn't an Armenian city at all.

Tomas. Tomas's face. In Yerevan, Dzovig hadn't needed the white carved façades of beautiful buildings.

In the Praça Rossio the cafés are still half empty. Men in white aprons are setting out chairs and ashtrays. She hasn't passed any corner shops, and one of the waiters signals to her with a napkin, presenting the surface of the table he has just wiped like an offering. She is very hungry. "Por favor, Menina," he says. After a time he brings her a steak with a fried egg on top of it, which she has understood to be a specialty, something he referred to as egg on horseback.

"A cheval?" she asks.

"A cavalo," he says, "sim, sim."

And she learns from him more Portuguese words: *obrigada*, thank you, and *manhã*, morning. She eats, watching the tourists gradually fill the empty seats while the Portuguese congregate at the counters, standing. She can see from her table the crenellated tops of stone walls, high up, overlooking the city. The waiter nods his approval: "Castelo de São Jorge," he says, kissing his fingertips.

She has to walk through the old quarter to get there. The Alfama, the waiter called it. The narrow streets twist and turn and rise, the houses lean against each other like a precarious stack of cards, with laundry lines strung across their façades and even from one side of the street to another. The stuccoed houses are faded and peeling but the air is cool and thin as if the country is new, or young, and she is not tired, walking up the hill, following signs that have the outline of a castle drawn on them. Turning a corner she stops, suddenly. At her feet is a woman on her knees, scrubbing the sidewalk with a brush and a pail of soapy water. Beneath the woman's body the cobblestones shine, black, wet and round, tiny rivulets of water passing between them and onto the street.

"Bom dia," says the woman.

Dzovig bends for a moment, stretches out her hand like a Christian at a font, before pulling back. Some memories are like this, sharp as new burns. She does not know what to say, except "Obrigada."

The woman looks at her, puzzled, but turns again to her washing. It is early in the day and there is work to do.

Dzovig's mother, Maro, liked to pray while she washed dishes. In Yerevan, in the apartment where Dzovig lived with her parents and sister, her mother could usually be found at the kitchen sink, or the stove. There wasn't really a kitchen, only a hallway where a few cabinets, the sink and stove were all aligned. Off the hall there were three rooms: a living room, and two small bedrooms. Dzovig shared a room with Anahid, her sister. In their parents' room the bed had been pushed up against the wall to make space for a small table, a makeshift altar where Dzovig's mother kept her saints: porcelain Madonnas gathered over the years from unknown sources, plastic crucifixes, rosaries. On the wall above she had tacked postcards and pictures of Christ, his head encircled in halos of gold, or thorns, some of them Christmas cards from years before. There was an illicitness in this, because Maro still remembered a time when the churches had been closed by the government and their lands given over to the collective farms, and baptisms were held in secret, at home. A time when communism was still new to Armenia, still alien. The time of Stalin. Perhaps she had been stashing them away since then, paper saints and plastic icons, hiding them in boxes like a subversive.

Maro would look up to these at the end of the day as if they had made possible the endurance of all her suffering, the vague misery of her daily hours at the stove, the silent war that raged between her husband and daughters. And then she would crawl into bed and lie in her usual position next to Arzas, oblivious to the familiar sounds of his body, already in sleep. When they woke, the next morning, neither one of them had moved.

Sometimes when Dzovig watched her mother at the sink it occurred to her that Maro had once been young, that perhaps she hadn't always been obsessed with Jesus. She wondered if this accounted for the strange affection Arzas still reserved for her, the way her parents held each other's hands on the rare occasions they walked out in public, like a young couple. Had she been older, Dzovig might have recognized this gesture as one of accustomed fear.

At home, Maro always wore a handkerchief over her head and layers of old dresses and skirts, her legs covered in thick nylon stockings, even during the hottest days of summer. Whatever she wore always looked torn from something, like the remnants of old sheets she used to cover pieces of furniture in order to preserve them. It was hard to imagine that anything in the apartment had ever been new, that anything in the building had ever been cared for, thought out with an intent towards beauty or ease for those who would inhabit it. To a stranger Maro could easily have looked ten years older than her husband, although she moved with a wiry determination, her upper arms hard beneath the beginnings of sagging flesh, scrubbing her pots with unnecessary fierceness.

"Ah, not even the water is clean anymore," she would mutter, "not even the water, Jesus."

Dzovig looked at her mother's hands then, the red cracked skin and the nubby fingertips worn to a strange gloss, like old stone, or wood.

"At least it keeps you busy, Mama," she said.

"You think you're so smart, don't you," her father said. "Look at her; you'll never have a body like that in your entire life."

Arzas laughed after he spoke. He always laughed as if there were an audience waiting to laugh with him.

But Maro simply stared out in front of her.

"When I was little," she said, "I drank water from a cabbage leaf——"

If she had turned then, she would have noticed a change in her husband's expression, a look that held some kind of forgiveness in it. But there were dishes. She only said, without turning, the words she repeated towards the end of every meal: "Eat some more, you haven't finished your meat."

The food she prepared always tasted and smelled the same to Dzovig. The apartment reeked of cooking: meat, onions, oil. There was always too much food heaped on each plate. Dzovig's sister, Anahid, was never hungry.

Dzovig's father ate with an arm folded between his plate and his chest. He held his fork like a spade. When someone spoke, he looked up. He had looked up at Dzovig on the day she had worn a green skirt, one that Rebecca had given her, for a party.

"A skirt," he'd said. "Look, Maro, she's wearing a skirt, for Christ's sake! What's the occasion? A skirt in February! You getting married?"

"Your legs will freeze," Maro had said.

That was the day Dzovig had met Tomas.

In the end there had been no party. Dzovig had stood with Rebecca in a crowded basement room where music was blaring.

"You look great," Rebecca said. She had taken it on as a personal mission to find Dzovig a boyfriend.

"I'm the only one dressed like a doll," Dzovig said.

Around them students were talking about the march that had happened in the town of Abovyan two days before, calling for the shut-down of a chemical plant. Dzovig could hear snippets of conversation through the music.

"They even sang some forbidden songs. My uncle was there."

"They won't shut it down."

"No, but maybe we can shut you up."

People were whispering into each other's ears, cupping hands around mouths. Something was passing through the room like a wave.

"They're talking about Karabagh," Rebecca said.

"I know," Dzovig said. She had heard students talking about Karabagh on campus, about glasnost and perestroika, the sense that grievances in the republics would be addressed.

Finally, the music was called off. A student climbed onto a table.

"They're demonstrating outside the opera house. I think we should go. We should all go."

There was instant agitation in the room then. A shuffling of bodies looking for coats.

"You'll freeze," Rebecca said, looking at Dzovig's legs.

Dzovig rolled her eyes. "Thanks," she said.

They found a pair of pants and she pulled them on, under the skirt. Everyone around her was happy, as though they were leaving for a carnival. Rebecca held onto her arm as they walked towards Theatre Square. "This will be interesting," Dzovig said.

"And there will be lots of men," Rebecca said.

At the edge of the square they stopped. They came upon a silence that was like an invisible wall, it was the silence of thousands of people standing together in a communist country, amazed with themselves.

Dzovig stayed with her friends, standing, sitting, listening to the speakers on the platform talking passionately about the

Armenians across the mountains in Karabagh whose territory should have always been part of Armenia, not Azerbaijan. Talking of solidarity. There were many, many people in the square. Towards midnight someone called for volunteers to march the streets, and Dzovig went because she was cold, stiff from standing. She started walking. She lost sight of Rebecca after a while. Doors were opening in the houses along the streets. Dzovig walked all night.

By morning the crowd had come to a stop. She looked at the man who was beside her.

"I've lost track of everyone too," he said.

"Doesn't really matter."

"No."

He smiled at her and told her his name, Tomas, and she wondered how long they had walked together, like this, without speaking. She felt pins behind her eyes.

"You look a little tired," Tomas said, as if he has known her for years.

"I'm not," she said.

"Liar."

"I never expected that there would be so many of us," she said, "I was supposed to be at a party."

"Armenians in Azerbaijan have been rallying for a week already. It's the least we can do. Anyway, it's started now, I don't think it will stop."

"The demonstrations?"

"I don't think I'll ever forget this night," he said. It took her a moment to realize that he wasn't referring only to the march.

☙❧

"I have something that I would like to show you," Tomas said.

"Now?"

"No. Now what I need is to sit down."

He took her hand. He asked her all sorts of questions. They finally stopped beside a building and he sat on the ground with his back against the wall. He looked at her pants, under the skirt.

"I was cold," she said.

"So it wasn't meant to look like that?"

"No." She was smiling, she was looking straight at him. He pulled her onto his lap. "Cover me," he said.

That's why she had kept the skirt. Because she had worn it as she had walked beside him, in the streets, because it had covered them on a morning when she had sat on him and he had looked at her with what seemed to be happiness.

Ptghni. What he had wanted to show her was a church in a village called Ptghni, a building she would remember because it had been the first, one of dozens of churches he would take her to. It was spring then, the demonstrations had stopped, the giddiness of the days when they had practically lived in Theatre Square, when they had hardly slept. Miracles had happened in those few days. And then the news had come at the end of the week of a massacre of Armenians in Azerbaijan, at Sumgait, of Azerbaijanis running through the streets of the town with steel rods and knives, of Armenian men set on fire. That's when Soviet troops had arrived in Yerevan to stop the demonstrations.

"I'd like to take you to Ptghni," Tomas had said, that first night.

The church at Ptghni no longer had a roof. Between the two longest walls a single span of arch still held, immaculate, intact.

"Look at that," he said.

Tomas thought that as long as the old churches were still standing, there would still be a country. He was studying architecture. Old monuments fascinated him. These buildings belonged to another Armenia, he said, a country whose faith had been spoken in stone. When Dzovig asked him what he would build after he graduated, he seemed almost offended.

"I don't intend to work for the government," he said.

"Everybody works for the government," she said.

"Not any more, Dzovig."

Dzovig's father had an opinion of his own. "Old or new," Arzas said, "there isn't enough money left to build a bloody chicken coop. Take a look around you, when you go on those trips with him. Take a look at the roads, the farms. It doesn't take an architect to nail a shack together, does it?"

But Dzovig no longer listened to the quantities of words that spilled out of her father's mouth. After that day in February she'd begun inhabiting a different planet, a sphere whose crust was as dazzling as the flecked blue centre of Tomas's eyes.

It wasn't very far, Ptghni. Sahag was Tomas's friend and he had access to a car. He was fond of reminding Tomas that Armenia was the Soviet republic with the most cars, per capita. "It doesn't change the fact that I need a lift," Tomas would say.

Sahag drove them there and back, stood smoking with his shoulder against a wall while Tomas circled the building. But

Sahag could drive only so far, and later Tomas would be pulling Dzovig onto the backs of old trucks, squeezing into cars with the friends or cousins of teachers at the university, taking her to all the old churches: Geghard, Haghartsin, Tsakhkadzor. They drove along roads that curled up the sides of mountains and led to no other place but a stone church that had stood there for centuries. There was often not enough fuel and they would have to walk for hours. Many of the churches sat in the middle of nowhere, surrounded by giant, brown hills, making it hard to envision that there had ever been people coming there to worship, or the throngs of hands that had built them. It was easy to forget that entire societies had flourished and died, that what bore testimony to their existence now were only these ruins, chiselled stones on a curve of earth. Tomas preferred the churches this way: the more ruined and remote the better. They walked through fields and villages and he described the workings of arches and domes, the properties of weight and resistance. Sometimes there was a priest or an old man who would appear to open the door and offer a few words on the history of the monument. But usually they were empty, stone churches sitting on mountains like hands on the ends of arms, pointing upwards, stretched between rock and sky.

Dzovig watched Tomas then: a body growing taut with energy, his breathing accelerated. She knew when to be quiet, waited for him in the grass as he climbed over sections of wall, or stood transfixed before an architrave. She often brought some food and water and ate alone while he sketched some part of the building. He was different here than he was in the city, everything about him was different. Sometimes, when he came back, he would lie with her in the grass and pull off her panties before spilling himself inside her in a few, frantic thrusts. But usually they just walked back together, his face rapt and silent as if he had just witnessed his own death.

The Castelo de São Jorge sits atop one of Lisbon's seven hills, overlooking the sea of orange rooftops that make up the city. The castle encloses a garden whose trees and vines have overtaken the walls, spilling between crevices, green and gold. Dzovig climbs the ramparts, placing her feet in the hollow centre of stone steps, their surface slippery as glass. She thinks, *Anahid would hate this.* She feels a phantom pull at her arm, her sister clutching, *Dzovig, wait.* Anahid hated stairs, hesitated whenever the level of pavement changed. Perhaps she had fallen, once, as a little girl, a kind of event that imprinted itself on the brain, but nobody remembered.

"Anahid should keep her feet in the brown dirt, where the cows are. Wouldn't that make you happy, Anahid?"

"Shut up, Papa." Dzovig said.

"You don't eat, that's why you're always so dizzy," Maro said. She seemed able to concentrate only on her daughters' physical well-being, ensuring that they were fed sufficiently in the way a farmer would look after his animals. Happiness was something that didn't occur to her.

Anahid needed very little. She went to school, stood in line, sat on her bed reading books. If she had had it her way, she would not have been born in a country that existed high above sea level, where the mountains stood sentry, ready to crush her at any moment. They were heavy, those mountains.

Anahid laughed when Dzovig would shut the door to their room and spread herself against it like someone dead from exasperation, or as if she were holding back an army of invaders.

Behind the door was Arzas, even though Arzas never came into their room. Dzovig did this for Anahid's benefit, Anahid knew, because Dzovig wasn't afraid of anything. She could stand naked in front of a mirror with a finger inside herself, asking "How deep do you think it is, really?" And Anahid would wonder then if that girl could truly be her sister. At night Dzovig slept like someone unconscious. Not Anahid. Anahid had a recurring dream, a dream that was made up of sounds rather than pictures. The sounds of boots climbing on steps, coming towards her in the dark, heavy as lead. Sometimes, when she woke from it, she had to crawl into Dzovig's bed before being able to fall asleep again.

Arzas liked the mountains. He had an icon of his own, like many Armenians: Mount Ararat, whose twin peaks now stood within the Turkish border, a persistent reminder of all that had been taken.

"That mountain," Arzas said, "that mountain will never be theirs."

"It *is* theirs," Dzovig said.

That was the only time he had ever hit her, and she had hated and loved the mountain ever since, knowing she could throw her father's soul against it and watch it fall, like a marble rolling down a slope.

"When Noah landed on Mount Ararat," Maro said, "he walked down the hill and planted a vineyard."

Up here, at the very top of the Castelo de São Jorge, Dzovig sets down her bag and slips off her shoes. The morning haze has begun to lift and ahead of her is the river Tagus, wide and blue, light bouncing off the water in a string of tiny sparks. The Tagus stretches out to sea and asks nothing. Dzovig smiles. She is light as air. She thinks perhaps she will stay.

II

VECIHE

We changed in that week. All of us changed, even Bedros, though he won't admit it. And most of all, Tomas. Twenty-four is the perfect age to be witnessing a revolution, to be making one, and Tomas was twenty-four.

I say we changed as if it had all happened long ago and we were now evaluating, claiming victory even, but we are still in the middle of it and no one knows. We have no reason to believe in ourselves or, if we do, we are still too unaccustomed to that feeling for any real efficacy. We believe we are determined, that's all.

It began on a Friday in February. Two thousand people rallied at the chemical plant in Abovyan, a town ten miles north of Yerevan. They could do it now, they thought, because of glasnost. Open the window. They were fighting for air, for the chance to breathe in our cities. They didn't know that over the mountains, in Karabagh, on that same day, forty thousand Armenians were rallying for the unification of their territory with Armenia. But there was a courier, apparently, who made it past the Azerbaijani roadblocks and out of the city. How soon would we have known, otherwise? We might have seen reports of the demonstrations on television, two, three months after the fact, with the stories cleaned up by the Soviet media, the numbers adjusted. But the courier reached Goris, within the Armenian border. Two days later, one hundred and fifty thousand people stood outside our opera house in Theatre Square, and by the end of that week all of Yerevan would be there. My son, Tomas. My husband, Bedros. We were all there.

I was at home that day, painting, when Tomas came rushing through the door. His friend Sahag was with him.

"They've boycotted all our classes," Tomas said. "You have to come, you won't believe it." Sahag was holding out my coat for me.

"You won't believe it," Tomas kept saying. And so I left with them, leaving my paint brushes in a glass of water. Tomas was almost running, dragging me by the arm.

"They won't disappear, Tomas, they've been there since yesterday," Sahag said.

It didn't take long; our house is only a few blocks from the square. I have walked there hundreds of times, in the evenings, with Bedros. But what greeted me was a different landscape, a sea of people standing side by side. At the back of the opera house there was a platform. Someone was speaking there.

"How many are we, do you think?" Tomas asked. His eyes were blazing.

I didn't know. Too many to count.

We made our way into the crowd a little, we didn't have to push. We just stood there, like the others. Different people went up to speak, some held up banners with pictures of Gorbachev. From time to time there would be applause, or singing. All of us in our coats, women holding purses. After a while Tomas left me; he said he was going to join some friends. I wouldn't see him again for three days.

We are a people accustomed to waiting. The hours passed. I left the square late in the afternoon to use the washroom, intending to go home, but a coffee shop on the corner had put up a handwritten sign that said *Washrooms Open*. Even this small act of generosity surprised me. I thought of Bedros, of the dinner I hadn't made, but I couldn't leave the square. I thought, ridiculously, *he will find me.*

The light was thinning but no one moved. A hush was over the crowd, an unimaginable quiet. No one argued, no one fought their way into position. There was no complaining, no spitting. We were all in awe at what was taking place, at the remarkable realization that we could stand together like this, by the thousands, for the single purpose of making our government, the Soviet government, act. That is what I remember most about that day, the silence that hung over us, so full of promise, a silence in which we weren't, for once, mute.

It was a little past ten o'clock when I returned home. The lights were on. Bedros came to the door.

"Where were you?" he asked.

"Didn't you hear? About the demonstrations?"

"Of course I heard. You could have left me a note."

"I thought you would realize. It's unbelievable, Bedros, I couldn't leave…. Did you have something to eat?"

"I ate. Where's Tomas?"

"He's still there. I went with him but then he joined some friends. He's probably still there. We'll go back tomorrow, you'll see—"

"I can't go, Vecihe, you know that."

"People were talking about a general strike—"

"Let's go to bed," he said.

I fell asleep almost instantly. Bedros told me in the morning that during the night hundreds had marched on our street, calling out for people to leave their jobs, to join the demonstrations. I'd slept through it. Later we learned that Tomas was among them. And that somewhere, in that crowd, was also Dzovig.

Today I am meeting her. Tomas hasn't said much, but I know that they have been together for the past month, ever since that night, something that has never happened to him before. One month has passed and we are waiting to see what will happen. After that first day, the crowds kept doubling in Theatre Square. By the end of the week there were a million of us. Bedros came after all; the ministry building where he works was closed. Tomas and I had been asking him to come all week. The city shut down. There were committees and emergency meetings, and Gorbachev came on television to tell us, *Go home, we will take care of everything*. He sent in troops to guard the government buildings, banned the foreign journalists.

"The hammer's coming down." Bedros said. "Didn't I tell you?"

"Are we supposed to be happy that you're right?" Tomas said.

All this went on, here in Yerevan. We were proud of ourselves. *Gha-ra-bagh! Karabagh is ours!* we said. But in Azerbaijan the crowds were a little different. Already there were a few deaths. Then, on February 27, Armenians in the city of Sumgait were pulled from their houses, killed with clubs by an Azerbaijani mob. The riots lasted two days. That's when it changed, for me. I stayed indoors. I painted. Bedros kept watching television reports, reading newspaper articles. "What are you looking for, Papa," Tomas said, "an apology from Moscow?"

Tomas left with Dzovig shortly afterward, taking her to see churches outside the city, his old obsession. He seemed different, suddenly, his mood had shifted. I thought at first that he and Dzovig must be dazzled with each other, with this whole fight, even though the government has banned the demonstrations and soldiers have surrounded the opera house. I heard a neighbour say that she had seen girls giving flowers to soldiers in the square, in mockery. I asked Tomas if Dzovig had been among them, but he didn't answer.

When I see Dzovig, I think that my daughter has arrived. Every woman must have a daughter, I have believed this for years, living with two men. I believed it even as I held my son in my arms when he was no bigger than a doll, and already so separate from me.

Her hair is short, round face, giant green eyes. There is no fear in those eyes. Tomas introduces her "Mama, this is Dzovig" and I feel clumsy because my hands are covered in flour from baking bread. Her eyes travel the room and she notices everything, my hands covered in flour, the dishes I haven't yet washed, the pictures on the wall.

"It smells good," she says.

"Would you like to eat something, Dzovig? I've been baking—"

"She a great cook," my son says.

I look at him in surprise. "What's come over you, Tomas?"

She looks at him too, with love, with an adoration that I recognize. Her hand is very small, next to his.

"Please, come and sit. Tomas tells me you are studying languages."

"Yes. English and French, mostly."

"And Russian, of course," Tomas adds.

"I already know Russian," she says.

"So, you will be able to travel anywhere in the world, Dzovig."

She looks for a moment as if the possibility of this has never struck her, or as if she had suddenly remembered a goal she had lost sight of.

"I used to dream about travelling when I was little," she says. "I always wanted to see those islands, the Bahamas; I don't know why. I'd seen a picture of them somewhere, probably. The ground looked so... soft. Real sand, no rocks."

"You'll have to marry a foreigner then," Tomas says, "because I'm staying. Or you could die, those who die also get to go."

"Oh, stop it, Tomas," I tell him.

Dzovig smiles. "Yes, stop it."

The corners of his mouth soften and I think, she is good for him. Maybe Dzovig will be the one to break Tomas's anger, an anger whose origins I have never been able to understand. What rages he had, as a baby, little fists shaking with fury before mountains of tumbled blocks. He wouldn't be comforted, even then. I look at her, at the small round breasts beneath her blouse, and I wonder if they have already slept together. I am ashamed to wonder: is my son capable of tenderness?

Dzovig looks at the pictures, the watercolours I have been painting this year. I hang them on the walls of this old house. I hang them up with yellow tape. It turns brittle after a while, leaving stains on the edge of the pictures. Those stains could be my signature, I think. Save me time.

Our walls are crumbling. We are falling to bits, like the rest of the country, but at least we are alone; our luxury is that we have space. When Bedros first brought me here I thought myself in a palace. All these rooms, all five of them, ours. This house must have been beautiful at one time; who remembers it now? There is a corner of the ceiling in the dining room, a tiny patch of bright green, some gold in it. It reminds me of Odzun, that green, of the large house where I lived with my mother, of the walls in our room there and the fields surrounding the village. Not ours, the house. As a girl I always assumed that it belonged to the Hagopian family, who lived there too. I didn't understand the subtleties of ownership in this country, then. My mother and I slept in a small room at the back, and my mother cooked and cleaned for them. We were very lucky, she used to say.

I wouldn't let Bedros paint over that tiny patch of green on the ceiling, years ago, when we still had the energy to try to improve things. Yerevan is a city without colour. White and grey stone everywhere, or else dark red, like old blood. Sometimes I think the layers of dust fall on Yerevan like rain, from the sky. *It's the bloody chemical factories*, my son tells me.

Bedros didn't paint over it, my patch of green. He could have. The house is more his than mine, a gift handed from the Communist Party to his father in exchange for services rendered. I don't know what my husband does all day behind the doors of the Ministry of Economy. But I know that I live here because of it.

The pictures are mine. They feed me, like the pattern on

a dress my mother used to wear, giant red and pink flowers on a yellow ground. I could stare at her for hours in that dress. Red and pink.

Tomas dismisses my paintings as any adolescent would: "This isn't a nursery, Mama," he says. Bedros is more charitable, or rather, more forgiving. When I showed him the first painting I had painted in years I felt like a woman putting on a dress that had cost too much. He said very little, holding back his surprise. Then he said, "It's taken you a long time." Now he tells me they are very fine. He assumes, like all husbands, that I need his approval. Still I am grateful for his little lie. This is the country of lies. But Bedros is a kind, tender man.

"Who painted these?" Dzovig asks.

"I did," I tell her.

She is incredulous. "You never told me your mother was an artist, Tomas."

She leaves the table and stands up close to a few of them, peering at the details, holding a finger to her lips. She reads my signature.

"Vecihe?"

"Yes, we mothers have names," I tell her, smiling at Tomas.

"What are they?" she asks.

"Just places, other places. Imaginary cities."

"There's a book like that, I forget what it's called, by an Italian; do you know it?"

"No."

"Full of places, like this."

"Now we know there is someone out there as crazy as you, Mama."

"It's very hard to find good paper," I tell her.

"It's almost as if a child painted them," she says, "except that a child could never paint like this."

She points to a row of houses sitting on a clothesline strung between two mountains. "This could be Ararat!"

"No, Karabagh," Tomas says.

"They're just houses, Tomas."

Dzovig says, "I've never seen anything more beautiful."

I put my arm around her and I kiss her quickly, on the temple, because I am happy. I am as happy as someone who has come home after years of exile. My son looks at me as if I were mad.

III

GORDINHO

The Alcobaça is the size of a small shop, its doorway no different from the other doors that line the steep and narrow street. A wooden sign hangs above it, the only indication that this is a place of commerce. Inside, the tables are already set, covered in plain cloths, blue and white china and thick wine glasses. The tables fill every possible inch of floor space and each has a different assortment of wooden chairs. Still, the place looks pristine with a carefully folded napkin and small butter dish set at each place. The cash register sits on a long wooden chest in the far corner, with bottles of wine and beer stacked neatly behind it.

A door at the back swings out and a woman holds it open with her arm. She is wearing an apron over a short dress, nylon stockings on plump legs and slippers on her feet.

"Estamos fechados, Menina," she says.

Dzovig asks, "Senhor Johnston?"

The woman looks irritated. "Um momento," she says, and the door swings back and forth a few times when she releases it.

When he appears he is younger than she imagined. Very tall and thin.

"Por favor?"

"I was told you are English. You speak English," she says.

His accent is British: "Someone's told you that, have they? Now who is it that has been spreading rumours about me?"

"Oh. German lady and her husband. They come here for lunch often, they said. They gave me your name."

"I'm sorry, love, but we only open at one."

"I don't come to eat," she says.

He looks at her curiously. She looks a little rumpled, he thinks.

"My name is Dzovig. I have been here for three days, in Portugal. I need a place to work. I would like to learn Portuguese."

"Dzovig, where is that from?" he asks.

"Armenia."

He rubs his chin. "We get a lot of tourists over here, not many Armenians. We get a lot of locals as well. We're not very fancy, as you can see. I don't think I have anything to offer you, I'm afraid."

Dzovig fixes him with her eyes. She looks tired. She stares at him with the persistence of a child who desperately wants something.

"I don't need money. Just to eat and learn to speak Portuguese. I can clean and serve the tourists, yes?"

He pulls a chair away from a table and motions for her to sit.

"Where did you learn English?"

"I learned in Yerevan, at the university. I also speak French."

"Do you have a place to live? You look like you haven't slept in days."

She doesn't answer.

"How do I know you're not going to rob me blind, Dzovig from Armenia?"

"Because I do not want anything," she tells him. "Only to be able to stay." She hesitates. "I need to have real work," she says.

"Here?"

"Yes. In Portugal."

He appraises her. For a moment she seems to be sinking, falling through layers. She is looking at him from very, very far away. He doesn't know why but something in him makes him want to pull her back, and in that instant he decides.

"Look. All right. Rosa isn't going to be happy about it, but she's always cranky anyway. There's a small room at the back, just a bed and a small bath. You can sleep there, if you want to. You can keep whatever you make in tips, but no salary for now. Anything you need from the kitchen, all right? Are you a good cook?"

"No," she says. "What is tips?"

He laughs. "Tips? Extra money that the customers give, for service. They leave it on the table, usually."

"And no one steals it?"

"No. You don't have tips in Armenia?"

"No. Only bribes."

"Well, just remember, good service, bigger tips."

She smiles for the first time. "Thank you, Mr. Johnston."

"They call me Gordinho."

"Gordinho?"

"You'll never guess. It means little fat man; it's the diminutive for *gordo*, fat. My real name is Gordon, so they figured it was close enough. The Portuguese are always going around making things smaller, you see; it's like an endearment. They say *Rosinha*, for Rosa. *Paulinho,* for Paulo. They'll even ask for a *bifinho,* instead of *bife,* when they want a steak."

"Bife a cavalo," she says.

"I'm impressed!"

"What does it mean, *Menina?* Everyone calls me this."

"It means little girl. You see? Small."

"They do this too, in Armenia. My mother she was called Maro, short for Mariam."

"I suppose it happens in most places," he says. "Come on, I'll show you the kitchen."

The woman who appeared before is chopping onions at a wide marble counter. In the sink beside her are large mounds of a green vegetable, already chopped into fine slivers.

"Rosa makes the best *Caldo Verde* in Lisbon," he says jovially, but Rosa doesn't smile. Gordon explains something to her in Portuguese and her eyebrows join together in a frown. Dzovig notices the fine black down that lines the space above Rosa's lips as Rosa eyes her suspiciously. They argue, Rosa and Gordon, and all the while her hands keep chopping the onions, mechanically, as if they were a pair of disembodied beings. Dzovig turns away.

"It will be fine," Gordon says, "she's a real lamb once you get to know her. Rosa has worked for me for twenty years. Sometimes it feels like I'm the one working for her, but that's just the way she is."

He leads her through a large pantry and towards a back door. Behind them Rosa is muttering, over and over, "Minha nossa Senhora, minha nossa Senhora...." The pantry is cool and stocked with large bags of potatoes and onions, cans of tomatoes and large sausages hanging from the ceiling.

"Chouriço," Gordon says, pointing. "Very tasty."

Behind it, a door opens onto a tiny room. Like the rest of the place, it is immaculate. The single bed is covered in a red wool cloth. Someone has placed a round, white doily on a table, next to the bed. Dzovig looks at the wall and is relieved that there is no crucifix.

"Rosa's son used to sleep here. He went off to America, some years ago. She hasn't heard much from him since, poor girl, but she keeps the room clean. Always hoping, I suppose." Gordon shakes his head. "He's a man by now, after all. Up there in Prazeres, the cemetery, there's a mausoleum some fellow built for his little girl, her whole bedroom intact inside it: slippers by the bed, dolls, everything. I've never seen much point in it, myself."

"No."

"Sorry?"

"No point," Dzovig says.

Gordon looks at her. There is kindness in his eyes. He motions to the room.

"Yes?"

"Yes, thank you."

"Right, then. I'll let you get some sleep. You look like you need it. You can get started in the kitchen this afternoon, after you've rested. We don't want you fainting on us. She won't bite, I promise you. You'll meet Francisco later. He's the other cook."

"*Obrigada*, Mr. Gordinho."

He chuckles. "Not bad," he says.

He closes the door and she hears the sounds of arguing coming from the kitchen. She lies on the bed, on top of the covers. She stares at the ceiling for only a few seconds before closing her eyes.

∞

She is with him, again, in her sleep. She is lying in a field with him. There is a church in a city—*Ani*, the word comes back to her. The city's name is like a human name, *Ani*, like a mother's call, imploring her. He's up on the roof now, waving to her. He is so happy he leaps off, still smiling. *Tomas!* His fall is long and graceful. His feet touch the ground and he is fine, fine, and she runs to him, her heart bursting out of her body; it seems like she is running forever.

When she reaches the church she hears his voice from behind a wall: I have it, he says. There are ribbons flying from the top of the church, long, multicoloured ribbons, tracing squiggles across the sky like the drawings of children. She wonders why she didn't notice them before, they are so festive. *Tomas*—she can't find him—*Tomas!*

She is carrying bread in her hands, the *lavash* her mother used to make in the *Toneh*, back then. *Tomas*—There are wine cups carved on the face of the church. That was at Ptghni, don't you remember? The cups of salvation. She remembers Saint H'ripsimé: her mother had a picture of her at home, hiding in the vat-store, where the wine presses were kept. She was wearing sandals. Anahid wore white sandals. She had long hair. *Tomas*—I remember Ptghni, I remember the wine pitchers on the north wall!

She can't find him. There are cracks in the stone floor at her feet. He is down there, tiny, like the boy in that fairy tale, at the bottom of the well—

Dzovig wakes up. There is a sound like rain. It is the sound of onions dropping into hot oil, from the kitchen. She has stopped relishing these dreams, by now.

IV

VECIHE

I started painting when I was six. I have very few memories from before the day my mother gave me the watercolour set. I started living on that day. "You were always making something," my mother would say, "your hands never stopped moving." I had never been in Turkey, the country of my mother's birth. My mother never spoke of it. But she insisted on giving me a Turkish name, and I knew from an early age that there had been another Vecihe—an angel, my mother said, who had saved us. For a long time I wondered why it was that if this angel came from heaven, it had to be Turkish. But my mother grew irritable when I questioned her about this, shaking her head in that gesture she had that meant I was too young to understand. On better days she made me feel that it was a point of honour between the two of us that I accept it, this Turkish name, and treasure it like a secret.

We were already living in the village of Odzun when I got the watercolour set. I had walked home from school, I remember, and found it sitting on the kitchen table, like a treasure left by some magical being. It was a flat, rectangular wooden box. The top of the box was dark green and on it was a word whose lettering I didn't recognize: *Aquarelles*. I touched the top with my fingertips; it slid open and, inside, the box was divided into several compartments. In the centre was one round porcelain dish surrounded by four larger square ones. Near the top were two long, thin brushes, and near the bottom, two long rows of watercolour paints in neat, square cakes. There were more colours than I ever believed existed. Best of all, in one corner, was a cake of gold paint: it was round, unlike the others, and so precious that in the coming months I would almost never use it.

My mother had her back to me. She was standing at the large sink, chopping or washing vegetables, something like that. But she could tell by my silence that I had seen it. Something in the softness of her shoulders made me feel as if she was watching me.

"Well," she said, "it's for you, Vecihe."

"Mama?"

She turned around.

"Don't you like it?"

My mouth stood open. I managed a nod, I think, and I remember starting to shiver, my knees knocking together. I was so thin then, I could injure myself with my own bones.

My mother smiled at me. "You're a good girl, Vecihe. You're my beautiful girl." She came and straightened out my hair, brushing it back from my face with her fingers. Her hands were warm and damp from the sink.

"We'll have to save up our paper, now. But here are a few sheets, they were in the box. Look how fine they are."

She held a sheet of paper between her fingertips in the same way that she would hold a piece of cloth, feeling for thickness and quality. I imitated her. The paper was as smooth as silk. And then I let out a squeal that made my mother jump, and she grabbed me and we both twirled around the kitchen.

It was at that moment that Mr. Hagopian walked into the room. He called my mother by her name.

"Zivart."

My mother stopped abruptly and began flattening the creases in the front of her dress with her palms. I wasn't afraid of him. He was very tall and thin; his gaunt face made him look as if he had once been on the edge of starvation and had never quite recovered. In our village, he was a a man of some power.

I rarely saw him in the house, his house, where I lived. He was away most of the time; I never wondered where or why. Sometimes I ran into him in various parts of the village, where he would be conducting some kind of business with other men. He always acknowledged me with a nod of his head or a wave of his arm. He had a peculiar way of waving his arm that made it seem as if he was beckoning me to him, and I always hesitated before running off with a childish defiance. Sometimes I heard his laugh, a warm, soft laugh, reaching me through the sounds of my footsteps hitting the pebbles on the road.

"Well," he said now, "are we having a celebration?"

My mother's eyes turned to the ground, and because I had seldom seen her like this, muted and fragile, I summoned up the courage to address him directly.

"Mama gave me a paint set," I said.

He stepped towards the table and held the box in his hands for a moment, examining it, before laying it back down carefully.

"That is a very special box," he said, looking serious. "I don't think I've ever seen anything finer. You'd better take good care of it, Vecihe."

I nodded. And then, because I noticed my mother's eyes meeting his for a flicker of a second in which both faces seemed to light up with laughter, I stood on the tips of my toes and said, not quite understanding this strange complicity between them, "Thank you."

In the house where I lived with my mother there were two other children, Hrach and Mida. They were Mr. Hagopian's children. Hrach was two years younger than me. He had a tricycle—a red, rusty creation with thick, flat wheels. The ridges on these wheels were always encrusted with tiny pebbles, and I often imagined picking them out with the sharp point of a stick, and wondering what sound the wheels would make then. It would have been difficult to notice any difference in the sound if Hrach was on the tricycle; he usually yelled at the top of his lungs as he rode it around the courtyard at the side of the house, swinging his body from side to side. I did try riding it once, but my knees bumped into the handlebars and I gave up before he had a chance to see me.

Mida was two years older than Hrach; we were the same age. She had wide, pale green eyes and was sometimes my friend. One of her favourite games was to take me around the house to the door of each room, in succession, and declare in her loudest voice which ones I could or could not enter. I followed her only because I was tantalized by the quick glimpse of some rooms, the ones I rarely, if ever, had ventured into. One morning she took me to the room where I slept with my mother.

"You cannot go in there," she said.

I stood confused, for a moment, and then I began to laugh.

Mida's eyes narrowed. "You cannot go in there," she repeated.

"Yes I can," I said.

"Even this room belongs to me. This is my house."

I brushed past her and sat myself on one of the beds. I crossed my arms.

"Girls don't have houses," I said, "only men do."

"When you grow up," she said, "you will be just like old Aghavnee, and everyone will spit on you!"

She stormed off, and though my instinct was to jump up and follow her I stayed where I was, surveying the contents of the room, this room where I slept with my mother, as if I had just seen it for the first time. The two narrow beds were pushed up against the walls, perpendicular to each other, and each one was covered with several layers of blankets and various cloths which we turned down or up when we slept, depending on the season. In the coldest of winter my mother covered me with a carpet as well, a carpet she kept rolled away during the warmer months. Our room was adjacent to the kitchen and, because there was always a fire going, we were seldom cold. On some days the walls were covered in a film of water, as if they had perspired from the heat.

There was a table in our room, and beneath it a small trunk where my mother kept the rolled-up carpet and some clothes. We had a chair and a mirror, and I assumed that they were ours, these objects, my mother's and mine, and that within the giant realm of the Hagopian house our possessing of them signified a measure of our freedom.

But I wondered now, after Mida's words, whether old Aghavnee had ever had such things. A bed, a chair, a rolled-up carpet at the bottom of a trunk. And whether the taking away of them had somehow brought her to her present state. I had heard someone say once that Aghavnee had come from Turkey, like my mother. We called her old Aghavnee because of the giant curve in her back that made her walk almost bent in two, like an old woman. She had large holes in her mouth where there should have been teeth and

her eyes looked like holes as well: dark, sunken orbs in the middle
of her face. From what I could tell she lived nowhere in particular
but spent her days wandering through the village, stopping here
and there, gathering food from various households. We children
ran from her as if from a plague, it was a game of ours. Being children, we were too young for pity. But I never saw any of the adults
in the village mistreat her. There seemed to be an unspoken acceptance of her presence, as if she were some element in the landscape, one of the minute vicissitudes of life in the village. She
carried around with her an old sack made of thick jute, and it hung
from her shoulder in folds, looking empty. She often talked as she
walked, to the trees, the insects. If someone passed her she smiled
at them. I seldom saw her in winter and never wondered where she
slept. But I wondered now, sitting on my bed, conscious for the
first time of the threat she represented, a symbol of what could be
lost, of what one could be reduced to. I wondered whether we in
fact did own the things that made up our room, and if we did, what
it was that could take them from us.

Mida's power over me dissipated when we were out of doors. I
understood that when we got farther and farther from the house,
as on our way to school, for example, our roles seemed to reverse,
that she needed me more than I needed her.

There were no strangers in Odzun. In spite of this a sort
of fear seemed to come over her in the village, as if the world were
populated with persons one was meant to be suspicious of. Our
school consisted of one room in a building adjacent to the market.
I'd heard someone say that it had at one time been used as a smoke-
house. Sometimes I thought I detected a smell of smoke coming
from the walls but I didn't tell anybody. We came there to learn

how to read and write the alphabet. We learned Armenian and also Russian. Russia was our mother, that's what the teachers said, even though we never spoke Russian at home, only in school. We did our sums with an abacus, an instrument I liked because of its colourful beads and the clicking sound they made when they hit against each other, like birds pecking at a piece of dead wood.

Mida hated school. She was nervous around the other children and when we all played she looked to me as if I was an interpreter between herself and a different species. *They're hitting the ball too hard, Vecihe, tell them!*

I wouldn't. The truth was that I was ashamed of her, that my living in a room at the back of her house was to me a kind of blemish, another circumstance setting me apart in the village, when what I wanted most was to be invisible. Not even the other children's cruelty succeeded in making me her ally.

"Princess Mida and her Turkish maid! The police will come and get you one of these days."

"Mida's mother is a witch. She has one eye of a different colour than the other!"

"Stop it!" Mida looked desperately towards me.

I would not defend her. I knew it was a lie that Mrs. Hagopian had different-coloured eyes. It was rather that one pupil was larger, making one eye look almost black in contrast to the other, which was blue. I had noticed this on one of the occasions that she had emerged from the sitting room, a room where she spent almost the entire day embroidering tablecloths. It was Mr. Hagopian who brought her the fabric from the places he travelled to, and she embroidered it with the most exquisite flowers and birds, vine leaves so intricate I wondered how they could be fixed there, in the weave of linen, and not grow out into three dimensions. Whenever she finished one, my mother would smooth it with an iron filled with hot coals, sprinkling drops of water onto the cloth that singed when the iron passed over them, bringing up clouds of steam. And then my mother folded it and placed it in a wooden cabinet that contained on its shelves a dozen other tablecloths embroidered by Mrs. Hagopian. I had opened that cabinet a few times, in secret, and run my fingers over and between the layers of fabric, feeling the raised embroidery like a blind man caressing the contours of a face. It was from that cabinet that I had stolen a handkerchief, a small square of white linen embroidered with a cherry, part of a set, whose disappearance I hoped would go unnoticed.

The Hagopian house where I lived with my mother stood near the edge of the village. The main road that traversed the village began at the church and ended at the house. On either side of it small roads had grown out of alleyways between buildings or paths traced by the continuous rolling of wagons on their trajectory between houses and fields. We rarely saw any cars, and I assumed that this was because they could not make the journey up the steep side of the mountain on which the village stood. Or perhaps they didn't know that when they reached the very tip, the ground would miraculously flatten like the top of a rich man's hat. I had asked my mother once what it was like, climbing up the road into Odzun. I imagined it as a straight line, top to bottom. It is a very long road was all that my mother said.

At one time the fields surrounding the house must have belonged to it, or to Mr. Hagopian. They were now part of the *kolkhoz*, the village collective, though most families still worked the piece of land that had formerly belonged to them. I had heard Mr. Hagopian explain this to Hrach. The fields were planted with different crops, some of them used for grazing. Some distance from the house was an apple orchard whose trees had the look of old hands. I was allowed to roam freely throughout the fields, following paths outlined by rough stone walls. In summer these walls were covered in patties of cow dung left there to dry, to be used as fuel in the winter. They gave the air a wonderful smell, a smell that was like waking up.

I had a secret place behind the orchard. No one came there. I reached it by following a path along the side of one field until it dissolved into open space, and then backtracking to the edge of the orchard from the outside, where no one would see me, until I came to a wide, rocky outcrop that was the very end of our village. Beyond it the face of the mountain dropped off into a deep gorge. The ground here was made up of wide, flat stones with yellow grasses growing out of crevices and different mosses that appeared in spring when the stones turned warm. It was hard to believe that anything else could grow there but to one side, near the edge of the gorge, was a small grove of trees, maybe a dozen in total, two of them curved out towards the precipice as if they had leaned over to see what was below.

The trees were not very tall. Their leaves were a silvery, pale green, and when the light turned blue, towards evening, they became almost incandescent. My wishing tree was here. I'd chosen one in the centre of the grove, a small specimen whose trunk I could easily climb. It was no different, really, than the other trees people had decorated outside the church, covering branches with remnants of old dresses, bits of lace or a child's shirt, each one a promise to God. Except that this tree was my very own. I thought that God might notice it more clearly, that he would see through to the centre of the grove and think me good.

It was here that I had tied my stolen napkin, thinking that my tree would be happy to have a cherry in it. And it was also here that I brought my paint set on the afternoon my mother gave it to me.

I hadn't decided yet where I would keep it. I was slightly afraid, after what Mida had said about my room, to leave anything of great value there. I'd never had anything of great value before. If I left it here the rains would get to it. I decided the safest thing to do was to carry it with me wherever I went.

I sat down in the grove and slid open the box. I don't know how I managed to guess that I would need water. I hadn't thought to bring any and so I put the tip of one brush between my lips and then licked a red cake of paint. The brush made the faintest mark on the paper. I needed more water and so I let drops of saliva fall onto the different squares of colour in the box, and slowly, I began to paint.

I painted my tree, a pale brown trunk with spidery branches, the rags I had tied to them small blotches of colour. I couldn't control the paint very well and some colours bled into each other so that the tree looked more like a flower in the end. Above me, the sky was turning pink and so that is the colour that I painted it, on the page.

I was finished.

I held my picture up for the tree.

I wondered then if pictures could also be wishes and, hesitating, I pierced one corner of the page through the tip of a small branch. And as I left the grove and walked towards the fields I could hear the paper rustling among the leaves, as if the tree were breathing to me its acquiescence.

V

FRANCISCO

There is another man standing at the stove in the kitchen. He is whistling through his teeth. Dzovig clears her throat.

"Ah! Do...Doo..." He can't pronounce her name.

"Dzovig," she says.

"Ah!" He smiles, and points a finger to himself. "Francisco," he says. Then he gestures with his chin to a bird in a tall white cage sitting on top of a cabinet. "Balthazar Rei de Portugal," he announces, and winks.

Rosa swings into the kitchen at that moment and examines Dzovig from top to bottom. She says some words to Francisco and signals Dzovig to follow her into the dining room. The late afternoon sun is streaming into the room and the white tablecloths look yellow, flecks of dust are floating in a golden haze. Dzovig reads the clock and guesses that they are ready for the dinner guests; she must have slept for six hours.

Rosa lifts up her palm and stretches out her fingers as she counts: "Um, dois, tres, quatro, cinco," all the way to ten. She then points to every table, counting again, until each one has been assigned a number. She does it a second time, pointing to tables at random and calling out their number until Dzovig is completely confused. They return to the kitchen and Dzovig is mumbling to herself the few numbers she has managed to retain. On one counter a plate has been set with a napkin neatly folded beside it. The plate is heaped with potatoes, onions, olives and some sort of fish. The onions are almost black and very soft. Rosa places three thick slices of bread and a glass of wine next to the plate.

"Bacalhau," she says, pulling up a stool.

Dzovig isn't sure if the meal is meant for her, but Rosa begins to look impatient. Dzovig sits down. "Obrigada," she says.

Rosa looks at her once more and then points to her hair. She makes the motion of running an imaginary comb through it before nodding towards the dining room and disappearing once more behind the swinging door.

The onions melt in Dzovig's mouth, and Francisco is whistling again, at the stove, through the wide black gap between his two front teeth.

The Alcobaça fills up quickly and soon she is passing from the kitchen to the dining room with plates of food in her hand. She is slow and clumsy and has to ask clients to point exactly to the items they want on the menu. She has never seen so much food in her life. Gordinho arrives after nine and takes charge of the wine and the bills. Rosa goes about her work, looking pinched, glancing at Dzovig now and then with complete disapproval. Gordinho watches her and smiles as if he were the proud instigator of a practical joke.

As she clears the tables Dzovig finds money, bills and coins tucked neatly under the rims of white porcelain. She takes them to the counter behind which Gordinho is standing.

"Haven't you any pockets?"

"No."

"I'll save it for you, then."

It is one in the morning when the Alcobaça closes. Rosa has left an hour earlier. Gordinho is fiddling with wine bottles and glasses.

"Not too much for you, Dzovig?"

"No. Not too much."

He opens a small drawer and hands her a stack of bills.

"Yours," he says. "It's less than it looks."

"Thank you. I will help Francisco in the kitchen to clean up."

"Good night, Dzovig."

Francisco is standing at the sink, this time, laughing and talking to his own hands as if he were cooing to a baby. The kitchen is all in order, everything cleaned and put away as if by magic. It is very quiet except for Francisco's soft singing and the steady trickle of water running from the tall spout over the kitchen sink.

Dzovig stands beside him without speaking. It is not his hands, after all, that he is singing to, but the bird—what was his name?—Balthazar something. The bird is hopping from side to side in the wide rectangular sink, flapping its wings under the thin stream of water. Francisco rolls the tips of his thick fingers over the top of the bird's head, laughing with his shoulders and the corners of his eyes.

Dzovig points to the water and says, "Água."

Francisco opens wide his mouth.

"Muito bem!" he says, and she understands these also, the words that mean "very good."

She repeats them to him, all the words she has remembered from the day: well, please, wine, red, white, soup, bread, water, and all the while the white bird is running across the sink, flapping its wings as if in jubilation, and Francisco laughs.

Finally, she points to the bird and says, "Balthazar."

"Não," corrects Francisco. "Balthazar Rei de Portugal!"

There had been a spring running through the chapel at Geghard. A spring of water running through ridges the floor and a bird, a white pigeon. The bird had belonged to a man who stood outside the monastery's gates. He owned three or four of them, all tied by their feet with coarse string. For a few coins he would let you set one of them free. Tomas hadn't noticed the birds. His eyes were already fixed on the cliffs above.

It had taken them three days to get to Geghard from Yerevan. They had walked for long stretches and taken rides whenever they could. They had slept the first night in a village whose name she didn't take note of. A farmer had offered them a cot at the back of his barn in exchange for chopping his wood pile. The farmer's wife brought them some water, and some dried plums that had been pressed into thin round sheets, their edges decorated with tiny, embossed symbols, crosses within circles, the same rosettes she had seen as a girl on a wall somewhere, a wall against which her father had stood. They had looked like stars to her then.

A little girl, the farmer's daughter probably, had stood timidly to one side as Tomas chopped the wood. She had almond eyes and braided hair.

"What's your name?" he asked her.

"Lilith."

"We're on our way to see a church, Lilith."

"Which one?"

"Which one? How many are there?"

"Three," she said.

"You'll have to show us where they are," Tomas said, but the little girl disappeared into the house and they didn't see her again.

That night, Tomas's hands were covered in blisters.

"You taste like plums," Dzovig said, "salty plums."

"You taste like the sea," he said.

"You've never been to the sea, idiot!"

"Nor do I want to."

"Why not?"

"Because I've already tasted it."

"Because you're an idiot. An idiot who likes churches."

"Yes."

"Why do you? Why do they mean so much to you, Tomas?"

"You want to talk about this now? Let's wait. Wait until Geghard. Then you'll know...I'm tired..."

"No you're not," she said, biting him.

Geghard. The monastery clung to the face of the canyon wall, a cluster of buildings overlooking the gorge of the Azat River. In the centre, the peak of its cathedral rose above its surroundings like the tip of a pencil, pointing to the mountain top behind it.

"You see that cone?" Tomas said. "Inside, it's a dome. And those flat walls, on the inside, are niches. It's as if there are two different buildings in one: the exterior is a grand illusion, see?"

Tomas was almost running, pulling her towards the entrance of the cathedral. They passed through a portal where the stone had been carved into lace, a filigree of pomegranates and vines, two doves on either side of the arch. Inside, the air was cool and dense, and her hand felt suddenly wet when Tomas let go of it.

In the half light it had taken a few moments for the shape of things to grow clear again: four thick columns, arches—a series of curved lines that converged beneath a dome whose surface looked like a mass of chiselled diamonds, a stalactite tent. At its zenith was a round, blue hole.

Tomas pointed to the inner wall of the sanctuary, where the outlines of individual stone blocks had disappeared: it was carved out of the face of the canyon wall.

"This is only the beginning," he said.

Beyond the sanctuary there were four other churches, all hewn out of the mountain itself. Cave chapels. Tiny passageways connected them, steep, crooked stairs, crawl spaces blackened by centuries of smoke. The oldest one, Avazan, had been carved on the site of a pagan temple that stood over a natural spring, and the water still trickled through it in snake-like ridges, in the floor. There would have been a purpose for it, Dzovig thought, a need to wash away the blood of sacrifices, to bless the slaughtered. And now it was as if water had covered every surface in the chapel, had passed over walls, columns, dome and floor like the hand of a giant, making it smooth. Only time and water could have done this. In the chapel, every stone was round.

Dzovig's eyes followed the clusters of stalactites that crowned the columns and lined each dome. It was as if the original caves had imprinted themselves in the minds of Geghard's makers, men who had chiselled in stone what centuries of water and minerals had done before them. The forms here were simpler than in the cathedral, bolder, as if they had been distilled to their essence, simplified yet augmented. Tomas explained it another way: "Less light, sharper profile," he said.

She knew he was away from her now, that he had stepped into another skin. She felt slightly afraid. Tomas ran his fingers slowly over the carvings on the wall: flowers, crosses, animals. He ran his hands over the walls of Avazan chapel as in a prayer.

Dzovig thought of her mother, of her mother's wet hands.

When she was three, she started to go away from me. That's what Maro had said about Anahid.

"I'm going to look around," Dzovig said. She remembered the birds she had seen at the entrance, their little feet tied to the ground. She couldn't stop thinking about them now.

When she was three she began to go away from me. I couldn't let that happen, Maro had said.

She returned to the main sanctuary and walked towards an open door, a rectangle of bright light that looked like the entrance to another world. She found herself outside, at the foot of a flight of stairs. She climbed the stairs and followed the curving surface of the mountain until she reached an opening, a corridor whose walls were entirely covered in *khachkars*, the carved Armenian cross. It led to another chapel, bigger than the previous ones, elephantine columns holding up the dome. She was alone here; she could feel the unevenness in the stone floor through her sandals. The smell of a grotto.

Dzovig made a sound, "Ah!", and the stones echoed. She looked up at the hole in the dome, the small circle of sky. A hole for breathing. She might see a pigeon flying by.

Tomas said, *Look, the bellies of seagulls have turned blue.* That was at Lake Sevan, on another day, a day that hadn't taken place yet, when they would go to Sevan and he would notice that the lake had painted itself on the bellies of seagulls as they flew over it.

Dzovig placed her back against a column and called out again, louder each time, and the mouth of the dome answered in waves, as if it were singing with the voices of hundreds, stored through the centuries within each stone. And then a whisper:

"Dzovig."

She turned around. It was coming from a corner, a hole in the floor the size of a watermelon. Through it she could see Tomas's face.

"I was looking for the birds," she said.

"Dzovig," he said, "we are inside the mountain!"

Afterwards, she waited outside for him, in the sun. She had money in her pocket and she said that she wanted to see the birds again. Tomas thought she was joking.

When she threw the pigeon up in the air, it flew into a tree and landed on a branch right above the man's head.

Tomas laughed then.

"You see, he's trained them. As soon as you turn around he'll get the bird back and wait for someone else to waste their money."

The bird didn't move.

Dzovig gave the man some more money for another bird and this time she held the bird in her hands as she walked away in the direction of the gorge.

"Hey, where are you going?" the man said. "You can't do that!"

But Dzovig ran and this time the bird flew high up, over the gorge, and disappeared.

When she came back the man was ranting but Tomas's expression had changed.

"I'm sorry," he said.

It had taken them three days to get to Geghard. They had taken some rides and walked for hours along the side of the road, and Dzovig recognized part of the road because she had travelled there before, in a white borrowed car that reeked of petrol, with her father. She remembered her father chewing his food as he stared at the lake, remembered a shower of pebbles hitting the ground, and clouds—and she said to Tomas, This is the road to Sevan, isn't it?

By the end of the week Dzovig has memorized all the items on the Alcobaça's menu. Someone, Gordinho probably, has left a book on her bed, *Teach Yourself Portuguese*, and she reads it at night, after everyone has left, before she falls asleep.

It is very quiet in her little room.

It is usually the sound of Rosa coming in through the front door that wakes her. Rosa comes by every morning, early, to drop off the fish she has bought in the Rua São Pedro. Rosa is noisy about the kitchen, on purpose perhaps. By the time Dzovig has dressed, Rosa has left again.

The Alfama, Lisbon's oldest quarter, grows familiar to her. She walks the streets and alleyways when they are still quiet, none of the restaurants or taverns yet open. It is women she sees mostly, women going to church or washing their front stoops, or hanging laundry from windows or cords strung between windows and between houses. The houses look like they have been painted in watercolours, colours that have faded and bled into one another as if the façades had been wet pictures that were held up too soon. And yet, for all the sun-washed colours, the houses have a solidity to them, the labyrinth of streets a permanence that seems to have evolved from some strange logic. Or perhaps it is the quality of the mornings, in Lisbon, the strange thickness of a sunlight so palpable that one can smell it.

She often stops in the Miradouro de Santa Luzia, a wide terrace beside a church whose outer wall is covered in blue and white tiles. There is a small fountain against the wall, a huge bush of bright pink flowers arching over it. She has never seen these kinds of flowers before. Below the terrace the orange roof-tops of the Alfama stretch out towards the Tagus. Above her are the ramparts of the castle.

She runs into Francisco, one day, on the terrace. He is playing cards with a group of men at a small table set up under a tree.

"Olá, Dzovig!" he says.

She waves, but Francisco isn't satisfied with this. He leaves the table and joins her on the edge of the terrace.

"É bonito, não é?"

"Beautiful, yes," she replies.

Francisco nods. He tries to explain something to her, something to do with the Moors, but her Portuguese is not good enough. Then he asks her about Armenia. Is it beautiful? He wants to know.

Dzovig turns to the men at the table, signalling that he should get back to his game. Francisco shakes his head.

"There's no hurry," he says. And then they are silent, together, on the edge of the terrace, as if they are waiting for something.

Francisco begins to speak. He gestures with his arms, drawing waves into the air with his hands and then pretending to swim across the terrace. The men from the table laugh. She still can't understand exactly what he means. Finally, exasperated, Francisco finds a piece of paper and begins to draw, first a train, and then a beach. At opposite ends of the train he writes two names, *Cais do Sodré* and *Cascais*. He points to the second name and then to Dzovig.

"A Dzovig precisa de praia," he says. His look is serious. "Dzovig needs beach."

VI

VECIHE

I left the house early this morning, hoping the wait would be shorter. I wanted some good lamb, and cheese. The man in front of me kept spitting on the pavement, and each time he did this the girl in front of him turned around, a worried look on her face. I almost asked her if she wanted to change places with me, who knows what kind of revolution that would have started? Our newfound sense of courtesy has been very short-lived, after all. People are still marvelling that no crimes were committed in Yerevan in February, during the demonstrations.

I've come away with lamb and yogurt. It has taken three hours. The yogurt is like water, so different from the kind we ate in Odzun, which was thick and opaque. *Madzoon*. When my mother said it, it sounded like the name of a loved one. She used to mix it with chopped mint and spread it on the *lavash* as if it were butter. It was heaven.

In Odzun we had no lines. This is what strikes me when I see young people now, like that girl, so much of their time spent waiting. Back then we worked for what we needed, even though we worked for the *kolkhoz*. We grew our food, we traded at the market, made things. It didn't occur to us to want what we didn't have. But there is something about standing in a line that fills you with wanting.

Classes have been boycotted at the university again this week, the one thing the students can still do now that the demonstrations have been banned. The soldiers still stand around Theatre Square, stiff, like miniature dolls stuck on a board. Apart from this, Moscow has given us, has given Karabagh, nothing.

Tomas and Dzovig have been going off together, looking at more churches. I don't give Bedros many details about these excursions; I know he disapproves of them, is irritated by them. I remember when Tomas used to draw pictures of churches as a boy, the buildings looked animated. Once he drew a church in mid-air, in flight. He said it had a motor for travelling. His fascination with them seemed so innocuous, then, so charming— what a bright boy we had, we thought.

How do you discern at what point an interest becomes obsessive? Tomas would say the unobsessed never accomplish anything, and maybe he is right. But I worry about him.

I was almost relieved, last month, when I saw him in the square, the look on his face, as if he'd been offered an unexpected chance, the chance to fight for something real, to be young, with others like him. To be joyous. He came home looking euphoric, full of arguments for his father, they were good arguments, *good*, I kept thinking. But he has been quiet again, lately, and I don't know whether he is simply waiting to see what the demonstrations have accomplished, or whether he has given up.

I worry about Dzovig travelling like this with Tomas, something that would have been unthinkable in my time. I told her, one afternoon, to be careful. You don't want to get pregnant, I said. She said it was very hard to find condoms. And then she told me of girls she knew, from school, who were having their virginity surgically restored before they got married. Some doctors are making a lot of money. Can you believe it? she said. I could believe that, and worse. We laughed about it, a little. Sometimes that is all you can do. The men in this country are as backwards as the politics, I told her.

I spent the next day travelling across the city. I found four boxes of condoms and paid a ridiculous sum for them. I placed them on Tomas's bed. He must have been taken by surprise; he said nothing at first. Later he grudgingly thanked me.

"I got them as much for Dzovig's sake as I did for yours," I told him.

"I'm not an idiot, Mama," he said.

Bedros doesn't know. He's meeting Dzovig tonight, for the first time. I've told him about her, prepared him.

"Something ordinary, finally," Bedros said.

"She isn't ordinary," I said. "She's not a flower, Bedros."

"That isn't what I meant," he said.

I know. I know this isn't what he meant.

I've found some good coffee. Lamb. Yogurt. I'll make stuffed vine leaves. Dzovig says that my cooking is very different from her mother's, but apart from this she has said little about her family. She has a sister, I believe. I asked her once if her parents would like to come for a visit, but she replied that her mother hadn't left the apartment in years, except to go to church. I wonder who shops for their food. I wonder about them. I would like to know from whom she inherits her green eyes.

Today, I didn't paint. The luxury of that thought feels so foreign to me still. To think of painting at all. I put that craving away so carefully, for so long, like a vow a nun would make, give up the incalculable. She would forget, over time, to crave a man's arms around her, a man's body, his smell. Forget a first love, the wet lips of a boy, that first taste of someone else's mouth. *I* would forget. Urges that, after a while, appear only in dreams. You wake from them with a vague memory of what it feels like to be truly alive.

I do remember one afternoon, though, a freezing, wet day in December. Tomas was two. He had been cranky for hours, and in desperation I had taken him out for a walk along Mashtots Avenue, walking towards the square. I didn't have a carriage then, we'd been on a list for one since his birth. (Some things even a bribe would not get you.) I carried Tomas for much of the way, pointing things out, trying to distract him. It was raining. Within an hour or two the sky would be black. I thought the fountains on the square—we still called it Lenin Square then—would make him happy, give us something to look at. They were still on; sprays of mist hung in the air in front of us, like a white curtain, moving, in the wind. Tomas was cold. I put him down but he kept pulling at me, his arms around my leg. I just stared at the fountains with the rain on my face. I must have looked strange, because an old man walked by and said "Ah, these winter afternoons are long for the children and long for the mothers."

I lifted Tomas up and took him home, made our dinner, put him to bed. You're very quiet, Bedros said. I kept thinking of the kind man's words with a strange sort of regret, as if I had been given an offering that I had failed to take advantage of. His words had turned me inside out. And then I realized that what I'd been longing for as I stood there, facing the fountains, was to paint, to paint the tiny drops of water in the delicate arch they made, a frozen filigree in the winter air. I wanted to remember that there was some beauty around me in this grey city.

Still, I didn't paint. By the time Tomas was in school all I wanted to do was leave the house. There was too much silence around me. When Bedros came home from work, late in the day, he seemed spent, wanting only quiet. Looking at it now I suppose I could blame him for not encouraging me, for not pushing me to paint. For not remembering. Sins of omission. I do not blame him. What use is blame, even towards one's self?

I went to work at the textile factory when Tomas was six. I joined the hardworking masses like a faithful proletarian. It felt good to earn some money, measly as it was, to hear other human voices around me, all of us complaining about the same things. I thought it would be temporary, that I would stay for just a short while. I stayed for twelve years. It's funny how some epochs in one's life often begin this way, as an interim measure, a second choice.

I was the thread lady. I placed spools of thread on the machines and watched them, making sure they were aligned. I could do it in my sleep after a while. Watch the threads through closed eyes. That was what I did. It never occurred to them to rotate our positions, to assign different tasks. Efficiency was not the issue. Bore us into submission, I suppose that was the aim. And perhaps they succeeded, because I stayed. After a while you do only what is safe, what you think you know. It was easier. All the same I was tired, working, going to collect Tomas after school, waking before dawn in order to beat the

queues for bread and milk. Waiting for Bedros to get home.
Waiting for a winter coat, a pair of new shoes. Cooking dinner
when the light outside the window was a sheet of black. Sometimes I bought flowers from one of the vendors outside the
subway station.

It's been two years since I left the factory. I was sitting in
the kitchen that morning, Tomas had already gone for the day.
Bedros was surprised to see me; I usually left for work before he
did. I'm not going to work at the factory anymore, I told him.
He said he was happy for me. That was all. Not a single question.
Sometimes, silence is the worst form of accusation.

That morning, I wandered throughout the house. I was
full of projects, I would clean this and that, repair some cracks
in the plaster, open some windows. It was spring. I was going
to paint again. I did some laundry, and then I fished out my
old watercolour box from the bottom of a cabinet, a place
where I kept a jumble of things, things I could no longer look at
but could not bear to throw away. Tomas's first shoes. A sack
made of jute. A yellow ribbon I had found in the house. A hair
ribbon.

The box was covered in a film of dust and the lid had
cracked. I passed my fingers over the word, *Aquarelles*, tracing a
brushstroke through the dust. There was very little paint left
inside. The cakes had worn away like dried up puddles, but the
colours hadn't faded, miraculously. The gold cake, practically
new.

I hadn't used the paints since I left Odzun.

I looked for some coloured pencils among Tomas's old toys.
The first picture I drew was a picture of lines, hundreds of lines
in all colours crisscrossing the page like the hundreds of threads

I had watched over the years, piercing the surface of my eyes like a million tiny needles. I drew those lines over and over, for weeks. And then I was able to paint.

We sit at the table, the four of us, like a tidy family, a little bit prim, more formal than we would be if Dzovig weren't here. Bedros is his quiet self, reserved around strangers, but Dzovig isn't afraid of him. She looks at him with open eyes, answers all his questions. She smiles at me as if to say that she understands, that we are all new at this. Tomas seems more nervous than usual, gulping down his food.

After dinner Bedros brings out a bottle of vodka, an offering. That's when Tomas makes his little announcement.

"We're thinking of taking a trip to Odzun, Mama, at the end of the month."

He's softening the blow, not addressing his father directly. He knows that sooner or later Bedros will have it out with him regarding these trips.

Odzun. A wave of dread washes over me when he says that word.

"It will take you days and days, Tomas. I don't know why you want to go so far."

"I want to see the basilica there, and we can see Haghartsin—"

"What about school?" Bedros says.

"What about school? For all we know there will still be a boycott."

"The boycott will be over in a few days."

"How do you know, did you get some secret information, Father? In any event, what difference does it make, boycott or not, nothing has changed. The Central Committee have handed out their little package of reforms for Karabagh, they'll repair a few roads, build a hospital or two and oh, my favourite, restore some ancient treasures of Armenian culture! That's what we got for Karabagh."

"Look at you, Tomas, disillusioned so quickly. Did you think you would change the order of things with a few weeks of demonstrations? You are like all those intellectuals, spitting out words with nowhere to put them. Did you think all this, all that went on was only about Karabagh? That people would stand there in the square, risk their jobs, out of simple solidarity with the Armenians in Karabagh? Are you that stupid?"

"Yes, I believed it. I think they did. I was there, remember?"

"Well, you're wrong. They were there because for seventy years they haven't had enough food on the supermarket shelves, because the air they breathe smells like a toxic dump, because the Medzamor power station could blow up at any minute, because the government officials are all busy fucking themselves and because for the first time people can say something about it! But in Armenia, we don't know how to say that we want democracy. The lost land, that's what we understand. That's what we have in Karabagh, that above everything else."

"What we have in Karabagh are the dead of Sumgait," Tomas says.

"Yes, another genocide, something to imprint on our skulls—"

"Which side are you on? You walked around like a good government official on the twenty-sixth, when everyone else stayed home in protest. What do you want, exactly?"

"I want you to do something useful with your life."

"If I wanted to be useful I would be in Karabagh right now, with a gun in my hands. But I'm doing what you asked me to do, Father. Isn't that what you've paid for, thousands of rubles in bribes so that I could get into architecture? How could I let all that go to waste?"

"I don't want *you* to go to waste, Tomas."

"Like you have?"

Bedros stares at Tomas and he looks infinitely tired. His voice is very low.

"You think I am a hypocrite, don't you? Does that surprise you? It shouldn't. One day you'll find that you have to make a choice. We all make it. You choose between fighting and living, because you can't go on fighting forever, fighting the system, the wars, the bloody history that you can do nothing about. And then you find out that you can still function, still breathe, and that what you want more than being happy is to go on breathing, to keep your children breathing. One day you'll have to make that choice, Tomas, and I wish you luck."

Bedros turns and leaves the room. Tomas stares at the table and says, softly, "Maybe I already have, Father."

Dzovig takes my hand in hers. She has been silent through it all. I am shaking. Tomas is biting the inside of his cheek.

"You never talk about Odzun, you know that? About my grandmother. I could have met her when she was alive, if you had told me about her. Why didn't you?"

"I thought it was the basilica you were interested in," I tell him.

"We're going, that's all."

"When are you leaving?" I ask him.

"I don't know, Mama."

"Will you be here on the twenty-fourth, at least?"

"I don't know."

"You know these churches, Tomas, these stone churches with their black interiors, these ruins that you love so much, they were full of colour when they were built. They were blasting with colour, Tomas!"

VII

MIGUEL

Dzovig doesn't go to the beach. She works at the Alcobaça seven days a week, from noon until closing time. After Francisco leaves, she lies on her bed and waits for sleep, and it comes quickly to her now, the deep, pure sleep of physical fatigue, a welcome coma.

"Everybody needs a day of rest, Dzovig," Gordinho says. "The customers are going to get tired of seeing you all the time, I don't care how pretty you are."

"It's all right, Mr. Gordon," she says.

Meanwhile, the coins and *escudo* bills accumulate in a cardboard box that Dzovig now keeps in her room. She uses some of the money to buy clothes at the Feira da Ladra, an outdoor market on the edge of the Alfama with stalls spread out under a canopy of trees. She feels more at ease in the market. The abundance of shops in Lisbon has ceased to be a novelty for her, though she is still not comfortable enough to enter most of them, feeling somewhat illicit when she does. She remembers her arrival in Paris, hours after leaving Moscow, millions of white lights beneath the plane and then the airport, like an internal city, and the smells and colours of shops and coffee shops assaulting her with all the violence of an exquisite and frightening dream.

At the market she buys a pair of denim pants, some shirts and two short dresses, all of them used. On one side of the market, women are selling old lace tablecloths and linens. They hang them from clotheslines strung between trees. At the opposite end, a few stalls sell African jewellery and statuary. One man, a tall African with smooth skin and long black tresses, has come to recognize Dzovig from her walks through the neighbourhood.

"*Linda*," he calls her; "Beautiful."

One day he gives her a necklace as a gift, dark wooden beads strung on a leather cord.

"Come to my *Taverna*, tonight, Rua do Paraíso."

"I have to work," she says.

"Where? Where do you work?"

But she has already walked on.

At the Alcobaça, the customers already know her.

"Olà, Dzovig," they say.

It has become a secret contest between Gordinho and some of the regulars to see who can make Dzovig smile first. Francisco is the only one who comes close, though he isn't in on the bet.

Francisco has a running dialogue with his bird:

"*Ai, Balthazar, esta menina, esta menina*...This girl, this girl... She's a good girl. She doesn't talk much. I know she's pale. What do you think, I haven't noticed? Sea air, to open up the lungs, I know...She needs a bit of sun on her face."

And then he begins to sing, something about a girl named Carolina who has a painted dragon on her skirt. Look out, Carolina, the dragon wags its tail...

"There's work to do around here," Rosa says to him.

She and Dzovig have evolved a kind of relationship, working the small and crowded dining room without ever colliding with each other. Rosa instructs, Dzovig learns. *Bom dia*, every morning, and sometimes, even, *Como estás?*

"Like mother and daughter," Gordinho says.

"Cala a boca," Rosa says: "Shut your mouth."

And yet, within a few months, Dzovig begins to find warm bread, every morning, left on the marble counter of the kitchen on a plate, after Rosa has dropped off the morning's fish. The bread is soft and thick in Portugal. Dzovig sinks her teeth into it. *Would you like something to eat, Dzovig? I've been baking—* That's what Vecihe had said, on the day she had met her. *She's a great cook*, Tomas had said. The Portuguese dip their bread in sauces, wipe their plates clean with it, use it as an utensil even, but never wrap their food in it.

The bread of Armenia: *Lavash*, thin as paper, or else loaves that crumble in your fist, like sawdust.

Late one morning a man arrives at the restaurant. Rosa has just unlocked the door, it is noon, still early for lunch, in Lisbon. The man takes a few minutes to decide which table he will sit at and Rosa grows impatient with him. In the kitchen she tells Dzovig, "You have a customer."

"Bom dia," the man says. He has removed his hat.

"Bom dia."

He orders a glass of red wine, waits until Dzovig has brought it before turning his attention to the menu. There is something very meticulous about every gesture that he makes.

"What are the specialties of the house?"

"Everything is a specialty here," she says.

"Ah, that makes things difficult. You must have a personal favourite, I suppose. What would you recommend?"

"I like the *Pargo*." His head is shaped like a perfect egg, she thinks. The front half of it is bald.

"Do you have tripe, by any chance?"

"Tripe? I don't think so."

"Are you absolutely certain?"

"Yes. We don't have it."

"Tripe Oporto, it's one of my favourite dishes. But one has to be in the mood for it. And it must be eaten hot."

"Hot?"

"Yes. It's impossible, otherwise."

"Would you like more time?" she asks him.

The man caresses his narrow moustache with his fingers. He doesn't look Portuguese at all. He looks a little like Charlie Chaplin, or Hitler.

"It is early. Yes, I think I would like more time."

Dzovig returns to the kitchen and fills small bowls with black olives, preparing to place one on each table. When she returns to the dining room the man has gone, leaving behind a neat stack of coins for his wine.

"Why do you? Why do they mean so much to you, Tomas?"

She was asking about the churches.

"Because they are all that's left."

"Of what?"

"No one knows about Armenian churches. Do you think they study us, there in the West, in Moscow even? And those who *have* studied us have got it wrong. They're all after their doctorates—"

"Not like you?" She smiled at him.

"Look." He tore a page out of a notebook and drew her a picture. They were sitting in a field outside the church of Saint Hrip'simé. "The central-plan churches are a mystery. They just appear in the seventh century, we don't know from where. They have no ancestry in Armenia or any of the bordering countries. So, the experts decide, Byzantium. That this type of church was already common in the Byzantine provinces and capital. But Armenian and Byzantine churches are totally different! Totally! In Armenia, everything is cramped, held in. Heavy with mass. I think that it was the other way around."

"You're not the first to think that."

"No, but maybe I'll be the first to prove it."

"Isn't it possible that different peoples could make simultaneous discoveries?"

"No. People always copy. Look at Hitler."

"I thought we were talking about architecture."

"Have you ever tried to find the name Armenia on a Turkish map, Dzovig? All those towns, cities, all their names have been changed. They never existed! Do you know how many of our churches were destroyed between 1915 and 1922 by the Turks? More than a thousand. There was a war, everything gets destroyed, I know all that, but what of the buildings that are left?"

"You mean Ani, don't you."

"Dzovig, the cathedral at Ani is a masterpiece of world architecture and what do we know about it? That Trdat, the architect, was called in to repair the dome of St-Sophia in Constantinople, *that's* what we know! The city of a thousand and one churches crumbling in the Turkish desert. No one is allowed to study it, protect it. Ani is like Rome, Jerusalem, it's an eternal city. They've reattributed all our buildings...The cathedral of Aght'amar is now built by the Seljuk Turks, even though these people didn't even exist at the time of its construction!"

"Tomas, you can't unmake history."

"Yes, you can. What is happening to our churches on Turkish territory is the continuation of history. It's destruction by neglect. Once they are gone there will be no trace left—it'll be complete silence."

"It's their silence, not ours, Tomas. Everything's changing, we were there together, in the square—"

"At first I thought it was, I really believed it, Dzovig. Not now. What will the Soviets do with Sumgait? That little package of dead bodies? Do you think we'll ever really hear that story, what really happened?"

"What do you want to do, Tomas?"

"You're sounding like my father. I want to see Ani. See it before it disappears completely."

"It's probably very difficult to get across the border, you know that. "

"I'll get in. I have no choice."

"Don't you think that happiness is a choice?"

"Those churches were built for Armenia by Armenians. No one told us to build them."

"So what?"

"*That* was our choice. That was when Armenia had a choice."

"Nothing you do can change it, Tomas."

"That's right."

"We're alive, aren't we?"

"Count yourself lucky."

When he spoke to her like this, Dzovig fell silent. The words spilled out of Tomas's mouth and, because she loved him, she said very little. She told herself that it would pass, that eventually her love would resuscitate him. She often imagined, when they were making love, that she could see a cross-section of his body entering hers, see through the web of blood vessels and muscle and bone how he fit into her, into her body.

At home, when she slept away from him, she clung to an old shirt of his as if to a dead child's.

In the second week of August, Gordinho closes the restaurant.

"Holidays," he explains. "It's too hot to be working. We'll reopen on the twenty-first."

Dzovig doesn't like the idea. "But all the tourists, we are so busy now, Mr. Gordon."

"I do it every year, Dzovig. Don't worry, they know when to come back. You'll have two weeks to enjoy yourself, without the witch looking over you." He rolls his eyes towards Rosa. "I can trust you with the keys, can't I?"

"Yes. I think so."

"No parties in the place, right?"

"No."

"You'll still be here when I get back, won't you, Dzovig?"

"Yes."

"Right, then. Rosa will be in Beira, she has family up there, but Francisco might drop in from time to time, he gets homesick for his kitchen. He knows where to reach me if there's any trouble."

"Where will you be?"

"I'm going home. England, I mean," he says. "Can't avoid it, you know, even if I wanted to."

Dzovig shrugs.

Later, before Rosa leaves, she says to Dzovig, "Boas férias," happy holidays, and kisses her on both cheeks without meeting her eyes. It is the first time Dzovig has felt a woman's skin touch hers, since Armenia.

The next morning, the Alcobaça feels strangely quiet. She wakes up at the usual time, even though Rosa has not come by to drop off fish, or bread. She showers in the small bathroom and makes herself a coffee in the kitchen. There is some bread and cheese left over from yesterday. In the dining room the curtains are drawn and all the tablecloths have been removed. Dzovig stands there for a few moments, passing her hands over the rims of chairs. She is nervous. It seems pointless to go out walking. She makes her bed. There is a film of dust on her bedside table and she wipes it clean with a rag from the kitchen. There are other things she could clean. A whole restaurant of things, in fact.

Dzovig pulls up her sleeves, draws open one of the curtains. Begins.

It keeps her busy for four days. She doesn't sleep very much. She scrubs every surface of the restaurant, walls, floors, counter tops. She oils every table and chair until the wood gleams. On the shelves behind the counter she dusts every bottle and glass, replaces every candle. She wipes clean the yellow bulbs that hang from the ceiling and scrubs the grout between tiles with a toothbrush and some bleach. The pantry takes her longest: removing every can of tomatoes or jar of dried spices, clearing bits of onion skins that have gathered in the corners of shelves like forgotten chrysalises. She polishes the marble counter of the kitchen with a special cream bought from a man in a corner store; after hours of rubbing a flannel cloth on it, in circles, it shines like the surface of a pool. She even takes down the curtains, when there is nothing left to do, and carries them in a bundle to Dona Lucinda's tiny house next door. Dona Lucinda has a washing machine and smiles widely. "Por amor de Deus!" she says, ushering Dzovig in. Together they stuff the washing machine and, while it washes, Dona Lucinda feeds her. "You're so skinny, *filha*," she says. In Portugal, every girl is a daughter.

Dzovig takes the curtains back when they are still damp, along with an iron she has borrowed. It takes her a while to get the hang of it, but by the end of the day the curtains are hung again, looking new and a little stiff. It is past ten o'clock when she has finished. Still too early for sleep. She sits on her bed thinking *I am tired, I am tired*, willing her body to go soft. She picks up her *Teach Yourself Portuguese*, even though she knows most of it by heart now, and reviews the last chapters, speaking aloud in her room. And then she reads another book, *What the Tourist Should See* by a man named Fernando Pessoa, a book she picked up at the Feira da Ladra for reading practice. It is a guide to the sights of Lisbon, complete with map.

At midnight she turns off the light. It is hot in her room and she can't get comfortable. She hears the voices of people walking in the street, sounds she has never noticed before. The restaurant smells of wax and polish and bleach. There is a tightness behind her eyes, a feeling she remembers from that night in February, walking the streets of Yerevan with Tomas. She is very tired, too tired for sleep.

Dzovig gets up with a sudden resolve, as if she were late for an appointment, and slips on a pair of jeans and a blouse. She goes out walking. There are lights in many windows still, and music pouring out onto the streets from bars and *fado* restaurants. Smells of cooking and smoke, the tips of cigarettes tracing squiggles of light through the darkness. She remembers the name now, Rua do Paraíso. She has to ask a few people for directions before finding it. It is quieter in this corner of the Alfama, there are fewer cafés. Towards the far end of the street she spots the word *Taverna*, a small sign in blue neon hung above a door.

It is a basement room. There are no tourists here, she can tell. A few people turn their heads when she enters, but their expression is one of curiosity, not of unwelcome. She stands there, by the door, waiting to see if he is around, the man from the stall who gave her a necklace and called her *linda*. She doesn't know his name. And then he appears from behind a door with a trio of glasses in his hand.

"So, you found me after all. Rua do Paraíso, you remembered!"

"Yes."

"Come in, come in. I'm so glad to see you!"

He holds her hand and sits her at a table. He signals to the bar and another man brings over a bottle and some olives.

"Now, you're going to have to tell me your name," he says.

"Dzovig. And you?"

"Miguel. It's not an African name, is it? We've been using Portuguese names for centuries, now. We're not a black country anymore."

"Your country?"

"Portugal, now. I was born in Mozambique. Dzovig—it's a strange name—where are you from?"

"Nowhere."

"Ah, I know the place well. Lots of beautiful women come from there."

He wraps his hands around a glass and takes slow gulps of wine, sways his shoulders a little in time to the music that's playing. His fingers are very long, perfect white ovals beneath his nails. His hair is long too; it falls in strange ringlets about his shoulders, some strands tied in a knot behind his back, holding the rest of his hair clear from his face. She has never seen hair like this before. His eyes are lighter than expected, a strange sort of yellow.

"Where do you work, Dzovig from nowhere?"

"I work in a restaurant," she says. "Where do you live?"

He laughs. "Here. I live here. Like I told you, this is my place."

"Where do you sleep?"

He looks at her now, waiting to see if she is serious. Dzovig doesn't blink.

She follows him up the stairs to a room at the back of the second floor. There are clothes and rugs and pillows everywhere, bowls filled with beads and some of the carvings she has seen at the market. It is very dark. He lights a small lamp and the shadows it casts are huge. The bed, a set of mattresses on the floor, is unmade.

"Do you want to smoke something?" he asks.

"No."

She takes off her blouse and starts to unbutton the front of her jeans. Her face has no expression. He holds her by the wrists and whispers, "Wait, what's the hurry?" He still doesn't quite believe it. She wants to undress and lie on the mattress and she wants him to fuck her, that's all, fuck her without thinking, quickly, fuck her to oblivion. But he has his own ideas, he won't be rushed through this. He runs his face against her neck, inhaling, and his lips are soft, large and soft and open on her skin as if the length of his kisses could hold her there, keep her from vanishing. He runs his hands along her arms, her legs, the curve of her waist, but it is with his mouth that he takes her, he wants to taste every inch of her. She keeps pulling at his shoulders, she wants him on top of her, she wants to be pounded. She hadn't planned on tenderness. And then before she can stop it she is coming, pressing his head between her thighs and falling, falling through her own body and his.

She cries out. He places his wide hands around her face and feels a dampness on her temples, her hair. He would enter her now, have his own turn, except that he can't. She looks very small on his bed. Instead, he turns out the light and covers her, and Dzovig sleeps.

The sun is already high when she wakes up. It must be close to noon, she thinks. She notices that her skin smells different. Miguel is sleeping beside her.

She gets off the bed and begins to dress, making no attempt to be quiet. He opens his eyes and pulls himself up on one elbow.

"It was very good," she says. "Thank you."

"Come back and see me?"

"I will."

He gives her a smile, even though he knows she is lying.

On her walk home, Dzovig stops for breakfast. She is very hungry and eats standing at the counter in the *Pastelaria*, as the Portuguese do. It is when she is reaching in her pocket for money that she finds it, the crumpled piece of paper with Francisco's drawing of a train on it and the names of two stations. Dzovig smiles. Beach.

The water in Cascais is blue, bluer than the Tagus, almost as blue as the lake at Sevan, except that there are no clouds. There are several beaches, a string of bays curling along the edge of the land. One beach is covered in fishing boats. Men in overalls and sweaters are untangling fishing nets there. Other beaches are populated with tourists or locals, mothers chasing after children with offerings of food, and girls in bikinis and half-bikinis, sunning themselves. The sand feels very foreign to her, thick and soft against her heels. She carries in her bag a small towel from the bathroom at the Alcobaça. She doesn't own a bathing suit.

At the far end of one beach is a small cove, a hollow in the cliff where the ocean pools. There is no sand there, only the sea and the walls of rock above it. A few boys are swimming, jumping into the water from boulders along the sides of the cove. The boys are squealing with laughter.

Dzovig takes off her dress and leaves it on a rock beside her bag. She is wearing panties, nothing else. The water is very cold, a thousand needles are hitting her skin and she sinks her head in. There is a silence beneath the waves, a silence she would keep, if she didn't have to breathe.

VIII

VECIHE

In the winter that I turned thirteen a young man came to live in Odzun. Mida was the first one to tell me about him. He had come all the way from Yerevan, she said, no one knew why. He was working in the *kolkhoz* as a farm hand.

Mida was excited. She had stopped going to school over a year ago and thoughts of marriage kept her busy. Her father hadn't said anything to her. Perhaps he hadn't chosen yet. She could refuse a man she didn't like, in any case. It was 1951 and the government had said so years before. In the city, we had heard, girls and boys could choose one another without their parents' help, but not in Odzun. Mr. Hagopian was a powerful man, he could take his time deciding for her. And while she embroidered the linens that would make up her dowry, closed off in a room with her mother, she dreamed. A stranger was as glamorous as a prince in a fairy tale, it didn't matter who he was. He was new. He was very tall, she said.

I didn't really care. I had started bleeding a few months before and I felt strange, reclusive, as if I'd been wounded by some strange fault of my own. I had first noticed the blood on an afternoon as I was walking home from the grove, a dark trickle running down my thigh.

"It will happen every month," my mother said.

She wasn't surprised, although she hadn't warned me about it. She had noticed, I suppose, the changes in my body, two small lumps on my chest that felt like olive pits under the skin. The hair on my arms had begun to darken, and on my head, mysteriously, it had started to curl.

My mother gave me a set of square cloths and a pin, and showed me how to fold them. "You can have children now," she said; "don't go looking any boys in the eye."

I wasn't quite sure what she meant. I had seen animals being born on the farm, the blood and liquids that spilled out of them, dogs mating in the fields. For a while I was afraid, every month, when I felt that strange pull at the bottom of my stomach: I thought that men would be drawn to me like animals chasing a scent. I was too ashamed to let my mother see my soiled napkins and so I took them to a stream near the gorge, in secret, and pressed them against the rocks, watching as the clouds of red dissolved in the water. Sometimes, when I was sure that no one's eyes could see me, I would lift up my skirt and splash water between my legs. I wouldn't have defiled the stream, like that, if I hadn't hoped that it would somehow stop the bleeding. It never did.

Unlike Mida, I still went to school during the winter months, although my mother wouldn't properly explain to me why my going there was such a necessity. I resented her for it, feeling as though she was inflicting on me yet another condition that would single me out among the other girls in the village, even though several of them still attended. But I would never dare question her on the issue. I knew this to be one of her unfaltering and deliberate decisions, a decision that carried the weight of a past so mysterious and horrific that to question it would be inconceivable.

She had found me one morning, the previous spring, planting cabbages beside the house.

"Why are you not in school, Vecihe?"

It was Mida's mother, Mrs. Hagopian, who had told me to stay home. There were things to do and learn at the house, she had said. I had obeyed her the way any child would obey her elder. The children in Odzun had grown up under the communal eyes of all the adults in the village. We had each been punished, at one time or another, by whomever it was that had witnessed our crime. One didn't ask for permission to scold a child, in those days. I had even heard old Aghavnee once, reprimanding a band of boys who had gathered behind a barn. I had heard her high-pitched voice, shrill, a voice that made me cringe. I didn't quite catch what they had been up to, though I saw them disperse shortly afterwards.

The first thing I thought when Mrs. Hagopian told me to stay home was that she had discovered some of my napkins and decided it was best to keep me away from boys, although I did not tell my mother this.

"She told me that I was to stay and work" was all I said.

My mother stared at me for a moment, then dropped the basket of clothes she had been carrying and stormed off, strangely, in the direction of the village and not the house. I took the basket to our room and folded the clothes carefully inside it. I waited, not knowing what else to do.

When my mother returned, her eyes were blazing.

"Get your things, Vecihe, you are going to school," she said.

Her voice sounded strange, disembodied and cold, as though it didn't belong to her at all. I couldn't move. I thought that any movement I made would unleash something terrible, an anger she was holding back like a closed fist. An anger that came from far, far away.

I looked at her hands. They were trembling.

"What is it, Mama?"

"Be quiet and get your things! You will go to school, do you understand me?"

Suddenly I hated her.

"And if I don't, the Turk will come and get me?"

She hit me across the face. I'd only repeated what I had heard many times, a bluff the adults used as a threat to keep children from disobeying them.

"What do you know about the Turks, Vecihe? Nothing. You know *nothing*. But this is your life, not mine, not my life. You will go to school. You will have that."

My mother looked very tired then and I did as she said, gathered my things with the imprint of her hand still burning on my cheek. She was wrong. I did know something of the Turks. I knew of another place, a province, Erzurum, a place my mother had come from that now belonged to them. There was a silence around it, the old Armenia. Cities, towns, villages that were never spoken of by our parents. And yet we children had managed to gather something through the silence, a kind of certainty that a horrible injustice had been committed, even if we did not quite understand how or even exactly when. Only that it had been committed by them, the Turks. And so, with all of my thirteen years of hating them without quite knowing why I concluded that my mother had been in school once, in a school she loved, in the old Armenia, and that because of them she had been forced to leave it, and march into the desert.

That night I heard yelling in the house. Mr. Hagopian's voice, and his wife's. Not my mother's. The next day I returned to school.

He was tall. He was standing outside the church when I saw him, leaning against the burial monument on the west side of the building. He had a long blade of grass in his mouth. I noticed, as I drew closer, that his hair was light and, forgetting to look away, I saw a flash of blue, his eyes. My mother had spoken of such people, once. Entire villages in the mountains between Odzun and Sevan, where all the children had golden hair and blue eyes. Perhaps he came from there, and not Yerevan, as Mida had said.

"He must have been up to no good, that's why he's here."

It was Hrach, Mida's brother. He had come up behind me.

"How do you know?"

"It's obvious."

"No, it isn't."

Hrach had grown up too. At eleven he looked like a miniature version of his father, thin and wiry, with an old look in his dark eyes. We often walked to school together, like siblings, though he had begun to spend more time with Mr. Hagopian on the farm. And he'd begun to sound like his father, with a gruff sort of kindness in his voice.

"Perhaps he's come looking for a wife," Hrach said.

"Don't they have wives in Yerevan?" I felt very clever.

"How do you know? You've never been there!"

"Neither have you, Hrach!"

"My father goes there all the time," he said.

"You'd better ask him, then."

"All I meant was, if I were a girl, I would not marry him, that is all."

I vaguely understood, now, that Mr. Hagopian worked for the government. His large house, the house where I lived with my mother, had once belonged to the *tanouter*, the village headman, who with his family had virtually disappeared from the village some twenty years before, I didn't know how. I guessed that it had something to do with the collectives, with Stalin. I'd heard people talking in whispers about families who had been deported because of their refusal to join the collectives, of the slaughter of animals on family farms, people who had killed their livestock rather than give them to the communists. Whispering about Trotskyites. I didn't know who they were—Hrach had said once that they were men who didn't follow the rules—though I suspected that Mr. Hagopian did, and that he knew how to avoid them. He spoke Russian very well. He often seemed infinitely tired. He had stayed in Odzun when many of the men had gone to fight in the war. A poster hung in the village then telling us that we needed to fight for freedom. The whole world was at war for the second time. I remembered that time because one day the government had suddenly opened the church, and a priest had come to the village and stayed. Stalin liked our priests again, that's what someone said.

From time to time Mr. Hagopian would ask me how my painting was coming along and request to see one of my pictures. I was always worried that he would keep them, confiscate them for some obscure reason, but he never did. Once, I showed him the portrait of a woman that I had drawn, an old woman, her back like a hook. To my relief he hadn't recognized her, though he seemed strangely saddened.

"Being an artist is not an easy profession in this country," he offered. And then, as if in answer to a question he had posed himself, he said: "But it's not as if you have a choice, is it?"

I assumed that Hrach would follow in Mr. Hagopian's footsteps. Whomever Hrach married would join the household as the young wife, better than a servant. My mother explained that in her own mother's time a junior wife would have remained silent in her new household until the birth of her first child, and sometimes for years beyond that. She would be permitted to speak directly only to the children, and sometimes through them, when addressing an older member of the family. She washed the men's feet. It was only with the successive dying of the elders and birthing of the children that she gradually earned the right to speak.

There were no servants now. Everyone was equal. We were told this in school, and even women went to work in the cities, in the factories, leaving their children in state nurseries. But my mother still cooked and cleaned in the Hagopian house, where I slept with her in a room at the back. We were very lucky, she said. Many years before the government had allocated two square metres of living space per person. The same as for a grave, she said. Look at us, how fortunate we were. Things were very different now. Still, I thought, Hrach's future wife would be a step above a servant. A step, really, above my mother. Mida would leave. So, presumably, would I.

I had asked my mother once if she would come and live with me when I married.

"Don't be ridiculous," she said, "you know that a daughter needs to leave her mother."

I could have asked her then, about her own mother and how she had left her. About the family I might have had. About my father. But I didn't dare. All the same I resented her for my own ignorance, just as I feared leaving her in that house, alone with Mida's mother.

"If a house has two mistresses," I said, "the floor will not be swept." This is what I had heard a woman say in the market one morning, and I had assumed, with a stubborn certainty, that she had been talking about my mother and Mrs. Hagopian.

My mother turned towards me with a puzzled look on her face.

"Have you ever noticed the floor in this house to be dirty, Vecihe?"

I felt ashamed. "No," I said.

"If you are endowed with intelligence, Vecihe, I suggest you keep it to yourself."

I didn't see the stranger again until the day after Easter. My mother had stuck seven feathers into an onion, one for each week of Lent, and I knew as I watched her pull them out that soon the stones in the fields would grow warm from the sun. Spring in Odzun made it easy to believe in miracles.

Many visitors would come to the house at Easter, bringing sweets, nuts, eggs. We all wore our best clothes, freshly cleaned and pressed. One of Mrs. Hagopian's embroidered tablecloths would be spread out in the dining room. My mother worked hard. She seemed more tired than usual lately, moving about with a lassitude that was unlike her. Mida and I helped with the baking, standing side by side at one end of the kitchen table. My mother stood facing the stove, boiling eggs in onion skins until they were a deep red. From time to time she rubbed her hands over the back of her hips, as if trying to erase an ache there.

"Do you think he will come?" Mida asked.

I knew who she was talking about.

"How should I know!"

"My mother made me a dress."

"Does she want him to come too?" I was curious now.

"She didn't say anything about it."

"He has blue eyes," I told her, regretting my words almost the instant that I said them.

"When did you see him?"

"I don't remember, what does it matter!"

"Did you paint him?"

"Of course not!"

"If you did paint him would you give me the picture?"

"Stop it, Mida! I'm going to tell your father!"

"Hrach said that he is twenty-three."

"That's old, Mida!"

We giggled. Mida's shoulders moved up and down when she laughed. She still had the same round cheeks she had had as a girl, and they flushed easily with happiness, excitement or anger. Her body had a softness to it, a roundness. If not for her cheeks she would have looked much older than she was.

Mida was far more accomplished in the kitchen than I was. Her small hands worked with an almost mechanical precision at chopping fruits or rolling out dough. When she worked she talked incessantly, about everything and everyone.

"Vartan and Elmas are engaged. Her mother is very ill, did you know that? They thought she would be in the ground by now. You're rolling it too thin, Vecihe. Look, like *this*. I don't think they make such a good match. Hasn't your mother taught

you anything? Is Mariam still in school? Did you see the stockings I made?"

"A man's stockings?" I asked.

Towards late afternoon Mida grew quiet. I was relieved, grateful
for some silence. We were walking towards the cellar when I
noticed something protruding from underneath her apron, but
I waited until we were alone, with the door closed behind us,
before asking her about it.

"What are you hiding?"

Her eyes glistened. She was bursting to tell me.

"It's for the stranger, the new one," she said.

"What is it?"

She pulled out a bottle of wine from a deep pocket in
her skirt.

"Mida, that's your father's."

"It's already half empty, no one will notice!"

I thought of the stolen napkin, embroidered with a cherry,
almost a rag now, on my tree.

"Notice what?" I said.

"If he comes tomorrow I'll pour this wine into his glass.
They say that it works, it really never fails."

"Mida, will you stop talking like an idiot!"

She looked at me then, standing completely still, and
as she spoke I could have sworn that I was six again, peeking
through a half-open door that she could slam in my face at the
slightest whim.

"I'll smash your paints against the rocks if you tell," she said.

I started to turn towards the stairs.

"Wait, Vecihe! I didn't mean it! Do you promise?"

I waited, but she didn't say anything. Instead, she reached up inside her skirt and pulled out a folded cloth. I recognized it immediately. White flannel, sodden with her blood, and to my horror and fascination I watched as she wrung several drops from it into the bottle.

Mida's day was a ruin. She didn't see him in church. Back at the house she was still hopeful, hovering near the door at the sign of any visitors, but by mid-afternoon her face had changed, all the anticipation drained from it.

"Mida is in one of her moods," Hrach said.

I kept my eyes on the floor, glancing when I could at the bottles of wine on top of the cabinet in the dining room, an uneasy accomplice. He didn't come, although the family he lived with, the Begian family, did.

Towards evening I relaxed a little. Most of the visitors had left. I could hear only the muffled voices of the men, drinking and smoking in the garden outside the house. I had almost forgotten about the wine when I passed by the dining-room door and saw Mida standing in front of the cabinet, polishing its surface with a cloth, the bottles gone. I didn't ask her about the wine. All the same she shrugged her shoulders and attempted a smile, as if she was resigned to the fact that a chance had been irretrievably lost.

In my room my mother was already asleep, one arm stretched out beneath her head, her palm open to the ceiling.

On the day following Easter, most of the families in the village gathered outside the church, in the graveyard. The women carried food and drink and, following prayers, we ate a meal among the graves. This was an old custom that had recently been put into practice again, since the end of the war. I had been to the church many times now, although I always felt ill at ease inside the basilica, its immense, darkened walls, the ceiling a distant blackness, a cold that hovered like something palpable, even in summer. Outside, it was a different building altogether, its stones golden, green mosses growing out of the clay roof, the peaks of the church and bell tower pointing to the sky. All around it was the purple haze of mountains; against them the church looked almost small. Safe, somehow. I felt it even then, the strange power that mountains have over us: the sensation, when you walk on them, of being more present on the earth.

The graveyard was on the north-eastern side of the church. That side of the building also had an arcade, a gallery whose horseshoe openings I had counted as a little girl. There were six, set between flat, square columns. Between the arches and the wall there were graves, what I thought of as the important graves, given their partial enclosure. As children we used to scamper over them, chasing each other while the adults ate. We hardly thought of them as graves at all, for in Odzun, as in all of Armenia, slabs of carved stone were more abundant than trees.

On that day we had been blessed with perfect weather, a warm wind. I sat with Mida and some of the other girls, not far from the older women. We ate little, knowing that the food we didn't consume would be left behind, on the graves, and that other families would come and retrieve it. They were not poor, really, there were no poor in Russia. I had caught a glimpse of old Aghavnee earlier that morning, circling the periphery of the church grounds, mumbling to herself, her head bent over her feet.

Hrach sat with his father. When I stood up with a jar of water in my hand and my paint set tucked under one arm he frowned in my direction. He was on the verge of yelling something at me when Mr. Hagopian smacked him on the side of the head.

Mida laughed. "Hrach is jealous," she said.

To my surprise she didn't ask to follow me. Perhaps she thought her chances of meeting the stranger would be greater if she stayed among the crowd. I didn't know yet what I was going to paint. I hadn't painted out of doors since the previous fall, but I still liked to do it in some seclusion, never having lost the slightly illicit feeling it gave me, as if my doing it were a privilege that could be snatched away.

On the west side of the church was a portal bordered with grapes and vine leaves. I sat down in front of it and began, vaguely aware at first of the sounds the villagers made close by, then falling into the growing stillness that always surrounded me when I painted, like a gift. It lasted until I sensed someone's approach and then heard the familiar, soft cackle.

"When the living look after the dead," she said, "God looks after the living."

Aghavnee. She had a half-eaten piece of bread in her hand, and nodded her head towards my picture.

"Yes," I said.

She seemed satisfied and walked on. And then I heard another voice, an unfamiliar one.

"You're the one who paints," he said. "I've heard about you."

"I've heard about you too," I said, trying to avert my eyes.

"You live at the Hagopian house, you and another girl."

"Mida. She is not my sister. Hrach is her brother."

He asked me my name, though I sensed that he knew it already. I was on the verge of asking him his when we heard screams, and I dropped all that I was holding and started running. There, making, his way between the graves, was Mr. Hagopian. He carried the limp body of a woman in his arms. My mother.

It took her several days to recover. No one would tell me exactly what had happened, only that she had fainted, that she needed rest. The village doctor came to see her, bringing a woman with him. An assistant, he called her.

I stayed home from school. The house was unusually quiet. I couldn't understand why everything suddenly felt permeated with shame. Even Mida said little as we worked about the kitchen, doing tasks that my mother normally performed. Mrs. Hagopian emerged from time to time to give instructions, sounding angry. She never looked at me directly.

My mother slept most of the time, her face drained of colour. Her hands, when I held them, felt cold. On the second day she opened her eyes.

"I will recover, Vecihe," she said. "You may go back to school tomorrow."

"I want to stay and help you, Mama."

"No."

Mida stood in the doorway to our room. "I'm here," she offered.

"I'm her daughter!" I said.

I stormed out of the house, furious. Instinctively I made my way to the grove, kicking at the dirt along the path. My heart was pounding. There, in the centre of the grove, I pressed my forehead against the tree until I could feel the rough bark indenting my skin.

"There was a lot of blood, you know."

I turned around. It was Hrach.

"There was blood on the stone where she was sitting, you can go see for yourself if you don't believe me."

"Get out of here!" I shouted. "Leave me alone!"

"I've seen you here before, you know! I know your little secret!"

I ran back to the house. I would ask my mother everything, I wouldn't leave her alone until she gave me an answer. Outside the orchard I saw Mr. Hagopian. He was walking across a field with a bundle in his hands. He didn't stop to greet me and I was glad of it.

Mida was standing outside the door.

"You look like you've seen the evil eye, Vecihe!"

She held a flat package in her hands.

"He was here, the stranger!" Her face was alight. "Look, he brought you this."

I untied the string, pulled back the brown paper. It was my paint set, the sheet I had been painting that morning carefully inserted under the lid.

I looked up.

"He said he found it outside the church," Mida said.

"Did he say what his name was?" I asked.

"Yes!" she said, as if she had won a prize. "Bedros. He said his name is Bedros!"

IX

TITO

Dzovig stays at the beach for the whole day. By mid-afternoon she notices that someone is watching her, a skinny man with the look of a boy about him. He sits at the top of the wall above the cove. There is something strange about the way he moves his body, as if he were staked to a pole that ran invisibly from his neck to his groin. He stares at her unashamedly, and after a while she begins to stare back. Towards evening she goes into the water once more, and coming up for air she sees that he has gone. She is almost disappointed. But he hasn't gone. He is waiting for her on the rock, by her bag.

"What do you want?" she asks.

The man says, "I want to go swimming with you."

"I've been swimming all day," she says. "It's getting cold."

"But you could take one more swim, couldn't you? I could use your help."

"Why?"

"Because I'm not good at swimming alone. It's dangerous for me."

Dzovig doesn't quite know what to say to him. He is holding onto the side of a giant boulder, steadying himself. He is very thin.

"What's your name?"

"Tito."

She hesitates a little. "What's wrong with you?"

"I have a muscular disease. Multiple sclerosis. A disease of the nervous system, actually. It started about ten years ago. It's not getting any better, or any worse. My body is a little fucked up, that's all. It doesn't hurt, in case you were worried. You, on the other hand, have great muscles. I've been watching you swim."

Dzovig begins to slip on her dress, suddenly self-conscious. "I know," she says.

Tito smiles at her with his eyes. "Come on, I won't do anything lewd, I promise. I just want to swim and I can't do it alone."

"What if I let you drown?"

"You won't. Can you help me with my shirt? That's it, just pull on the sleeve."

"I haven't said yes, you know."

Tito waits.

"All right," she says, finally. She takes off her dress again.

"You have beautiful breasts and I don't even know your name," Tito says.

"My name is Dzovig. If you try to touch me I'll really let you drown. So, what do you want me to do?"

He moves towards her, dragging one leg a little behind the other, and reaches for her arm.

"Just holding hands might be enough," he says.

She leads him to the water, holding out her elbow as if she were supporting an old lady across a street. He's heavier than he looks, and because his limbs go off in different directions she finds herself pulling at him. It gets easier once they are in the water.

"There aren't so many waves here," she says. "Are you all right?"

"Yes, I'm fine. I'm great!" he says. "You can let go now."

"Are you sure?"

"Yes, Dzovig."

The water is up to his shoulders and she notices that his movements have become less jagged. He closes his eyes for a moment, relieved.

"I feel almost normal when I'm in here," he says.

"Do you want to swim now?"

"Yes, please."

She grabs his hands again and starts to pull, the way you would pull a child in the water, saying, "Try and kick your legs!"

He makes a lot of noise, splashing water in every direction.

"Just your legs. Don't move your hands!"

Inadvertently his hand goes flying and hits her on the side of the head.

"Oh God! I'm so sorry!"

But Dzovig starts to laugh. He looks so ridiculous, she can't help it. "Come on," she says, "don't stop!"

After a time she loops her arms around his waist and pulls him that way. "It's safer for me like this," she says, still laughing.

"You're an angel," Tito says. "Thank you, thank you."

"Just swim, Tito."

They are all alone in the cove now. The boys who had been jumping into the water have long since gone. In the lengthening shadows the sea turns dark blue.

"You're starting to shiver," she says finally. "We should get out."

They reach the rock and sit down, water dripping from their bodies. She lends him her towel.

"I'll never bathe again," he says, rubbing it against his cheek. She puts her dress on and notices him struggling with his shirt.

"Who dresses you?"

"My father." Tito points towards a tall, modern building farther along the shore. "You see that hotel? My father manages it. He doesn't like me hanging around the pool too much, he says I frighten the guests. What about you? I've never seen you in Cascais before."

"I've never been to Cascais before. I live in Lisbon. I've lived there for seven months."

"Your Portuguese is amazing, for seven months."

"Not really."

"And before that?"

"I lived in Armenia."

"Communist country?'

"Yes."

"There was an earthquake there, a couple of years ago. I think my father sent some clothes."

"Thank you," she says, smiling, "for the clothes, I mean. It wasn't near Yerevan, the city where I lived. Farther up in the north. I was already gone when it happened. It was horrible. Twenty-five thousand people died. It was the middle of the school day."

"We get earthquakes here too, you know. Most of Lisbon was razed in 1755."

"I didn't know."

"Too late," Tito says. "You're here now. What's it like, living in a communist country?"

Dzovig looks at the sea.

"I didn't really know until after I left," she says. "It's like being a child your entire life. Being told what to do, getting only so much. You always want things, but not the way people here want them. You don't go shopping for fun in communist countries. You get used to waiting. Some people are happy just doing their job, having their friends. They don't care about living in a different house, or reading different books. Even when they know that there is something more out there, something better. Maybe they feel protected."

"Why did you leave?"

"Because I couldn't go on there, I couldn't live anymore...," she says. "Are you going to get worse?"

"One day you'll tell me why you couldn't go on," he says.

"You didn't answer my question."

"I don't know. It's a disease that goes in cycles. You get sick, then better, then sick again. I could stay this way for the rest of my life, or get suddenly weaker. I've been this way for a long time now."

"It must be difficult."

"Well, it's a little like living in a communist country. You feel trapped, helpless, you get told what to do. You can't get what you want." He pauses. "I don't know anything about Armenia, Dzovig."

"Why should you? It's a tiny country."

"And I'll bet that it was great, once, wasn't it?"

"Yes. And then we were conquered, over and over. Massacred, actually."

"Oh. Well, we Portuguese were great conquerors, but we lost everything."

"What's your national holiday?" she asks.

"April twenty-fifth, when we overthrew the dictatorship. They call it the Carnation Revolution, because there was no blood. People stuck flowers into the soldiers' guns."

"Ours is April twenty-fourth. We remember the genocide. The Turkish government assassinated all our leaders on that day in 1915. Then they killed two million of us, did you know that? All the Armenians in Eastern Turkey were deported, marched into the desert. It was women and children, mostly. The men had been shot first. We have carnations too, we bring them to a memorial—it's called Tsitsernakaberd—on that day."

"Were there many Armenians in Turkey?"

"We had lived there for thousands of years. Historic Armenia covered a huge part of Eastern Turkey."

"I think we have a lot in common, Dzovig."

"You're ridiculous," she says.

"I know," Tito says. "Will you come back tomorrow? We could go swimming again."

"Maybe."

"You could sleep with me one day. I'm a virgin you know, no one has ever slept with me before."

She shakes her head. "Can you get up the beach on your own?"

"Sure." He kisses her on both cheeks. "Come back tomorrow, Dzovig."

It is just past eleven at night when Dzovig gets home. The door is unlocked and she has a moment of panic before she recognizes him, sitting at a table in the dark. Francisco. She lights a small lamp. He looks strange sitting there, immobile, staring straight ahead.

Dzovig kneels in front of him.

"What is it, Francisco? What happened?"

"Balthazar. He died this morning. I woke up and found him lying at the bottom of his cage. Just like that. He wasn't even sick. He didn't look sick—and I've been sitting here like an idiot ever since, because of a stupid bird—"

She puts her arms around his neck. "Oh, Francisco—" and before she can stop herself she is crying with him, unashamed, like a little girl. "Don't cry, Francisco...I went to the beach you know, it was lovely. I liked it very much."

She reaches into her pocket and pulls out the crumpled note he had given her.

"Ah, Dzovig," he says, wiping his face and hers, "I'm glad you got a little sun on your face....You needed a bit of sun."

X

VECIHE

Tomas and Dzovig have been gone more than a week. I think they must have arrived in Odzun, by now. Sahag was driving them as far as Dilidjan, he has some cousins there that he hasn't seen in years. Sometimes I think I should be paying that boy a salary, the number of times he has driven my son across the country. I haven't been sleeping well since they left; neither has Bedros, though he pretends that he has. During the day Bedros is oddly cheerful, it's a deliberate cheerfulness, something defiant about it. Perhaps he is simply protecting himself.

    Odzun. I have never been back in all these years. I never wanted to, even when I knew that my mother was dying. I had sensed her death for days before the letter came. At the factory, my spools of thread rattled on their posts. In a way it was not unexpected, just the inevitable shut-down of her body. The real death had happened much earlier, before I had even left.

    You know that a daughter needs to leave her mother, Vecihe.

    I tried to make a phone call. It was pointless.

    I had written to her a few times, over the years. I wrote more often at first, when the newness of my leaving still seemed like a reversible act, when we still allowed ourselves the possibility that Bedros and I might one day return, even though I had run from Odzun, from her, with such desperate defiance. My letters were always full of good news, how large the city was, the house, Tomas's first tooth, an opera we had managed to see. I sent photographs, of Tomas mostly. She seldom wrote back, not out of any anger, but simply out of acceptance. It was I who was the coward. My mother could acknowledge an ending when it came. Thinking of this now, I suspect it is the lesson we are all meant to learn.

I never asked her about Odzun, about Hrach and Mida, what happened to that house I had lived in or the people in it. Perhaps Hrach never returned either, after that summer. He'd gone to Moscow, to study: what kind of man has he become? What kind of woman has he married?

Years ago Bedros learned of Mr. Hagopian's death through some connection, a friend of a friend at work who had known him. Cancer in the lungs. He had died some years before my mother had, which surprised me. I'd always assumed the reverse. When I first came to Yerevan I couldn't remember him clearly; my thoughts of him always intersected with other memories. Pebbles hitting the road under my shoes, a bundle of old sheets, brown with blood, hauled up from the earth in which they had been buried through the heaving of many springs. And that picture I couldn't erase, of my mother leaning against the stone wall, and the ridges of shadow between the stones like an alphabet surrounding them, and his wiry body pressed against my mother's with an ease so unlikely that one had to stand in awe of them, in spite of everything. For years I carried that image with me, like a stone in my stomach.

I can remember him now, the weary kindness in his face and that irony in his voice, his mouth in a half-smile. I can remember him as the man he was in my childhood, not a father, but in some strange way, an ally. Did he and my mother ever have one last moment of tenderness, I wonder?

I can't stop thinking of them now. I can't stop thinking of Tomas and of what Odzun will make of him. Of what he will bring back. It won't take long for the whole village to know that there are visitors. Perhaps he will stay only near the church, he's obsessed enough for that. Still, someone will find him.

Tomas was almost manic before they left. He was hardly ever here. Throughout the summer he had been eating less and less. He is so thin, now, almost skeletal. Bedros spoke very little with him since that dinner we all had, as if anything else would be superfluous, useless. But I know that he is as worried as I am.

I screamed at Tomas when I saw him leaving in a heavy rain, one afternoon. I yelled at him for not helping me enough, for not eating enough. "Go stand in a line instead of a church!" I told him. "Don't you know that this is a communist country?"

He just laughed.

This is one of the surprises of parenthood, that we have to learn about our children obliquely, that what they hide from us we search for, also in hiding.

I asked Dzovig if she had any clues, if Tomas was any different when they were alone. She was waiting for him to arrive, one afternoon; he was late, and I was glad. I had her to myself for a few moments.

"He hates having doubts," she said. "He wants to be absolutely sure."

"About what?"

"Everything. His theories about architecture, his role. He wants to save the churches before they disappear completely. To restore them, not physically.... I think he wants to set the record straight. I can't argue with him about it, I can't tell him to slow down—"

"Dzovig, he's not going to join the militias in Karabagh, is he? He hasn't said anything to you?"

"No. Sahag discouraged him. It was the idea of eating mice that did it, I think." She smiled. "I wouldn't let him. I'd kill him first."

I said something then, words that I had no right to say. "I'm afraid for you, Dzovig. I'm afraid that he will make you unhappy."

She looked at me. "When you love someone, it's who they are that you love, not what they do, isn't it?"

"Yes." *Yes.*

I packed some food for them on the morning they were leaving. Dzovig arrived early, with a bag hanging on her back. Tomas twirled her in his arms as if they were going to the moon, even I had to laugh.

"Make sure that he eats," I told her, "and you too, Dzovig."

"Don't worry, we will."

"The Ossian family lives near the church. I'm sure they would put you up if they are still there. They're a good family."

"But not your family?" she asked.

"No."

She looked at me, waiting, sensing that there was more. "Do you want me to bring something?" she said finally.

"No," I said. "There isn't anyone, really. I haven't written to anyone in years. They have all probably left by now, it's so hard in the villages.... The house was at the end of the main road. It was painted yellow, then, the garden was to the left. Ask for the Hagopian house. Mida might be there. She was the daughter. No. She is married, of course, we were the same age. She married the Assadourian boy, Artashes, she must live somewhere else. There was a grove of trees at the back of the farm, overlooking the gorge.... It's silly, never mind—"

"No," she says, "tell me where it is."

"I used to go there and paint. Across the fields. Leave it. It was like a secret place."

"I'll look for it," she says.

"No, leave it." *Leave it.*

I kiss her on both cheeks. Sahag waves to me from the car, a cigarette between his fingers, honks the horn. And as they pull away, my son turns around and blows me a kiss through the glass.

Tomas did stay here until the twenty-fourth of April. I don't really know why I had asked him to, why I felt it important for him to be here on our day of pilgrimage to Tsitsernakaberd. I knew there would be hundreds of thousands of people there, there always are, every year. I thought, perhaps stupidly, that it would put the light back into his face, restore something to him.

Maybe the true meaning of Tsitsernakaberd is lost on Tomas. He was only a baby in April 1965, on the fiftieth anniversary of the genocide, when thousands of students protested for formal recognition of what had happened, for the millions of deaths. They were talking about Karabagh then too, about our lost lands in Azerbaijan, in Turkey. What they got, finally, was Tsitsernakaberd, a memorial monument on the western edge of the city. I had been in Yerevan for eight years then, eight years away from my mother. I visited the memorial, that first time, with my mother's face before me, with songs ringing in my ear. I didn't find it beautiful. Near the centre, I tripped and fell. And then I sobbed like a child. I couldn't explain to Bedros then, or later, to Tomas, what I was atoning for. But I wanted them with me as I went, year after year.

I didn't know this time if Tomas would be going. Bedros and I left the house together. It was a warm day. We didn't see any soldiers. "At least they've had the sense to stay away," Bedros said. We joined the procession with our flowers in our hands. I could see in the crowd the photographs of men mounted on placards. We all knew who they were. Up near the monument, someone (a group of students, we learned later) had placed a thousand-pound *khachkar*. It was one of the simpler ones, not too much carving on it, but lovely nonetheless compared with the stark lines of the memorial. The *khachkar* was surrounded by mounds of flowers and more photographs. I read the inscription on it as I walked past: *SUMGAIT*. A name that was read that day by every one of us.

Tomas came home that night.

"I was there," was all he said.

Bedros and I are calm. We sit, eating our dinner. I hear the sound of his feet rubbing against one another, in their socks, under the table. He asks me if I have done any painting today. I haven't.

"Tomas hasn't called," I tell him.

"Well, he doesn't usually, does he?"

"I know, but I asked him to, this time."

"It's probably completely different now, Vecihe. Half the village has probably left. It's been over thirty years, you know."

"But the other half is still the same, isn't it?"

"What does it matter? People are busy living their lives. People are always leaving."

"Maybe Dzovig will remember to call. I'm sure she wouldn't forget."

Bedros shifts in his chair and stops eating in exasperation.

"You put too much trust in that girl," he says finally.

"What do you mean?"

"I mean that we don't know who she is. She's just the first."

"Bedros, don't be infantile!"

"He's just going to become more and more involved with her and it's too early, don't you see?"

"Yes, I see. I see with my two eyes!"

I start to clear the table, to do something with my hands. The dishes clatter in the sink.

Bedros says, "She's just part of it, Vecihe, it's a big romantic struggle all of a sudden, going nowhere."

"Do you really believe that?"

"I believe that no one knows what they are doing, that we are underestimating Moscow, or overestimating them. People have no idea what kind of shape this country is really in, the economy.... What I believe is that many more people are going to die."

"And what has this got to do with Dzovig?"

"He might do it, Vecihe, he might just pick up and head for the border. He's not rational right now, he's blind."

"But she *isn't* blind, Bedros. And we are lucky for that."

"I don't know. There's no softness in her," he says. "She's hard."

I look at him, at Bedros. My husband with his blue eyes. When I first saw them I believed he'd come from one of those villages my mother had spoken of, between Sevan and Odzun.

All the children were blond in those villages. Russian. But the blue of his eyes had come from much farther away, from Lake Van, in Turkey. Blue as the lake.

There is something poignant about it, his inability to say it clearly. What he really means is, she has no fear, and for those of us who were born under Stalin, a person without fear is somewhat alien. Our children are different, born under other regimes. Until recently they have been resigned rather than afraid, and of the two, I don't know which is worse.

The evenings are getting longer now. Tomas hasn't called. We take a walk through the streets after dinner, as is our custom. Some of these old apartment buildings are beautiful, the red tuffa stone, soft with age, the curl of iron railings. The summer nights are delicious in Yerevan. Seeing people, seeing families walking in the light of evening makes it possible to believe that there is a reason for being here, for staying. We don't hold hands, not out of any residual anger but because it has never been our habit.

Later, in bed, Bedros runs his fingers through my hair, a gesture that used to be a kind of signal for us. I read it now more as an offering, not really a truce, but the reclaiming of a memory.

"Do you remember that train ride, Bedros? Our hands under the blankets?"

"We were crazy," he says. He rearranges himself, turns onto his back.

"We were leaving."

"Yes."

"What I never expected," he says, "was that I would have such a small understanding of my own son. I never thought it could be possible."

I can barely make out his profile in the dark.

"Maybe it's the same with all of us, Bedros."

He doesn't answer me. My eyes grow heavy and I am thinking of Odzun, again, the path along the edge of a field and the plum trees that grew there. They would be coming into fruit about now, I think. Small, yellow plums. *Yellow.*

XI

ARZAS

At Sevan, the clouds hung very low, like a second row of mountains suspended over the first. This is how Dzovig saw them, giant balls of white mist, then the mass of brown hills that surrounded the lake in folds, and then the water, still and wide and blue. Despite the clouds the sun was hot that day; by the end of the afternoon their skins had turned bright red, except for Maro, her mother, who had stayed wrapped in her dress and stockings, a shawl over her head. Her father wouldn't wear a hat.

They had driven to the lake in a borrowed car. One of the men who worked with her father at the rubber factory had lent it to him for the day. The car was tiny and white, and Dzovig could feel the vibrations of the wheels beneath the back seat. In the back of the car was a plastic bottle filled with petrol and an old blanket that Maro had rolled up. She had also packed the food, bread and cheese and some leftover meat from the day before. To Dzovig it looked like there was enough food to last a week, but it was always like that with her mother's cooking.

They had never been in a car before, the four of them, as far as she could remember. She had never seen her father drive although it hadn't occurred to her that he might not know how. He'd learned in the army, maybe. She had heard her mother say once that he had been in the army, all men had. Perhaps it was

Dzovig who had never been in a car before, she was only six, after all.

Her mother sat in the front seat next to her father, looking grim, as if someone were pinching her arm for the length of the trip. Her knuckles clutched at the armrest on the inside of her door. Arzas also held onto the car: his fingers touched the roof while his elbow stuck out of the open window. Dzovig had the wind on her face.

Her mother's lips were pursed.

"I don't like borrowing other people's things," her mother said. Her lips were pursed. Arzas ignored her. Arzas was excited. His eyes kept darting across the road. Once in a while he laughed to himself or tapped with his other hand the top of her mother's thigh. She pushed his hand away and threw it back at him saying, "The road, Arzas."

Anahid was quiet. From time to time she looked out of her window, or at Dzovig. She was five. She wore white sandals on her feet.

Arzas said, "When you see how blue it is, you won't believe your eyes. You've never seen anything so blue."

"When will we be there, Papa?"

It seemed like forever. The backs of Dzovig's thighs were wet and stuck to the seat of the car, and she found it hard to keep her eyes open in the wind. And then the wind grew faint, suddenly, and Dzovig noticed that the car was coming to a stop on the side of the road. Her mother looked more worried than before.

"Just let me do the talking," Arzas said.

A man walked up to the car. He had a hat on his head and a set of keys dangling from his belt. Also a stick in his hand. He bent down a little and looked at everyone in the car.

"Your licence," he said.

Dzovig watched her father pull some papers out of a compartment in the front of the car, on her mother's side. The man took them and walked away.

"Bastards." Dzovig's father was reaching into his pocket.

"Is that man in the army?" Dzovig asked.

"I said to be quiet," her father said.

The man came back. Anahid looked at her feet.

"This licence has almost expired. You'll have to apply for a new one."

"Thank you, I will."

"These things have to be done in advance, you realize that."

"Yes."

Dzovig's mother shifted in her seat a little and smiled. Dzovig couldn't understand it. Her mother sounded strange now, happy almost.

"We are on our way to Sevan," she said, "for a picnic."

The man didn't seem to know what to say for a moment. He looked at Arzas.

"Three people were killed on this road yesterday, you wouldn't want that to happen to your lovely family, would you?"

"Oh, how terrible," Maro said.

Dzovig's father didn't smile. The man had grown impatient now.

"This permit," he said, "you have to display it like this," and he reached inside the car, slapping a piece of paper under the windshield, in front of her father.

"We didn't know," Maro said, "It's not our——"

"There are fines."

"I understand," Dzovig's father said. He stretched out his

arm and gave the man a crumpled piece of paper. "Thank you for your help."

The man seemed satisfied and walked away. The car started moving again. Her parents didn't look at each other. Her mother's mouth was a straight, dark line.

"How much?" she asked.

"Why don't you ask him yourself, since you find it impossible to keep your mouth shut?"

They drove on. Dzovig and Anahid looked out of the windows at the hills on either side of the road. Some of the hills were green. Along the way they passed more of the men in hats, and Dzovig and Anahid smiled at each other when they did, without quite knowing why. The back of the car had begun to smell like petrol.

Finally, after a long turn in the road, Lake Sevan appeared, a wide stretch of water that had no end to it, like a sea. On one side a narrow piece of land jutted into the lake like a finger, pointing to its centre. The end of the finger had a mountain on it, like all land in Armenia. Dzovig could see the peaks of two churches on top of the hill. From the road they looked like toy houses. It was for the churches, she knew, that her mother had come; Maro would light candles there.

When the car stopped and they all got out, Anahid bent over and threw up on the pavement. Her body was shaking. Maro wiped her face with a rag. "Look at your sandals," she said.

Dzovig tried to sound cheerful: "Look, Anahid, we can build something on the beach."

Her father was already walking up the hill, in a hurry, as if he hadn't really arrived yet.

"Wait, Papa!"

The climb up to the churches was steeper and longer than it had appeared from the road. There were many stairs and Dzovig's legs were stiff from having sat in the car for so long. Anahid was still whimpering as Maro dragged her by the hand. Midway along the stairs a woman was sitting to one side with her hand outstretched. Dzovig thought she looked somewhat like her mother, with shawls and layers of different clothing covering her body in the hot sun, except that the woman had very dark skin.

"What does she want, Mama?"

"Nothing," Maro said.

"But, Mama——"

Inside, the church was dark and cool. Dzovig saw her father place some coins in the hand of a man who stood by the entrance. The coins were for candles, thin, yellow strands of wax that her mother would light and place on a table. The table was shaped like a shallow box, filled with sand. Dzovig stuck her finger in the sand.

"Dzovig!" Maro said.

Dzovig went to find her father. He was back outside, smoking, leaning against the church wall. He blew the air out of his mouth as if relieved of something. In the wall there was a window, a narrow slit beneath a small arch, and over the arch, a flower carved within a circle. Or a star, maybe.

"This used to be an island, you know," he said.

"An island? In the middle of the lake?" Dzovig asked.

"Yes."

"With water all around?"

"That's what an island is, Dzovig."

"How did they attach it to the land, then?"

"The lake is drying up. The government uses it for power, electricity."

Dzovig didn't understand.

"Every year the water gets a little lower. Every year."

"Yes. But how do they attach it?"

"It's already attached, beneath the water. You just couldn't see it before."

"Why not?"

"The water was covering it, I just told you!"

"How did the churches get here, then? Before or after the water went away?"

"Before," Arzas said. He laughed to himself again. "They must have dropped from the sky, right onto this hill, like Noah on Mount Ararat."

"You're lying," Dzovig said.

There was no sand on the beach, only stone. The shore was covered in small grey rocks that burned like hot coals when Dzovig walked on them, barefooted.

"Come to the water," Dzovig said to Anahid. "It's cold!"

Anahid wouldn't move. "I don't want to," she said.

Maro had spread the old blanket from the back of the car on the ground and was unpacking the food. Now that she had been to the churches, eating seemed the only important activity left. "Come and have your lunch," she said.

Dzovig's father was wearing short pants and had taken off his shoes. Dzovig noticed how white his legs looked, sitting on the blanket. White and surprisingly thin. Two round pieces of bone stuck out to one side of each big toe, like noses, but Dzovig decided not to ask about them. She liked her father better when he had been sitting in the front seat of the car, with his elbow pointing out, before the man had stopped them.

"I'm not very hungry, Mama," Anahid said.

"You'll eat," Maro said.

"My stomach hurts."

"You have to eat."

"I'll eat her piece, Mama. I can do it," Dzovig said.

Maro rubbed her hands together.

"Fine," she said.

Her father didn't say anything. He chewed his food and looked at the lake.

After eating, Dzovig walked along the edge of the shore, looking for shells or stones, gathering the pebbles she liked into a small pile. Anahid followed her, holding the pebbles.

"Maybe we could give her some rocks," Dzovig said.

"Who?" Anahid said.

"The woman on the stairs. We could ask her how the churches got on the island."

"What island?"

"She would know," Dzovig said.

There were other families at the beach, families with children and women and men, some with grandparents. Dzovig's grandparents had died in a desert, in the war, that's what her parents had told her. It was the men who went into the water mostly, the men and some of the children. After a time Dzovig noticed that her father was also in the water, in his short pants. He had taken off his shirt. He was swimming. And then he was coming towards her and Anahid, dripping water from his head and the ends of his pants.

"How about a swim, Anahid?"

Dzovig didn't like the sound of his voice. "We're making a collection," she said.

"I don't want to," Anahid said.

"What did you say?"

"I said no thank you, I don't want to, Papa."

There was a sound then, the sound of Arzas's hand slapping onto Anahid's wrist, and all the pebbles she had been holding hitting the ground like shards.

"I don't want to, Papa, please!"

Arzas was laughing. "Come, my little baby, my little sissy."

And then he was pulling her sister away, lifting her into the air by one arm, and Anahid screeched as if she were being burned, *No, Papa! Please! No, no no!*

Dzovig gathered the pebbles. She wouldn't watch her sister's body, flailing, Arzas's hands pressing her head under. She didn't listen to the screams, the coughs, her sister's lungs gasping for air, her sister vomiting again, at the water's edge. The crack of her father's knuckles against her sister's skull. She didn't look at her mother in supplication. She only gathered the pebbles, and after a while it was as if Sevan had ceased to exist, with its beach and families, her mother wrapped in layers in the hot sun, her father's skin, white and dripping like the skin of a fish and her sister's terror, all of them engulfed by a strange silence. Dzovig didn't say anything. She kept quiet even as she sat in the back seat of the borrowed car at the end of the day, and reached slowly for her sister's hand without ever taking her eyes off the back of her father's neck. And as they drove away she saw the clouds again, saw them tumbling down the mountains, and imagined what sound they would produce if they could crash into the lake.

XII

VECIHE

It was after Aghavnee died that my mother became unwell. I did-n't notice the link between these two events at first, Aghavnee's death and my mother's slow descent into madness, a death of its own kind. Several months had passed following Aghavnee's death before I understood, although the passing of time had lit-tle to do with it. During those months the old sack Aghavnee used to carry lay shoved in a corner of our room. Mida and Mrs. Hagopian might have been horrified to find it there; they would have ordered its contents scattered, so that Aghavnee would not come looking for them. But no one came to our room and I never questioned my mother about it. I never, out of curiosity, wanted to look inside it.

It was winter when Aghavnee died. The ground was frozen. It was Hrach who found her, and as the men from the village gath-ered around the body their mouths threw up clouds of steam. We had been at the house when Hrach had burst through the door, calling for his father. I had only come because my mother had immediately ran from the house, with no coat on. I ran after her with her coat in my arms.

Aghavnee was on the ground. They wouldn't let any of us near her. By that I mean any of the women. Bring a blanket, someone said. What had happened was this: someone, more than one, had raped her, and left her naked on the frozen ground, except for a pair of boots she still had on her feet. Her clothes were never found, not even the following spring, trailing in rags on the banks of a stream or hung from the rocks down below, in the gorge. Perhaps they had been burned, or torn to shreds, and then tied perversely on bushes or trees as offerings, or as claims to forgiveness maybe. Even I thought this impossible, though I could imagine it.

A blanket was brought and there was some argument then, about where to place the body. My mother was standing beside me, the skin of her neck had turned red from the cold. No one had touched Aghavnee's body, which was still on the frozen ground behind an outbuilding, a shed where tools and implements were kept, and food stored for the winter. The men who stood in a circle around her argued. Then I saw the familiar flash of resolute irritation pass across my mother's face and her sudden push through the circle of bodies to where Hrach's father stood. I did not know what strange sort of power she had over him. I wasn't sure if they knew I had seen them, that day, kissing against the stone wall, kissing with the sun on them as if this were an act the world was meant to witness. I would never question them about it, but I knew it all the same. I knew it as I watched my mother speak to him, her lover, in the circle of men that surrounded Aghavnee's body with clouds of steam hanging above them, and his nod of acquiescence, the decision made, a dispersal then, and three men lifting Aghavnee's body into the air. That was the moment when I caught a glimpse of Aghavnee's skin as part of the blanket slipped from one of the men's hands, just beneath her ribs. White, hardened as wax.

Hrach came up to me.

"It's horrible, what they did to her," he said. "You don't want to see a thing like that."

"What do you mean *thing*, do you mean her body?" I said these words with some venom even though I knew that Hrach was trying to be kind.

"They're taking her to the house," he said.

"I know."

"Your mother, Zivart——"

"I know!" I said.

My mother was still standing near the spot where Aghavnee's body had been found. She seemed frozen there, staring at the ground. I looked too. I searched for her, following her eyes, but there was no blood in the dirt. Not a trace of anything.

Someone called her, "Zivart, do you want this?" and it was only then that my mother lifted her eyes and began to move.

Hrach said, "Come, she'll want your help, Vecihe."

There was more discussion at the house, although my mother was not a part of it. She seemed to be in a world of her own suddenly, where the usual rules of her existence no longer applied. She gave orders. Mida and I followed her into a room beside the kitchen where the muffled voices of Mida's parents could be faintly heard. Perhaps they were arguing their daughter's presence here, in a room where Aghavnee's body, still covered by the blanket, had been placed on a table. My mother was oblivious to them.

"Go and heat some water," she said.

My mother began to wash the body. There was no hesitancy in this, no attempt to shield us from it. My mother lifted one of Aghavnee's arms.

"Hold it like *this*," she said.

The arm felt very heavy in my hands and it was then that I saw them, the cuts and bruises. Part of one breast had been ripped off by teeth. Elsewhere there had been a knife, or knives. Mida turned away but I held the arm. I didn't move. Aghavnee's thighs were encrusted in brown blood, but the cloths my mother used to wash them came away bright red. My mother did not flinch as she pulled at folds of flesh and pushed them carefully into place. She wiped again and again at blood that kept surfacing as if the body that had contained it were still pulsing. I did as I was told. I felt a sort of numbness after a while. I didn't speak.

Mida and I emptied and refilled large bowls of hot water.

"We should close her eyes," Mida said to me in the kitchen, "or she will know who buried her."

But Aghavnee's eyes remained open, black as coal, staring at nothing.

A bolt of linen had been left in the kitchen, by one of the men, I presumed, or possibly by Mida's mother, whose voice I could no longer hear through the walls. My mother began to wrap Aghavnee's body. She wrapped it in layers until nothing could seep through the linen and the cloth remained white.

We were covering her head when Mida said in desperation, "Her eyes," and my mother stopped.

"If God had closed her eyes...," she said. "Let God look into them now."

And then my mother bent down slowly and placed her lips on Aghavnee's face, and without being asked I did the same.

The men buried her in the graveyard. We women did not go to the interment. I don't know what words were said. There was a coffin, and, because the ground was too frozen for digging, dirt was piled over it and then covered with stones. Hrach told me this. I saw it for myself the following day when my mother took me with her to the grave. My mother brought food.

"The dead are hungry," she said.

My mother refused to cook after that day. Instead, she gathered what food she could find in the kitchen and brought it every morning to Aghavnee's grave. I had seen this done before, in the village, by very old women mourning their dead. I didn't think it that unusual: in time, I thought, my mother would return to her cooking and cleaning, to the quiet steadiness of her life. To her silence. In time it would be spring and she would be hanging sheets in the sun and pulling cabbages from the earth. She did do these things again, eventually, and I was thankful for it. I wanted my life to continue as it had before, with only its minor irritations. I'd grown accustomed to the safety of not questioning and therefore I kept my eyes closed. I wouldn't look at my mother's altered face, at the manic flutter of her hands.

My mother began to wander aimlessly, to forget things. She no longer combed her hair. Sometimes Mida combed it for her, sometimes I did. Everyone in the house noticed, but there was a sudden kind of deference towards my mother, as in that time years before when she had collapsed in the graveyard, leaving her blood on the rocks. I didn't want to look at her now, pretending as everyone else did that her behaviour was part of some natural progression, an outcome of events that was tacitly understood, that warranted some kind of protection.

I did not understand it. I did not want to. I kept to myself until the ground split open beneath my feet and then I needed her again.

And what I needed was for her to speak.

I no longer went to school. I was eighteen the winter Aghavnee died and beginning to feel very old. Mida was to marry the Assadourian boy at the end of the summer. Artashes was his name. She had given up all hopes of marrying Bedros months before; Mr. Hagopian had approached him, to no avail. I still saw Bedros occasionally in the market or in the village. He was quiet. He seemed always perfectly alone and never in need of anything or anyone. I envied that.

I read whatever books I could find. There were not many. Mr. Hagopian brought some to the house from time to time and Hrach made sure that I knew about them. Hrach had come to the end of his schooling in Odzun as well. In the autumn he would be going to Moscow to continue his studies. His father knew many people in Moscow, he said. He always spoke to me like that now, his tone a funny mixture of boasting and offering, as if anything he received carried with it the possibility of somehow benefiting me, though he could never articulate how. I'd grown accustomed to dismissing him. I felt stronger than him, in the way I had felt at school with Mida trailing behind me.

I hadn't yet forgiven him. I hadn't been to the grove again, not since Hrach had found me there years before. He had ruined it for me. I painted very seldom now, and usually indoors. I painted images that were in my head, not in front of my eyes. My pictures made no sense. If others had seen them I believed they might have thought me mad, like my mother. They could have sent me to one of the Soviet asylums. But no one saw them. In the spring following Aghavnee's death I stopped. I decided I would never paint again.

Preparations for Mida's wedding were well under way at the Hagopian house. Mida had grown suddenly more serious, as if she had made a deliberate decision to leave girlhood behind forever. Even Mrs. Hagopian came alive again, emerging from her room to give orders in the kitchen. I did as I was told alongside my mother, relieved in a sense that I was there to watch her, and save us both from shame. But I could find no joy or excitement in any of it, not even when Mida showed me her dress. Then one afternoon my mother woke suddenly from her stupor and asked: "What will become of you, Vecihe? Who will you marry?"

And with some cruelty I replied, "What will become of you, Mother?"

I don't know if Hrach overheard this exchange. Perhaps he'd been planning things all along, and suddenly found the courage. Or it may just have been one of life's coincidences, that he chose that very same day to speak to me.

"Why don't you come to Moscow and study at the university?" he said. "We could ask my father."

I was too stunned to reply at first.

"He knows many people in Moscow," Hrach continued.

"Since when do girls go off to study, Hrach?"

"You could study painting. Lots of women do it."

"I don't paint anymore."

"You could. You used to."

"No."

"I'll ask my father."

"No!"

"And then when we come back—"

"What makes you think I would come back?"

"Because we would get married, and your mother—"

"No!"

"Who is going to take care of her then? Do you think they will want her in some other house, someone who is not right in the head like that? Do you think you can take her with you when you go?"

"I will not marry you, Hrach, and I'm not going anywhere!"

Hrach's eyes were burning with tears, but I threw my words at him all the same, because he had presented me with the possibility of obtaining something I hadn't realized I wanted, a freedom I could barely contemplate. I looked at that possibility now as if it were spread before me in the pages of a book, a book of unexpressed and forbidden longing, and in my anger I cursed him for having opened it.

Mida's wedding lasted for three days. Everyone came. My mother looked presentable; we had bathed and wore our best clothing. Mida seemed like another person, serious, with gold coins dancing about her head, dark eyes looking out beneath her veil. Perhaps she was afraid. I watched from a distance as she stood with the groom, their foreheads and noses touching, palms pressed against palms and a cross held over their heads. It was beautiful. I felt nothing.

There was a banquet at the house, mountains of food and endless visiting. I wanted only to get through it. My mother worked hard, serving and cleaning up after the guests. I almost dared to think that she was fine, that truly, she was coming back—but she began to sing. No one took notice at first, a slow hum at the bottom of her throat as she cleared away trays of pastry. But slowly the song grew louder, it was a song I had never heard before.

"Mama," I said, "everyone can hear you!"

But she kept on. Heads began to turn in our direction.

"Mama, please!"

I pulled at her hand but she jerked away from me, still singing. Mida lifted up her eyes. I looked around me in desperation and saw Mr. Hagopian patiently making his way through the crowd. How would I defend her? My face was burning with shame. And then I did what the shameful do, I ran.

There was another church in Odzun, Tsiranavor-Tsakhkavank, on the eastern edge of the village. It was a ruin, two intersecting pieces of wall, their crenellated tops like the jagged edges of a torn piece of paper, overgrown now with mosses. There was no ceiling left, only one small arch, which had once spanned the doorway. The arch and the fragment of wall behind it made a kind of frame through which I could see bits of mountain, bits of sky, blue and green and black.

I was alone. I sat on the ground with my back against the wall. I sat there until the light began to change, and then I saw the outline of a figure walking towards me, someone I vaguely recognized. It was Bedros.

"They will be looking for you soon," he said.

"I'll go back."

"I come here, sometimes. It's quiet."

"I should go," I said. I stood up.

"It was very hard for your mother, what happened to Aghavnee. People know these things."

"But she hardly knew Aghavnee," I said.

"I heard someone say they knew each other in the war, your mother and Aghavnee. Maybe they came from the same place. Did she tell you?"

"She never tells me anything. I don't even know who my father is."

"None of them want to talk about it. It's hard. I only know because my father was there too, in the desert. He came from Van. Everyone he knew died."

"Nobody knows about you," I said.

"My father sent me here. He wanted me out of the city for a while. I think he was worried about something. He thought it best I should not show my face for a while. It was arranged."

"Why?"

"There are a lot of changes in the government right now. People come and go."

I didn't understand.

"It's complicated," he said. "Never mind."

"Does he know Mr. Hagopian, your father?"

"I don't know. Maybe."

"Did you fight in the war?"

"I went at the end, it was practically over. My father pulled some strings. But he is dead now. They can do what they want with me, I guess. I'm going back to Yerevan at the end of the harvest. My father had a house there."

"And you will live there?" I asked. "I'm sure it will go well for you. I wish you luck."

I began to walk away.

"Wait, Vecihe," he said. I felt strange, hearing him say my name like that, as if I were someone else entirely.

"I want to show you something."

I followed him around the ruined church, to the corner of a wall. He pushed a large stone away with his foot.

"I think this has something to do with Aghavnee," he said, "but I haven't shown anyone yet. I want to be certain first."

It was a bundle of cloth, half buried, brown with old blood and blackened with earth. A pattern, along one of the folds, tiny dots, a pattern I recognized.

"It's not Aghavnee's," I said. I was looking at Bedros's face but what I saw in front of my eyes was someone else. I saw Mr. Hagopian as I had seen him that day, walking across a field with a bundle in his arms, an afterbirth wrapped in sheets. And I understood.

"Vecihe?" Bedros said.

I started running for the house.

"Tell me, Mama."

"Leave it."

"Tell me why you were bleeding at the graveyard. I want you to tell me."

"Leave it, leave it."

"Bedros showed it to me, I saw the sheet buried in the ground!"

My mother was looking away from me. She wouldn't answer.

"Tell me about Aghavnee. You have been so different since she died and I'll go mad watching you, Mama, if you don't tell me. I'll go mad."

"It was a lovely wedding."

"What was that song, Mama? Where is it from? Sing it to me. Sing it again."

"There was a woman, Vecihe, an angel—"

"I don't want the angel! I want to know about Aghavnee! I want to know where you came from, who my father is. I want you to say something, Mama!"

"Mr. Hagopian is very kind. He took care of me, you don't have to worry—"

"Please—"

I was on the floor, pressing my head into my mother's knees, pulling at her hands. My mother rocked her body back and forth. She would not tell me anything. She lifted my face up towards her own and wiped back my hair.

"Leave it, Vecihe," she said.

Then, that night, I stood in our room undressing for bed, and as she watched me, she began to speak. Her voice, the tip of a needle, etching words onto a piece of glass.

XIII

ZIVART

"We sang songs in the orphanage, in Kharpert. They wanted us to sing. Many of the younger children had forgotten Armenian, they had become little Turks. But after the war the English wanted all the Armenian children to be given back.

"At the orphanage, we ate bread and soup. At night we ate raisins and nuts. Sometimes beans. We were hungry. They taught us how to write and how to sing. There was a lot of learning in the orphanage.

"Vecihe tried to hide me at first. You are my daughter, she said. She gave me good food to eat. Then, one morning, Vecihe said to me, I must take you to the orphanage. All the Armenian children go there. They will take good care of you. You are only a child, you cannot stay with me.

"You are my mother, I said. I was crying pitifully. I was crying and crying, because all the sorrow had come back into my life.

"You are only a child, Zivart. You are Armenian.

"At the gate she left me. I screamed for her and the people there held my arms. I screamed for two days. I was thirteen. After that, they made me sing. I sang."

"We lived near Khnus. It was not far from Erzurum. In our village, the authorities had pasted papers on all the walls, telling us we must leave in five days. They gave us one cart, and a horse. My mother was packing everything. I was nine years old. I kept asking her, who are we going to visit? My mother didn't answer. One afternoon, my uncle came to the house. It was the day before we left. He was dirty. He had been running. Grandmother closed all the windows. Hide all the gold, my uncle said. He had a wild look in his eyes. My mother began to wail and I was afraid. My father did not come home that day. We will meet him on the road, my grandmother said. She put gold coins in my hair. You must walk like a princess, Zivart.

"When we left, there were no men on the street. Only mothers and grandmothers—and old men. And other children, like me. Babies. The *Zaptieth* were on horses. There were two of them. They yelled at us to keep moving. Where are we going? I asked. No one knew. It was the summer.

"The first night, we all slept under the cart; my mother, my grandmother, my sister, my younger brother and me. I counted us. We were five. We never slept under a cart again. In the morning, our belongings from the cart were scattered on the ground. The carts were turning back. There was no room on the road for carts, they said. We began walking, carrying what we could. We will come back later, for our things, my mother said. We must keep walking. We walked and walked. My legs were hurting. We must not stop, my mother said. That night she covered us with a carpet. There were so many of us on that road, with nowhere to sleep. We just stopped when it was dark, we slept on the ground, there, in the spot where we had stopped.

"I don't know how many days we walked. There were more and more people walking, there was no road anymore. The earth was full of rocks. We had no more food. We didn't drink.

There was a valley, one day, where the *Zaptieth* made us stop. Men came down from the hills with knives. Kurds. All the women were screaming and running. I was on the ground, with my brother. My grandmother was on top of me, hiding me with her body. I could not see anything, only hear the screams. I was crying for my mother. After a while it was quiet again. We looked up. I couldn't see her at first. I was calling for her, Mama! Then she found us. Her hands were covered in blood. My sister, Azniv, was gone. They had taken her, put her on a horse. They had taken our blankets. My mother no longer spoke, after that day. She only looked out in front of her, there was nothing in her eyes.

"Get up, the *Zaptieth* said.

"We hadn't eaten in days. People around us started to die. Some would fall by the road where they were walking. The *Zaptieth* kicked us when we did not move fast enough. We never passed any villages, only near them. I held onto my grandmother when we walked. I'm so tired, I kept saying. I wanted water. In the mornings, we sucked the dew off our clothes. We pulled at the grass with our nails.

"There were wells. You don't know about the wells. The first time I saw one, I was so happy. We started to run but we couldn't run, all our strength was gone from us. The *Zaptieth* were shouting and then shooting their guns, but some women ran to the well. I saw the women climb the well and then I saw them jump, they were so thirsty. They died like that, jumping into the well. But we were thirsty too. We tied our clothes together, someone had a cup and we drank from it, from that water where the women had died, I will never forget it—

"After many days, we came to the river. The *Zaptieth* would not let us drink—they wanted money. I had no more coins in my hair, but my grandmother had some. She had sewn them into her clothes. She paid for us. The river was like a giant well, with women running towards it to die. Many threw themselves in it, with babies in their arms. Sometimes it was the *Zaptieth* who shot them, when they were in the water. I saw my mother staring at the river with a strange look in her eyes, staring at the river like a loved one, with a longing, like that.

"At night, my mother rubbed dirt on our faces. She wanted us to look ugly, so that they wouldn't take us. They took lots of children away, and the young girls. There were almost no young girls left. Sometimes, the mothers asked the Turks to take their children. Take my babies, please, they said. Take my babies. There was no food to give them. One day, my mother gave me some clothes, a boy's clothes. You will be a boy, she said, they won't steal you away.

"Now, when we walked by the river, we saw dead bodies floating by, babies and women and even men. It was a river of blood. There were bodies everywhere, on the road. We saw them but we did not feel anything. We had lost all our feeling, by then. We wanted only to know where we were going, where we could find food. My brother, Yacoub, was very sick. He could not walk anymore. His eyes were too big. That day, he said, I want to die now, Mother.

"My mother wanted to carry him. We must walk, she said, we will soon be there.

"My brother was on the ground. I want to sleep, Mama. I want to sleep, here.

"My mother was pulling at him, shouting at him. We must go, Yacoub. We must go. I was crying. I can't leave you, she said, God help me. But my brother could not move anymore.

And then my grandmother sat on the floor beside him. I will stay with him. Go. We will die together, here. I am old. You go.

"My mother started walking with me. Her head was always turning back to look at my brother. My grandmother had his head on her lap. My mother was crying for the first time. My God, my God, she was crying. She was looking at the sky and shouting, My God, can't you hear us? Can't you hear us?

"I don't know for how many months we walked. Or weeks, or days. We had no clothes left. Our skin was black, we were all black. I stayed close to my mother. We didn't speak anymore. One morning, she was dead. I got up. I was nine years old. I followed a family of three. They let me sleep beside them. The aunt pulled the lice from my hair. I had lice in my eyes and in my mouth. When the men from the hills came at us with knives I ran. Someone grabbed me from behind but I bit his arm and struggled free, and then I saw him grab the little girl of the family I had slept with. She was screaming.

"We were near Kharpert when there was a big fight. Many Kurds came down from the hills and the *Zaptieth* were shooting. I didn't know if they were shooting at the Kurds or at us. Everyone was screaming. The Kurds were on top of the women. I did not know where I was. I just sat on the ground. I sat there. Someone picked me up and we were bouncing on a horse. I did not understand what the man said. I was bouncing with the horse, like a rag doll. When I woke up, I was on a bed, and a woman was looking at me.

"A woman, she was looking over me. She said her name was Vecihe."

Vecihe's husband was a rich man. He had brought her a servant, he said. But I was not her servant. She gave me food and cut my hair. She took me to the bath house and cleaned me. She patted my face with her hands. She taught me Turkish words. I was happy, I had a mother again. At night, I screamed in my dreams and Vecihe came to me, don't cry, Zivart, you are safe now. I didn't think anymore of my mother and father, of Yacoub and my sister, Azniv, who had been taken away on a horse, and my grandmother who put gold coins in my hair. I was happy again. I lived in Vecihe's house for four years. And then I went to the orphanage and all the sorrow came back. I remembered everything, but I could not speak. When we talked about the marches, about our mothers and sisters and brothers who had died, the workers at the orphanage punished us. You will not talk of such things, they said.

"They taught us songs. I sang. I put my memories away."

"After some years, our orphanage moved. The Turkish government did not want us in Turkey anymore. We travelled in carts, over the mountains, in the desert. We thought they would be taking us to Armenia, the bit of country that had declared its independence after the war. But the English missionaries took us south to Aleppo, in Syria. I was sixteen. I helped in the orphanage, teaching the little ones. Later we learned that Armenia had joined the Soviet Union; it had been a country for only four years. And they told us that people there were starving and sick.

"I met a man in Aleppo. He would come by to see me, he brought me fruit to eat. He had come from Trebizond, on the coast of the Black Sea. I liked him because he had the same name as my brother, Yacoub. Yacoub Kazanjian. He worked hard, he said. I married him.

"I worked as a servant, washing clothes. Yacoub did many things, he was always working. His hands were black but he always washed his hands. We lived in a room, I kept it clean. I spoke Armenian and I remembered Turkish, from my years with Vecihe. There were many Armenians in Aleppo, at that time. We even had our own schools, newspapers.

"The first time I got pregnant, I bled and bled. I bled each time. We saved our money, but we had very little. We had a roof over our heads, and four walls. We were not cold.

"When I had you, a daughter, I was thirty-two years old. It was like a miracle. I named you Vecihe. Yacoub said, she will be beautiful like her mother. He bounced you on his knee. You were only one when he died. I buried him with our money. I was alone again.

"Something happened after you were born. I felt different. I started to think about my mother. I looked at you and I saw her face, I saw her eyes staring back at Yacoub, my brother, when he was dying, staring at the river like a loved one. Rubbing dirt onto our faces, to save us. Looking at me. She was your grandmother. I had nothing to give you. I remembered that I had a sister, Azniv, who had been taken away on a horse, who knows what had happened to her? I started thinking of her more and more, she was all I could think of after a while. I had not seen her die, that was all I knew. In Aleppo, there were stories of people who had found their brothers and sisters, or aunts and uncles. The orphanages placed notices in the papers. I wanted my family too. I wanted an aunt, for you, someone. I began to look for her. Do you know what it is to look for someone, Vecihe?

"I had a little money left, not much. I took you with me, from place to place, I asked everywhere I went, I stopped in all the orphanages. I climbed onto trains when no one saw me, like a thief. How could I find her? It was impossible, of course. So many years had passed. I got as far as Mush, more than half way to Erzurum; did you know that? It took many weeks. I think I had forgotten what I was looking for. I was begging in the streets for bread. I slept in doorways, with my body curled around you. You don't believe me when I say there was an angel who saved us. You don't. But I will tell you that someone nudged me awake one morning and when I opened my eyes I saw Vecihe standing over us.

"Zivart, Zivart, she said, is it you? Yes, yes, it's me, and the water poured from her eyes like rain.

"It was Vecihe who sent us here to Odzun. She told me about Russia. The Russians were asking Armenians to go to Soviet Armenia, they needed more bodies. But the Armenians who went there had nothing, and the government had nothing to give them. Vecihe knew a family in Odzun; she wrote them a letter. She gave us money for the journey, and food and clothing. And a carpet, *this* carpet, she gave it to me, to keep us warm on the road. You will have a home, Zivart, and food for your daughter, and no one will take you away.

"And so, we came here. To Odzun."

"When we walked in the marches, Vecihe, with the *Zaptieth* behind us, we were starving. We were dying from hunger and thirst. Thousands of us. We were no longer human. In the daylight, we picked through the manure of animals, looking for grains to eat. The *Zaptieth*, they were not starving, but they looked through shit as well, the *Zaptieth* and the others; they were looking for gold in our faeces. They took all the young girls, all the pretty ones first. They tore at all the women. Leave it——

"There was a girl, once. She must have been about fourteen, like my own sister who had been taken away, so quickly. This girl was picking at a pile of manure. They started to laugh at her, to hit her with sticks. What's your name? they asked her. She told them. Aghavnee. *Pigeon.* They tied her hands behind her back and threw her on her knees. Now pick at it, they said, like a real pigeon. She's even more ugly than a pigeon, they said. Who cares, as long as she lays eggs? And then, they raped her, right there, her face——leave it——I saw this with my own eyes, each one had his turn. And they just left her there, to die.

"No one helped her. How could we? Leave it, leave it—— We wanted to live. We could have said something, yelled at them, but we didn't. We didn't say anything, Vecihe. *We couldn't.*

"When I came here, to Odzun, I saw a woman wandering the streets. Aghavnee. *Pigeon.* She would not stay in one place, everyone said. She could not stop wandering. She had been wandering for years and years. That was how she lived. Then one day she came by the kitchen door.

"She said, Is the gate open? Is the gate open?

"I looked into her face. I looked into her black eyes. My God, my God, Vecihe, do you think I would ever forget that face?"

This was the story that my mother, Zivart, told me in the year that Aghavnee died. I was eighteen.

XIV

TOMAS

Sahag had taken them as far as Dilijan. He had some cousins in that town, two young girls who had jumped into his arms with a mad joy moments after the car had pulled up to the house, and an aunt who wept as she welcomed him. Sahag himself seemed almost unrecognizable as he kissed and kissed them. Dzovig had never seen him so plainly happy. Inside, Sahag's aunt made some coffee and brought out photo albums, and sat with a bowl of nuts in her lap. She peeled each nut individually and offered them, one by one, to her guests. Tomas seemed ill at ease. Dzovig could tell that he was itching to leave.

Dilijan looked like it belonged in another country altogether, with its painted wooden houses and the mountains around it covered in mist. This part of Armenia was green, lush almost, the air was cool and moist and, perhaps because of it, the people seemed happier, they had painted their doors and eaves. Dzovig and Tomas walked towards the fruit market in the town; Sahag had told them the chances of finding a ride would be better there. Sahag would remain in Dilijan; they would join him there again at the end of the week.

Dzovig and Tomas accepted a ride to Odzun from a man who was half-drunk. He had two children in the back seat of his truck. Dzovig had to close her eyes at every turn in the narrow road as it crept up the mountain in a giant zig-zag; one mistake and they would all have gone flying into the gorge. The road was bumpy, full of holes. The little boy kept asking, "Are you dizzy?" In exchange for the ride the man insisted that Tomas should come and have a drink with him. His driving was getting more and more erratic.

"I think we can stop here," Tomas said.

"Here?"

"Stop the car, my friend."

Dzovig and Tomas got out and the man drove off, throwing out of the window a chocolate bar that Dzovig had given the children.

"Those kids," Dzovig said.

There was no one on the road.

"I think we are not far from the monastery of Haghartsin," Tomas said. He looked at his map. "I think we can walk there."

He held her hand. The road was black and wet, it seemed suspended under a giant green canopy; the air was thick with mist.

"I could walk for days on this road," Dzovig said.

"You might have to," Tomas said.

She was thinking about the night when they had walked together for hours like this, without knowing each other, without knowing that they would become lovers, and she felt overwhelmed with gratitude at her luck, at the fact that she was with him, now, on this road. But Tomas had his own thoughts.

"We Armenians are very good at walking," he said.

At last they came to an opening in the trees. *Haghartsin.*

There was a stone courtyard along the length of a rectangular building with a cluster of three churches behind it. The building was a thirteenth-century refectory, and they entered it through a wide arch, an opening once used by pilgrims.

"Imagine eating bread in here," Tomas said.

Dzovig stretched out her arm across one of the window openings, trying to reach the outer edge. The walls were four feet deep.

They thought themselves alone until an old man appeared, one of the elusive keepers of Armenia's treasures, or that's how she thought of them, these men, ancient souls who appeared quietly, as if they had been sleeping within the stones themselves, guarding them, waiting for someone who could be told the story.

The man gave them a tour, jiggling a set of heavy keys in his hand. He showed them the graves of Bagratid kings and a sundial by which masses were timed. In one of the churches there was a movable column that had been used to hide weapons in times of invasion. The man seemed very proud of this particular feature. Afterwards, he pointed to a tree just outside the church door, a magnificent oak, seven hundred years old, he said. The tree had half its trunk hollowed out, and Dzovig wondered how it could survive, like that, half-empty. Perhaps this is what happens to human bones as well, she thought, a gradual hollowing until we are standing on nothing more than the shells of bones, half filled with sand. And then the concave hole in the trunk appeared to her as a kind of house and she thought that she would tell Vecihe about the tree, that Vecihe would understand about it because of that place she had loved, the grove. And then she remembered that they should telephone Vecihe, from Odzun, and she turned, looking for Tomas.

"Tomas?"

She went back inside but found only the old man.

"He's gone round the back," the man said, "don't know why, nothing there."

Tomas was crouching by a wall, staring at an inscription of some sort. When she came closer she noticed that it wasn't an inscription at all, only a series of vertical marks, not letters, which Tomas was tracing with his finger, over and over.

"What are you doing?" she asked.

"Counting," he said. His fingers wouldn't stop moving.

"Counting what?"

"The dead."

In Odzun, Dzovig hadn't asked the woman about the grove. She had wandered around to the back of the house and found some buildings that were dilapidated but nevertheless looked like recent additions. She had followed the outline of what had once been a low stone wall, she had followed it until she could see the gorge, but there were no trees there. In the village, there was a smell of burning wood and chestnuts. There were yellow flowers, sunflowers, growing in a line beside some broken-down cars, car parts rusting in the grass like metal carcasses.

Odzun was the kind of place whose configuration you could memorize in a day. Tomas had probably memorized it already, the architecture of it, even though the houses and the short roads would have told him nothing of what went on here. They had passed small groups of men in the village, idle men who stood with their cigarettes, young men who had looked at them with a vague curiosity before turning their eyes back to the tips of their own boots. And they had seen children playing, two boys pulling tape ribbons out of cassettes and holding them across an intersection like some line of defence, a demarcation of property. Dzovig had stopped when a piece of tape had blown against her knee, not wanting to cross the imaginary barrier, but the boys had scattered almost immediately, leaving dark ribbons on the ground. Tomas hadn't spoken to the boys, or the men. In a way, Dzovig understood how he could accommodate his love for the old churches so easily; they were inanimate, they didn't talk back. Or if they did, they spoke only as emblems, proof that some things were capable of lasting. Perhaps he held this fascination in common with those who had built them, men who had carved infinite patterns on slabs of stone, the world concentrically divided until the very idea of cessation seemed an impossibility.

Earlier, at the church, Dzovig and Tomas had sat under an arcade, eating the fruit and bread they had bought in Dilijan.

"Your mother must have come here a million times as a girl," she said.

"Maybe."

"I think she used to paint here."

"She never told me that."

It was the end of the day and the sun was low. Around them the mountains were immense, purple and black. Dzovig looked to the edge of the grass, the line where the earth suddenly dropped off and she felt herself unsteady, held up on a plate by some invisible hand.

"It's beautiful here," she said.

"In twenty years, there won't be a dog left in this village, only this," Tomas said, pointing with his chin towards the church.

"Do you want to look for the house?"

"What house?"

"Where your mother grew up."

"Not now," Tomas said. "Do you suppose anyone has ever had sex in the church?"

"In ten centuries? Probably."

"The priest, most likely."

"With himself."

He was laughing, finally, and she felt grateful. She couldn't quite remember the last time he had laughed.

"It's getting pretty late, you know, we should probably look for a place—"

"Let's just wait," he said, "wait a while. I don't feel like seeing anybody."

But there was somebody: a woman, walking towards them from the direction of the village. She was wearing a dress, and a cardigan that she held closed with her hands, as if she had put it on in a hurry. She was walking towards them, and she was smiling.

Dzovig and Tomas were driving with Sahag now, returning to Yerevan. They would stop for a while at Sevan. Of course, she saw the clouds again. They were the first thing she saw as Sahag drove towards the lake, clouds hanging there as if there had never been a wind strong enough to move them.

"I'll meet you on the beach," she said.

She had had enough of churches. She walked with Sahag towards the water while Tomas visited the two churches on the island, which, she remembered, was no longer an island.

Sahag said, "Whatever it was that happened in Odzun, I hope he gets over it. He's looking sick, Dzovig."

"He hasn't slept. He hasn't slept in three days."

"You keeping him that busy?"

"I'm not joking, Sahag. Look at his eyes."

"I know, I know."

Sahag took off his shirt. The sun was blaring.

"We met a woman in Odzun, she knew Vecihe. She told him stories about his grandmother. He didn't expect it, that's all. He just wanted to see the church. He couldn't sleep afterwards."

"But it's been a while, Dzovig," Sahag said.

Dzovig was about to say something when she saw Tomas waving at them from one of the churches, waving madly, gleefully.

"I don't know what you mean," she said quietly.

Tomas was walking down the hill now, coming towards them.

"Yes you do. You know that he's been different. Since Sumgait. He's up and down, you never know. But that's when it started."

"He's coming," Dzovig said.

"I thought you were going to wave at us from the roof of the church," Sahag said.

"I did wave," Tomas said. "You didn't wave back."

"Not from the roof."

He sat down beside them, leaned back on his arms.

Sahag pointed with his chin at a cluster of white, modern-looking buildings in the distance, perched on a hill overlooking the lake.

"We should all become artists," he said, "and move in there. Treasures of the state."

Dzovig thought suddenly of her sister, Anahid, of the room she shared with her in the apartment where her mother and father lived, an apartment at the top of a grimy stairwell where the light fixtures had long ago been stolen or broken and never replaced. Anahid, who had worn white sandals on her feet.

Sahag pulled off his pants. "I'm going in," he said.

Dzovig looked at the water in front of her. She said, "I hate this country."

Tomas turned towards her.

"I came here with my parents when I was little. It was horrible."

"Why?"

"Never mind. You know, I asked my mother once why she had ruined my sister's life, never letting her go anywhere, always afraid, *you're going to fall, Anahid, you can't do it, that bruise will kill you one day*...You know what she said? She said, 'When she was three years old, she started to go away from me; I couldn't let that happen.'"

"What did she mean by that?"

"I think she meant that she wouldn't let Anahid turn out like me, a kid she couldn't understand, a foreigner in her own family. I used to pull my scabs off when I was little, even if it hurt—it drove my mother crazy but she couldn't stop me."

"But what did Anahid *do* when she was three?"

"I don't know! Put on her own socks, maybe. Nothing my mother says ever makes any sense."

"What about your father?"

"My father's a bastard."

"Anahid has had you, Dzovig. One day something might happen in her life, something might change."

"You don't know that."

"No, I don't know anything," Tomas said. Flecks of light bounced off his eyes.

I would know you anywhere, the woman in Odzun had said to Tomas, *you have the same eyes as your father, so blue.* It had taken her a while to say Vecihe's name. *Vecihe, we grew up like sisters, she and I. She was always a good student, always painting. Her mother, Zivart—*

"The Soviets have increased our territory by four hundred square metres of land," Tomas said.

"What?"

"Because the lake has shrunk. Four hundred square metres. And the *khatchkars* the communists threw in the water in the thirties are all reappearing, like skeletons."

"I want to leave," Dzovig said. "Let's leave, please. I don't want to spend the rest of my life here, in this country."

Sahag swam in front of them and called out.

"Come in!"

"You can't leave," Tomas said. "You're stuck with me and I won't let you. We're both stuck here, with glue."

Let me tell you about Zivart, the woman, Mida, had said, holding her hands against her cheeks.

"Tomas—"

"I can almost *see* her, Dzovig. Zivart. It's not that long, seventy years...it's almost nothing. The roof needed some repairs—"

She couldn't follow him anymore, the trajectory of his thoughts exhausted her. She looked at her feet because it was easier than looking at the water, and with a sudden tenderness Tomas pulled her hair back and pointed to the air above them.

"Look," he said, "the bellies of the seagulls have turned blue."

XV

VECIHE

This, the day in which Tomas has died, is a day of bright, bright sun. A brilliant autumn day.

There is a knock at the door, a soft knock, as if the officer who is standing on the other side of it is afraid of waking a sleeping baby. A few questions, did we have a son called Tomas and was he born on—and then, Your son's body has been found at Ptghni, in the church. He had a gun with him. He took his own life.

I hear Bedros sobbing, ranting. I hear the click of the officer's boots on the floor, grains of dirt being crushed between the floor and the soles of his boots. Blood is pounding in my ears. I am not crying. I am asking for my son's body, for his body, where is it? I want it with me. Outside, it is bright daylight, the middle of the day. This morning he wore a white t-shirt that was already slightly dirty and I asked him why he was wearing that shirt. He is dead.

Everything shifts. They take us to him. They will not let me see his face. This is his shirt, these are his shoes, but this is not my son, Tomas. How could it be him?

There are people in the house. Night comes. Another day. The sound of water, of rain on the pavement. Bedros is sitting in the chair, staring at the air in front of him. I cannot go near him. I want my son, Tomas, I want his limbs on my lap.

Dzovig comes to the house. It is raining outside. Her fists are on the door. Bedros is shouting, Don't you let her in! Don't you come into this house!

I want to tell him: didn't you know? Didn't we always know that one day our son would kill himself, that he would shoot a gun into the roof of his mouth? Of course not, we didn't know. We couldn't have. We are, all of us, liars. This we know.

I am at the window, looking at Dzovig. She is outside, standing in the rain, looking at me, asking for me. This is the moment when God holds me suspended, with sheets of glass crashing all around me, my son dead and Dzovig, my daughter, backing away. Except that I do not believe in God. For many years I have known that God does not exist, and therefore, for a moment, I feel almost nothing.

PART TWO

*This is my morality, or metaphysics, or me: Passer-by of
everything, even of my own soul, belonging to nothing, desiring
nothing, being nothing—abstract centre of impersonal sensations,
a fallen sentient mirror, reflecting the world's diversity. I don't
know if I'm happy this way. Nor do I care.*
Fernando Pessoa

I

TITO

"This has been very expensive you know."

Tito is sitting calmly at a table in the Alcobaça, looking up at Dzovig.

"I've been eating in every restaurant in Lisbon. Do you know how expensive that is? I'm very lucky that my father is a rich man."

Dzovig smiles in spite of herself.

"You didn't come to the beach," he continues; "you said you would."

"I'm sorry. I've been working."

"I've been waiting for you all this time," Tito says.

"I didn't ask you to. Are you going to order something?"

"Yes."

"What?"

"I'll have the *Caldo Verde* and then the *pescada* and then I'll have a dessert, *pudim flan*, and a cup of coffee, please."

Dzovig disappears into the kitchen. The truth is she has hardly given Tito any thought since the day she came home to find Francisco sitting alone in the dark. Francisco came to the restaurant every day, after that, and Dzovig asked him to teach her how to cook, just to keep him busy. He would sigh, but nevertheless roll up his sleeves and tie an apron behind his back.

Francisco's love of food was irrepressible; soon the kitchen was smelling of clams cooked in wine and coriander, fish stews steaming with garlic and poached eggs floating on beds of green peas. He taught her several ways of preparing *bacalhau*, salt cod, what had once been considered the food of the poor but now sold for two thousand escudos a kilo. And Francisco confessed secretly that his *Pargo Deliciouso*, red snapper, was far superior to Rosa's, though he would never tell *her* that. He baked it in the oven on a bed of chopped onions and tomatoes, having salted it hours before. The secret ingredient was a single banana, sliced very thin and soaked in wine. Dzovig had never eaten so much in her life. One night they stayed up past midnight making *Bolas the Berlin*, balls of white pastry that rose like bread. Francisco was back the next day before dawn to fry and then roll them, still warm, in coarse sugar.

"What are we going to do with all this food, Francisco?"

But the food never went to waste. There were neighbours, old ladies, beggars down the street who accepted it gratefully. The *Bolas* they had simply placed on a tray, outside the front door, with the steam rising off them into the limpid morning air.

Towards the end of the holiday Francisco seemed recovered, though he still looked up wistfully to the spot where Balthazar Rei de Portugal's cage had stood. He never thanked Dzovig for her company. He never asked anything of her. All the same she understood that Francisco's goodness was intrinsic.

When Rosa returned from her holiday she had stepped through the door and looked at every inch of the restaurant with an air of deep suspicion.

Francisco said, "Don't look at me. It was *Santa* Dzovig here who did it."

Later that day Rosa placed in Dzovig's hands a green and yellow ceramic mug filled with *café com leite*, and busied herself aimlessly, waiting for Dzovig to drink it. As Dzovig drank the last of the coffee, her eyes grew wider. There, jutting out of the bottom of the mug, was a little porcelain penis.

"I'm going to have a heart attack," Rosa said, she was laughing so hard. "It's a present from Caldas, *a minha terra*, it's our specialty!" And then she laughed some more.

Gordon said, "Well, you're doomed now, Dzovig, there's no escaping it," and Dzovig smiled and placed the mug on a shelf in her room.

When Tito has finished his meal he gives no indication of leaving. The restaurant is busy, though not quite full.

"We are going to be needing this table," Dzovig says.

"Will you come to Cascais on the weekend?"

"I don't know."

"I'm here now, you know. I'll know where to find you."

Dzovig says, "I'll talk to you outside, please." Tito gets up, shuffling between the tables of the restaurant until they are both outside on the narrow sidewalk.

"Tito, I work here. I don't want a boyfriend. I want to be left alone."

"Why?"

"It doesn't matter."

"I think you're fascinating," he says.

Dzovig is suddenly angry.

"Look, if you want me to sleep with you, if that is what you want I can do it, I've done it before when I needed to get some money. Is that what you want?"

"No."

"No?"

"No."

"Then, *adeus*."

Tito comes back every day, after that. Gordon rolls his eyes at first, then raises one eyebrow every time Dzovig passes in front of him. Gordon has looked pale since his return, Dzovig thinks. By the end of the week he is bringing liqueurs to Tito's table, on the house.

Tito says, "They're beginning to pity me around here."

Francisco says, "Look, Dzovig, he's not going to eat you alive, for heaven's sake."

She finally agrees to meet him in Cascais, on Sunday.

"Only because I want to swim," she says.

When Dzovig gets off the train, she sees him immediately, standing by a small newsstand in the corner of the station. He has a wide smile on his face.

"Olà," she says. "Did you wait long?"

"No, only a few hours," he says, "it wasn't so bad. Someone even gave me money. They were very insulted when I gave it back."

They start walking towards the beach, along pedestrian streets lined with restaurants and shops. The pavement is a mosaic of black and white stones in a harlequin pattern, but rounded, as if the whole surface were undulating.

"I like the streets here," Dzovig says. "They are so typical, so Portuguese. It's as if they are leading you somewhere."

"And they last forever," Tito says. "In Sintra, they paved over the old cobblestones years ago and now the asphalt is crumbling, wearing away. But underneath it, there are the old stones, still intact. Harder on the feet though, high heels in particular."

"Is that where you grew up, Sintra?"

"No. I grew up in a village not far from here, a small place, on a cliff overlooking the sea. Azenhas do Mar. I'll show it to you one day. It's beautiful. You're not afraid of heights are you?"

"No."

"The beaches here, they're not that great. Cascais is like a big swimming pool for tourists. I thought we could go to Guincho, it's only ten kilometres from here, the waves are great there."

"Tito, you can't swim in big waves."

"No, but I could watch you. Did you bring a bathing suit?"

"Yes. I bought one."

"Pity," he says.

"I would prefer to stay here."

They walk to the beach and Dzovig pulls off her dress. She helps Tito remove a towel from a knapsack and stretches it out for him on the sand, next to hers. It is early September and the beach is less crowded than when she first came, but still busy. Families with children are clustered around giant parasols. She leaves Tito on the towel and walks into the water, swims until she is farther out than any other bather. There are small boats bobbing in the distance. She'll be safe, Tito thinks. He watches her. He could watch her forever.

Later she pulls a book out of her bag and lies on her stomach, reading. *Lisboa: What the Tourist Should See.*

"You're reading Fernando Pessoa?"

"It's a tourist guide. I bought it because it has both languages, see, English and Portuguese. I look in the English section when I don't understand."

"It's by Pessoa. You don't know him?"

"No."

"He's one of our most important writers. He's a famous poet. He was strange; he wrote as several different people, not under different names but in a specific style for each one. He called them heteronyms. Very brilliant. After he died they found a whole trunk full of thousands of pages of his writing and all the time he had been working as a bookkeeper in some small office. They are publishing all his papers, bit by bit."

"It's just reading practice," she says.

"Look, you should read the preface," Tito says.

"Can I have my book back, please?"

Towards midday Tito disappears for a while and returns with a basket of food, grilled sardines and potatoes, *Pasteis de Bacalhau*, olives and salad. Two beers.

"Caught this morning," he says.

"How do you know for sure?"

"Fishermen never lie," he says, "that's why we are such an honest race."

"Really?"

"You're very suspicious, Dzovig."

"No. I believe you."

Close by, a family is also preparing to eat, the mother is unpacking two large coolers full of sandwiches and salads. She calls to her son, a boy of about three who is poking a stick at the edge of a tide pool. Like all the small children on the beach he is naked except for a hat.

"*Oh José*," the mother calls, "come and have your lunch."

"We could go sightseeing next week if you like," Tito says, "I could show you some castles or churches."

The father scoops up the little boy whose legs are kicking in the air now, and sits him under the parasol.

"I don't like churches," Dzovig says. "I prefer the beach."

The mother holds a plate of food in her palm and feeds the boy with a spoon. She holds the spoon up in front of his face while he chews, as if she is waiting in ambush to enter his mouth again.

"Stop fidgeting," she says.

"Where did you learn to swim like that?" Tito asks.

"I don't know," Dzovig says. "I don't remember."

Sitting there, eating on the beach, Dzovig realizes that Tito has a beautiful face: wide, dark eyes, curly hair, full lips. With a beard he would look like a sailor, she thinks. Close by, the boy starts to protest, tries to squirm away from the circle of shade he is sitting in. "'*Tá quieto*," the mother says, "sit still."

The boy's father is lolling on his back, in the sun. His round stomach protrudes from the plane of his body like something inflated. "Open your mouth, José," the mother says.

"You don't remember how you learned?" Tito asks.

"No."

The boy is crying now, his mother pulls him back by the arm, "Sit down," she keeps saying. The spoon is in front of his mouth again.

"All right," Tito says. "Let me ask you something. I've been wondering about this. What I want to know is, how did you get out of a communist country?"

But Dzovig isn't listening anymore, she is walking straight into the water. Her movement is so sudden that even the woman stops to look at her, long enough for the boy to squirm out of her grasp.

She did leave. It hadn't been that difficult. In the end it had been easy, really, anyone could have done it.

The day after Tomas died, Dzovig went home to the apartment where her mother and father lived. It had been raining. It had already been dark for hours.

Maro, her mother, put her arms around her and brought a towel. "You're all wet," she said, "where have you been?"

She had gone to see Vecihe.

Anahid looked very frightened. "Dzovig, Sahag phoned," she said. "He was looking for you."

Anahid followed Dzovig into their room. She closed the door.

"I don't want to see anybody, Anahid. If anybody asks, tell them, please, I don't want to see anybody!"

"I'll tell them, Dzovig. I'll tell them."

The following day, Dzovig left the house at dawn and waited in line outside the immigration office for several hours before being told that she was at the wrong office. At the next office she waited some more. There were two desks. The woman behind one of them looked at Dzovig as if she had just asked her for a ticket to the moon.

"Impossible," she said.

"Please," Dzovig said.

Behind the other desk was a small man who kept shaking his head from side to side and muttering the word *no* over and over, like some kind of tic: *Che, che che*. He did this every time he filled in a line on a form. He wrote extremely slowly, like a child practising his letters, saying *che che che* all the while. His breathing was shallow and quick and from time to time he wiped his forehead with a yellowed handkerchief.

On her way out, at the bottom of the stairs, Dzovig heard breathing behind her, *che che che*, and the man offered her a piece of paper with an address on it. He might be able to help her if she came there.

"Ten o'clock," he said, "*che che che*."

She sucked him in the bedroom of an apartment where an old couple sat watching television on the other side of the door. He would get her a visa, he said, he would get her to Moscow. The way things were going in Karabagh, everybody was leaving the country. Armenians dying in Azerbaijan or else taking off.

"Believe me, you're not going to want to be around. This blockade they've started is only going to get worse. And we need the room," he said, "for refugees coming into Yerevan from Karabagh. It all evens out in the end."

A group of students was leaving in two months. "They're sick of sitting in the square," he said. She would need to bring her passport and a large sum of money, *che che che*.

Dzovig went looking for money, borrowed some from Rebecca, from Sahag.

"I tried to reach you." Sahag said.

"Please," she'd said. "I just need some money."

"You're not the only one, Dzovig, who lost—"

"No, I'm not."

"You're leaving, aren't you?"

"I've always hated this country, Sahag. I've always hated it."

"No you haven't, and neither did he, Dzovig."

"No, he loved it here, Sahag, he loved this fucking country, look at all the great things he's missing!"

She went to the bank with her mother. *I need some rubles for the cemetrey, Mama, for flowers.*

She began standing on street corners, each day a different corner, wearing lipstick. Sometimes she went to a bar. It was easier than she had expected. She felt nothing other than nausea, at first, and even that passed. Around her, in the city, demonstrations on behalf of Mountainous Karabagh were still going on; someone had begun a hunger strike in Theatre Square. The trials of those accused in the massacre at Sumgait had resulted in one man being condemned to death. The government had announced the closing of the Medzamor nuclear power plant and had reshuffled some of the local leaders, events Tomas would have paid attention to when she first knew him. Not after their trip to Odzun. Not after that.

Dzovig walked the streets now thinking only of money, of days passing. When she came home, at night, her parents were already sleeping. She washed herself in the bathroom, she scrubbed her skin until it was bright red. Anahid would be waiting on her bed. When Dzovig crawled into bed next to her she could feel relief wash over Anahid's body. *You shouldn't wait for me, Anahid*, Dzovig would say. Anahid's body felt hot, as if she had a fever, and the bed smelled of her, a smell Dzovig had known since childhood, a smell she couldn't separate from this girl that was her sister, this body against which she slept.

By the end of one month she had more money than the man had told her to bring. She knew she would need it for bribes.

The plane was leaving in a few days. Dzovig couldn't find her passport. Maro was always in the house, but on Sunday morning her parents left for church. Anahid didn't feel well, she would stay home, she said. Dzovig was frantic, looking through stacks of papers, in kitchen cupboards, under the makeshift altar that Maro kept in the bedroom. She couldn't find it anywhere.

Anahid stepped silently into the room. "I think it's here, Dzovig," and she held out a stack of papers she had found in a shoe box, like an offering.

Dzovig looked at her sister then, at her sister's plain face, at the strands of hair that fell across her eyes like a curtain. Behind the curtain Dzovig saw a girl whose understanding of things, suddenly, seemed infinite.

"I'll be fine," Anahid said.

"Anahid, he's not *you*, Papa. Don't let him crush you."

"I know that."

"I'll be back——"

"No. But I'll be here. I'm worried for you, Dzovig. Where will you go? Where are you going? I'm scared, for you."

"I'll be all right. Don't be scared, Anahid."

"Will you write to me, Dzovig? Write to me, please. You know how I love getting letters——"

"Tell them I have gone to stay with friends. Tell them that I said that, all right?"

The man got her to Moscow. She had spent two days at the airport, hiding in the washroom or simply sitting on a chair, checking her plane ticket every few hours, reading every last letter on it. When the time came, the process of getting on the plane took hours, with a series of forms to be stamped and read over and over again, and airport officials scrutinizing her repeatedly and arguing among themselves as to whether she had all the necessary documents. *This visa is useless*, one had said. *This fare is not registered.* But I have my ticket. *Please step aside until we call your name. I said step aside.* In the end, she paid for a new fare, in cash.

On the plane, Dzovig stared out the window. Her seat was near the back, opposite a washroom that reeked of urine. The door to the washroom didn't close properly and swung open when not in use. The luggage compartments above the seats rattled and squeaked as the plane took off but Dzovig didn't notice. Below her, in the December dark, Yerevan grew smaller and smaller with its scattered lights. She watched as the lights became a series of dots, so tiny now they practically didn't exist at all. In a few days, an earthquake would strike Spitak, in the north-east of Armenia, killing twenty-five thousand people. But she would be gone. She would read about it in a Moscow newspaper.

In Moscow, Dzovig spent months moving around the city. She used the Russian she had learned in school. She made enough money to buy food, slept in men's apartments or in rooms they took her to. She didn't have to hide anymore. Sex in Moscow was like a new drug, with hookers standing openly in front of shops or in parks, and cars stopping for them.

A prostitute named Tatianna passed her on the sidewalk one day and said, "Hey, you should look better than that if you want to get work."

Tatianna was seventeen and lived in an apartment with her mother. They had come to Moscow several years before, when her father was still alive. Her mother didn't ask her where she got her money.

"I think she knows," Tatianna said, "but she needs it too much, the money. Better not to ask."

Tatianna took Dzovig to a particular bar. "This is where the rich ones come," she said. "If I were you, I would dye my hair."

"How much do you ask for?" Dzovig asked.

Tatianna's cheeks flushed a little. "Depends," she said. "If you meet me here in the morning, I'll take you to my place. We can do your hair. My mother will be at work."

At Tatianna's apartment, Dzovig sat on the sofa but couldn't keep her eyes open.

"You're tired," Tatianna said. "Why don't you sleep a little? My mother won't mind."

Dzovig slept until Tatiana's mother woke her. She had slept for fourteen hours.

"You need some food in you, and a bath," Tatianna's mother said. She didn't seem surprised at all, as if she was used to finding young women sleeping on her sofa.

"I'm sorry," Dzovig said. "You are very kind. I'll be out of your way. Tatianna—"

"Tatianna has gone out with friends," the woman said. She seemed a little tired herself. "She will be back later. Have some dinner at least, we can wait together."

"Thank you, I should go."

"No, you can stay. You're not from Moscow, I can tell. But your Russian is good."

Dzovig did stay, eating the meal that Tatianna's mother had prepared and sleeping again, afterwards, for the rest of the night. And she returned to the apartment and slept on the sofa for several weeks, leaving part of her earnings on the kitchen counter for Tatianna's mother. Tatianna dyed Dzovig's hair.

"When I was a kid, I wanted to be a hairdresser," she said. "Now I think it doesn't pay enough."

Many of Tatianna's clients worked in government offices. They bought foreign perfumes for her, and nylon stockings. One had even given her a leather jacket.

"You can buy anything you want," Tatianna said.

"What I want is a plane ticket," Dzovig said.

"You mean, a foreign husband?"

In the end it was all done legally by a Mr. Hagopian, an Armenian, who was tall and thin and who was not even a client of Tatianna's, only the friend of one. Dzovig sat in his office and told him that she wanted to study in France, that she wanted to be a translator. He appraised her with his eyes.

"If I believed you I might not be so eager to help," he said. "Whatever it is, it's got to be better than this, right?"

He had given her a four-year student visa, and the name of a travel agent. She thanked him. As she turned to leave he asked her what town she had grown up in.

"Yerevan," she said.

"Will you ever go back?" Mr. Hagopian asked.

And because she trusted him, she answered truthfully, "No, I'll never go back."

In the water, Dzovig holds her head under as long as she can.

"Bad for your digestion," Tito says when she comes out again. "Didn't they teach you that in Armenia? All that food in your stomach will make you sink."

Dzovig begins to laugh.

"I suppose you're not going to tell me then, about your great escape."

"It wasn't very exciting. I became a prostitute to make some money. And when I had enough money I left."

"You're not here legally, then."

"I'm supposed to be studying in France. Gordon was looking into my papers here. We haven't heard anything."

"You probably won't. It takes years to get anything done in this country."

"You have no idea——"

"That was dangerous, you know. You could have been killed."

"That's what my father said. Are you shocked?"

"No. It doesn't matter."

"I didn't die."

"No, you didn't. And now you're here, in Cascais, with me."

"Are you always like this, Tito, smiling at the world?"

Tito looks at the sea. "I can tell you are from an inland country. You know, it's the same with people who come from cold countries, although I should probably move to one. I should live in a place like Canada, or Finland, it would be better for my condition. But they take things much more seriously in those places, they hold it all in. Look at this, this sea, we stare at it all our lives. There's nothing we can do about it, about the tides, the waves…. We're nothing compared to that. We last less than a grain of sand. So, we think, why fight? You might as well leave it up to fate and be happy. In Portugal we're even happy when we're unhappy, because the sea laughs at us, in our faces."

"Like walking in the rain when you've forgotten your umbrella, and you don't care anymore, you're so wet...." Dzovig is surprised at herself, because she cannot remember a moment of happiness in the rain.

"That's it," Tito says. "That's exactly it."

II

VECIHE

A child's frailty is in his arms. The legs always seem the strongest, jumping, running at amazing speeds, and then the hands that grasp, hold on with such force. But the arms have no strength, their flesh is rounded and soft. When I think of Tomas as a baby it is his little arms I crave, stretched upwards, the tips of his fingers barely reaching beyond the top of his head.

I have lost my sense of time. I used to think it important, like so many other things. I used to measure my life in days, weeks, years. Now there is only one time, it is all of a piece, it is all the time after my son's death. And the day in September, a number on the calendar that will now be the only day, the only anniversary we will remember, eclipsing even his birthday. Death takes no notice of our human plans, and we did have them, didn't we? Like all parents we had plans for him, even if they were, in the end, partly for ourselves.

Months have passed. I have stopped counting. It is winter. What a difference an absence makes to the sounds of a house. Looking at it realistically I know that Tomas wasn't here that often, but now my thoughts seem to reverberate against the walls, amplified by the silence. I go into his room but I can no longer tell if it is still his smell on the sheets, or my own. It is only recently that I have begun looking at his things; every drawing, every scrawl on the inside of a book I invest with such importance. Death does this: turns the mundane into the sacred. I ask myself, is this simply a remembrance or am I looking for clues? What can I make of these drawings of churches, notes, of some pages with nothing on them but a series of vertical marks, copies of old inscriptions, maybe, but no, these aren't letters, only marks. And even if he had left a note, what could he have said that would be enough? What explanation could I give to convince the world that my son was not insane, that he was not stupid?

I try to move more slowly about the house. I try not to break things. I haven't stopped painting. I throw paint onto the paper, soaking it until it rips, and then I start again. The paintings are nothing, just something to do with my hands. The other day I drank a cup full of paint, not deliberately. I only realized what I had done when I noticed a metallic taste in my mouth.

I know that Bedros wonders how I can still paint. Perhaps he thinks I should stop, do nothing. All our lives we are told how to behave, how to love, obey, stay silent; how to forget God. And now I find that my husband has his own expectations of how I should grieve. When I look at him I see a different man, a transformed face. Of course, he might say the same thing of me. One has to assign blame and we have each other for that, and our own selves.

I think of Dzovig. A rush of panic overwhelms me when I see her standing outside as she was that day, when I hear again Bedros's senseless, misplaced rage. For weeks after Tomas's death I didn't dare call her for fear of what it would do to him. *For fear.* When Bedros returned to work I searched for her number— Tomas hadn't written it anywhere—and finally spoke to a man who said that she was not there and asked that I not call again.

There are days when Bedros and I hardly speak. At first there was no need. It was enough to hold onto his body, to hold him, it didn't matter who was on the receiving end; we were in it, both of us, in the horror of it. I think that there must have been moments when his hands were on my face, when for a second he felt, apart from his own pain, sorrow for mine, but I am unsure of even this. Perhaps I was invisible to him all along. What a fallacy it is to assume that a shared loss automatically brings into being a larger closeness. Now, when I am desperate for him and he sits there, not two metres away from me and as if he were behind a thick, glass wall, I curse the selectivity of his grief, how normal, how businesslike he sounds in his dealings with other people, saving his rage and sorrow for the moment he steps through our door. I too have expectations, I suppose. The sound of his voice on the phone when he talks to others, the ordinariness of it, makes me cringe.

We strive to be normal. This is the great miracle of death: that living goes on, that we keep on eating, shitting, sleeping. I think of those animals I have seen on television, in landscapes that always look too beautiful to be real, leaving the carcasses of their young in the dirt with apparent indifference in order to hunt, migrate, survive. I never fathomed, really, with what agony they must have witnessed the moment of death, with what fear. I know now that it is an agony you feel first in your body, in every nerve: a physical wrenching. It is only later that the mind absorbs. But the body remembers. Sometimes, when I am going about my day, it shocks me to realize that for a few moments I have not thought about Tomas. Sometimes I forget that he is dead. I tidy up his drawer, fold a t-shirt. And then all my memories come rushing back and the irreversibility of everything stares me in the face. That's when I feel it. A blow to my stomach, like a kick.

There will only be memories from now on, of course. I should almost be used to it. So much of parenthood is a leave-taking, a series of endings one has to witness, and beginnings. I watched with fascination as Tomas became a man, but like any mother I was nostalgic for the boy I'd lost, for the baby. I remember one night. Tomas was recently out of diapers when he woke up crying and I went to him, as I always did. I carried him in my arms with his head against my neck and his legs around my waist, letting him drift back into sleep. I walked with him to the bathroom and sat down to pee and when I did, he peed also, wetting my stomach and my nightgown with his urine and never waking, as if we were still one body. Of all the moments this is my favourite.

There is a sequence to things.

What would I say to you now, Tomas, if I had known? What would I say to you? That I adored you, adored you, that I rail at you for having taken from me what was entirely mine, which is the right to die before you, the right to die first.

III

PESSOA

The summer ebbs. It hesitates, sending out days of exquisite sunlight as if it were reminding the place of its essence. The intense heat has lifted, it rains now for days at a time. The sea is cold, much too cold to swim in, and no longer of the same blue. Dzovig and Tito don't mind this, they still meet at the beach, at various beaches, walking on the sand in their bare feet.

Most of the tourists have gone and the Alcobaça now feeds the locals, families, men and women who are noisier, more demanding, and more joyous. Dzovig works five days a week now, for a salary. A small salary, because she refuses to leave her little room at the back of the restaurant, where she keeps the ceramic mug that Rosa has given her and a stack of books in Portuguese, insisting that rent be deducted. Tito also makes a salary working in the accounting office of his father's hotel, where he can't frighten the guests, he says. But in the evenings and on weekends Tito becomes a sort of fixture at the Alcobaça, letting himself in the kitchen without asking permission, to see what Rosa and Francisco are cooking today.

"His father should be putting us all up for a holiday in that hotel of his, the number of times his son eats in my kitchen," Rosa says.

Gordon has been working a little less, claiming that he is unpopular with the locals, a blatant lie. He isn't well and they all know this. Rosa seems irritated by his presence, as if his pallor were an affront to her and to the work she needs to get done. Perhaps only Francisco knows why Rosa leaves the restaurant at eight o'clock on the days when Gordon is not there, carrying stacks of warming pots filled with food and returning two or three hours later. If Dzovig has noticed this, she hasn't asked about it. Dzovig believes herself at peace, setting tables and serving the guests, her favourite time the hours late at night when she and Francisco are closing up for the day, the silence of the dining room then and Francisco sighing before patting her shoulder and saying, *até amanhã*, Dzovig, until the morning. As Dzovig's Portuguese has grown more fluent she has begun to dissect it with some fascination, in particular the phrases that have no accurate translation or those that, if translated, would sound more like poetry than ordinary speech, as when Rosa spoke of the place from which the ceramic mug with a little penis at its bottom came, calling it a *minha terra*, meaning, in a sense, it's from my home town, but more precisely, *it's from my earth*. Dzovig remembers her first conversation with Gordon about the Portuguese propensity for diminutives. *You'll never guess*, he had said on that day; *it means little fat man*.

On her days off Dzovig goes to the beach with Tito. She is comforted by the routine of this, and she has grown slightly addicted to the sea now, to the smell of it. On the sand she adjusts her pace to Tito's. He takes her to Azenhas do Mar, the place of his childhood, a village of small white houses clustered in a labyrinth of tiny streets, courtyards and gardens, all of it perched on a promontory overlooking the sea, with stairways leading down to the shore. On the beach a swimming pool that has been carved out of the rock fills with sea water at high tide.

"Sometimes that pool is the only beach there is," Tito says.

"Is that where you learned to swim?" Dzovig asks.

"I don't know," he says, "I don't remember," and he smiles. He points out the house where his father was born.

"I only lived there until I was four," he says, "why should I love it so much? It's silly, I know. I love it because my mother died here. You see, I have a few tragedies of my own, Dzovig."

"You never told me."

"Ah, it doesn't matter. I was just a baby. I was well looked after. It's the missing of her, when I was little, that's what causes me pain now, when I remember it. I used to pray to her, at night, when I was a kid, I used to say *Mother, if there is such a thing as you*—and then I would ask her to send me a bicycle or something. Can you imagine, a bicycle on these streets?"

"Do you have a picture of her?"

"At home, we have some. My father wouldn't put them up. *I don't need a photograph to miss her*, he used to say."

"When I was small I used to place a ball at the bottom of a long stocking and I would bang it against the wall of our building. And I would lift up my leg and bang it under my knee, like that, and over again. I don't know why I just remembered that. I loved that game."

"Sounds dangerous."

"Yes, my legs were all black and blue."

They drive one day to another beach, farther south along the coast. Dzovig hasn't driven in ages; the Portuguese drive like madmen, she says. It is November, grey and cold, the sea is the colour of slate. The beach is deserted, rough and raw. The tide is out but the waves are still crashing in the distance. They keep their shoes on.

"This place is a lover's paradise in the summer," Tito says; "let me show you."

He leads her to some caves at one end, hollows in the cliffs, their walls encrusted in black shells.

"Listen to the echo," he says, and he calls her name, cupping his hands around his mouth. "*You* try."

"No."

"Say something bad, come on," and he hurls profanities at the cave until she is laughing again, repeating everything he says.

He notices that her jacket is open and she is shivering.

"You're cold," Tito says, and he grabs hold of the button at the bottom, manages it eventually.

Halfway up her belly he stops. He places his hand on her breast, feels her nipple against his palm. He opens her shirt and places his mouth there, without asking, and she doesn't move. And then he loses his balance and Dzovig tries to grab him before he falls over.

"I love you," Tito says, "you know that."

"I wouldn't recommend it," she says.

"Of course you wouldn't."

"Tito, so much can be taken from you—"

"Can I kiss you now? I've already kissed your breast—"

"Yes."

In early January, Lisbon begins to feel different to her. The white lights of Christmas still hang in the streets, and the dark comes very early now, a black sheet suddenly tossed over the city. Dzovig and Tito are lovers; they have been lovers since Christmas Eve, the night Dzovig met and dined with Tito's father, at the hotel, and later undressed herself in Tito's room. On that night Tito's body had felt to her like any other body, soft and hard and fluid, when he moved. He had come inside her utterly and completely, holding onto her afterwards as if she had just rescued him and he was grateful. She hadn't stayed, that night; she had walked along the silent, carpeted hallways of the hotel and returned to Lisbon. But she has stayed with him since, sleeping on the large white bed and waking to a view of the sea, far beneath the room's balcony. Standing at the railing she can hardly believe it.

"I only come here for the view," she says.

If Tito is hurt by the half-truth of this he doesn't tell her so. Tito is a happy man, whistling at his desk throughout the day, knowing that he will see her at night. He can hardly eat. When he takes the train to Lisbon, a train that travels along the coast, he closes his eyes. When Dzovig takes the train to Cascais, she stares out the window at the rain on the sea. Tito wants her with sheer abandon. She can do this, make him happy in this way.

In the Alfama the stuccoed houses look drenched, tired, more beautiful perhaps. The pavement glistens in the rain. Every morning, before work, Dzovig walks the streets around the Alcobaça, on her way to other streets, other addresses. She fixes her eyes on specific houses, memorizing them. One street literally consists of a flight of stairs and Dzovig counts these as she climbs them, out loud. A stranger observing this might be reminded of a little girl playing hopscotch. But Dzovig wants to make sure. The stuccoed houses in their washed-out beauty, the stairs, the doorways... all these could evaporate.

Before Tito she owned these streets, she owned them because she belonged to no one, and it occurs to her that that she isn't singular in this, that others have lived this way, with houses, streets, cities etched onto their brains like maps, like those black lines on phrenological heads, the skull divided into sections until every human trait had an explanation, an answer. She has read somewhere that dreams of houses are actually dreams about the body. Fernando Pessoa, she thinks, was very fond of dreams.

Dzovig doesn't know who lives at the addresses on Largo do Carmo, Rua Passos Manuel, Rua Dona Estefânia. She doesn't know at what point she decided to retrace Pessoa's steps, all the places he inhabited in Lisbon, in chronological order. She'd begun by visiting the places in her book, Pessoa's book *What the Tourist Should See*, as a kind of self-education, but she had tired quickly, having no patience for monuments. She picked up a book of his poetry at the *Feira*, out of curiosity. It had poems in it by the three heteronyms: Alberto Caeiro, Ricardo Reis, Álvaro de Campos. Three different books of poetry in one. Three selves in one brain.

Now, she stands in front of buildings where he once lived. She doesn't ring the doorbells. Sometimes, she stares up at a window, counting vertically to make sure she has the right floor. Sometimes she assigns a particular building to one of the heteronyms. Did Pessoa do this, she wonders, give dwelling places to his three poets just as he gave them histories, professions, particular deaths?

Dzovig doesn't believe in ghosts. Nevertheless she feels

accompanied, as if Pessoa were standing there with her, like an accomplice.

Tito buys her some earrings one day, pulling her into one of the many jewellery shops that line Rua Augusta and pointing to a pair that have stones the colour of emeralds, outlined in gold and surrounded by silver marcasites.

"Those," he says, "they match her eyes."

Something in the delicate curls of silver surrounding the oval gems reminds her of home, of the petalled crosses of Armenian *khachkars* with their ends all pointing towards one another. She thinks of her sister, Anahid. A sudden heat rises to her face, a series of memories tumble through her, moments and faces of the past two years—more than two years, she realizes. *Write to me, please.*

Dzovig lingers, her head bent over the paired jewels under the glass counters. When she looks up again her eyes are pale, the colour of rushing water.

"Are you all right?" Tito asks.

"They're beautiful, Tito. I will wear them."

She returns there the next day, without him, buying a pair of earrings identical to her own but with red stones instead. Ruby red.

January 24th, 1993.
Dear Anahid,

I am living in Portugal. I have been here for almost two years, it's hard to believe. I spent some months in Moscow after I left, and then in France. I'm sorry it has taken me so long to write. I should have written earlier, for your sake. I just couldn't. I'm sorry.

*These earrings are for you. I have a pair the same. Please tell
Mother and Father that I am fine, I am working in a restaurant, my boss
is English. I have a room and I eat well. I can speak Portuguese! The sea
is beautiful here, maybe you will see it one day. I would really love that.
I hope that you are well and the winter is not too cold this year. I know
the country is all fucked up, but maybe for the better? We don't hear very
much about Armenia here.*

*I hope you wear them. I'll try to write more often. I think of you,
Anahid.*

Dzovig

Dzovig and Tito walk along the streets towards the Elevador de Santa
Justa, a tower made of black iron with an elevator in it that links
the lower Baixa with a neighbourhood up above, the Bairro Alto.

"It looks like the Eiffel tower," Dzovig says.

"You've never been on it?"

"No."

"You've never been to the Chiado?"

"No."

"Jesus!"

Stepping off the elevator they pass a ruined church
whose skeletal arches she recognizes, having seen them from the
Baixa. Up close they look as if they were always meant to be this
way, gothic outlines in the sky.

Tito points to the church with his chin. "My aunt has a
saying. She says, 'In us, the only real thing is the skeleton.'" They
walk along the Rua Garrett and there is construction everywhere. "We had a huge fire here two years ago. They are rebuild-
ing it now. Many beautiful buildings were lost."

The street is a mess, the air clogged with dust. Nevertheless the people walking here seem contented.

"I've been thinking," Tito says. "Soon it will be spring again, people will be going to the beach.... It would save us a lot of travelling if you lived at the hotel. My father could use someone like you, who speaks English and French, at the reception desk. You could make some money."

Dzovig stares straight ahead.

"The real reason is, I can't bear those train rides into Lisbon anymore, waiting to get here, my stomach can't bear it. It's bad for my health."

Dzovig looks at him. "Tito, the man I loved, in Armenia, his name was Tomas. He killed himself. Shot himself in the mouth. I'll never love anyone like that again. I can't."

"I'm sorry."

"Why should you be? It has nothing to do with you, Tito."

"I want it all to do with me. All that has ever happened to you."

"Well, it can't."

"Look, I know you've run away from something, something that I can't compete with. And it may be that for the first time in my life I'm being completely selfish. But I don't care. I don't care if I'm not the one. I only care about today, about being with you now."

"And Gordon, Rosa, at the restaurant. They have been very good to me. Francisco just found himself a cat, it drives Rosa crazy. I don't know if I can—"

"We could still see them, they could be like your relatives; we would come every Sunday—"

"No," she says. "We wouldn't. But they would understand."

"They would. Definitely."

"You already asked your father?"

"I did. I'm sorry."

"I will think about it."

"Good."

They pass a café where a few tables have been set out front, with some tourists bravely taking in the sun and noise. Among them is a strange figure, cast in bronze. The man wears a fedora and bow tie, and leans his elbow on a round table. Beside him, also in bronze, is an empty chair.

"Who is that man?" Dzovig asks.

"It's Pessoa. Remember? Your tourist guide? He used to do a lot of his drinking here, at the *Brasileira*. I think he even did some writing here, on a napkin or something."

"Not on a napkin. On loose pieces of paper."

"How do you know?" Tito asks.

"I read the preface, remember?" she says. "I've read about him." Her heart is beating. She can't believe she has missed this. And she doesn't know why exactly she has kept them from Tito—her little excursions through Pessoa's Lisbon.

Dzovig turns her head to look at it once more, the figure of Fernando Pessoa with one leg crossed over the other and a right hand paused in mid-air. Paused at a thought, as if in hesitation.

It's taken you longer than I thought—

She almost smiles.

IV

VECIHE

September 1991. We are a country again, at last. Our independence has been declared. It is momentous, terrifying. It has been
two years since Tomas died, two horrible years. And we know
that there is worse to come.

Last year we witnessed the collapse of the Soviet empire,
republics breaking away in succession even as we struggled to
do the same. We watched, open-mouthed, with the rest of the
world, young people sitting on the Berlin wall, shouting with joy.
Here the leaders of the Armenian National Movement have been
imprisoned, released, elected, all within the span of a few months.
We went on strike, we demonstrated again until we were told
that the law had been changed, that finally the republics could
secede. In all, three different governments have since declared
jurisdiction over the area of Mountainous Karabagh. And our
young men have been sent there to fight the Azerbaijanis.

The irony of all this is that the one objective we began
with is the one we haven't been able to achieve. We begin our life
as an independent country, but already at war. Since August of last
year a blockade has cut off rail service and fuel shipments from
Azerbaijan. All our industries are failing. Yerevan is full of refugees
from the earthquake and from Karabagh, and the shortages have
begun. I think back sometimes to those weeks in February, three

years ago, when it all started. How astounded we were at our own power, how hopeful. We didn't free Karabagh but in the end we have freed ourselves, and perhaps we couldn't have without those weeks, without that revelation.

Sometimes I think I should be thankful that Tomas is not here. I should be thankful for not having a son to send to war; how long could we have prevented that inevitability? (I'm not thankful. Do I envy the mothers of war? Of course I envy them.) Our system of special favours has vanished. Money will now be the only thing left to bargain with, but what use is money when there isn't a pound of sugar left on the shelf to buy?

Thousands have already left the country. We are a decimated population, and what's more, we are inept from inexperience. We have spent years in the system at jobs whose purpose fulfilled only some obscure, communist logic, and now that the logic is gone, we don't know how to place ourselves. The other day I sent a poor woman clerk into a fit of anger because I laughed out loud when she told me to stand in a line several metres away from her. I'm your only customer, I said, and then I did what she asked, to show her the absurdity of it.

Bedros is still working at the ministry, I don't really ask for details. Perhaps he will at least feel that he is a part of something that can be reinvented. There are days when we hardly speak. We watch news reports of the fighting along the border, how tired he looks then. With our eyes fixed on the television I hear his voice again, saying *More people will die, more people will die.* And then I think, if we didn't do this, what would we call ourselves? And how different are we from those who took on a tiny piece of land in 1918, with a starving population, and called it a country? That was the last time we were an independent country.

In the aftermath of a war where millions of us were killed, when borders were being drawn and redrawn like a series of lines in the sand, by Turkey, by Russia, our little republic lasted only four years. And how much have our chances improved?

I ask myself, as all the events of these months unfold, what those on the outside make of us. That word, *diaspora*, it's a beautiful-sounding word. A word, for us, so heavy with implication. I would have been part of it, that whole other country scattered across the globe, had my mother not gone to Odzun. How would our lives, mine and hers, have been then? They would have been another story.

When I say *that whole other country*, it is my own desperate bias speaking. An imagined solidarity just in case one has to leave. Years ago, what I so wanted to leave was not my country, but my marriage. I used to fantasize about leaving the way one dreams of a lover, with the same thrill and fear. What if I didn't go home that day, after work? What if I just disappeared? In the end my courage failed me, or perhaps it was the opposite. Perhaps it was more brave to stay. If we knew the ramifications of every choice we made, how could we possibly make them? Sometimes I think that life is as random as a coin spinning madly along the floor, coming to a stop *here*, showing *this* face. And then there are moments when I think that we know it all, we see it all in advance before us, that we understand the possibilities even as we choose....

Mida used to say that Aghavnee's star was unlucky. Did she say this before, or after Aghavnee's death? Mida. How many times has she remembered my face in all these years?

Months after Tomas died, I went looking for Dzovig. I spoke to Tomas's old friends, what few I could find. Sahag told me she had left the country but that he knew no more than this. Then, as I was leaving, he asked me to wait and admitted that he had seen her at night, on the street.... He couldn't bring himself to say it openly.

"She was out of her mind," he said, "after Tomas. She wanted money, she needed to get out."

I kissed him. "Tell me where her parents live, Sahag." I didn't care anymore if I would offend them. I needed to know what had happened, what she had said.

The building was not too far from the university, one of those crumbling structures that might at one time have been beautiful. Now, bits of balconies seemed to hang on the walls as if they were held there with string. I climbed the stairs. There was no answer at first. I knocked again, I had a feeling that some- one must be inside. A man opened the door, her father. The type of man who, in his own household, is always the one who opens the door.

"I'm sorry to bother you," I said. "My name is Vecihe Abajian. My son was Tomas."

We both stood there for a moment, waiting, with the half-opened door between us. I heard a voice from behind him in a kind of whisper saying, "Arzas?" Then he shook his head as if he'd just been reminded of his manners and he extended his hand to me.

"Please. Come in."

There was no friendliness in his voice, only a kind of muted resolve, as if he had decided to get through this, whatever it was, as quickly as possible. As I stepped inside I caught a glimpse of Dzovig's mother, rushing into the bedroom with her hands behind her back, untying some sort of knot. A young woman was clearing cups and newspapers off the table.

"This is my daughter," he said.

She greeted me with a nod and a timid smile. Her hair was black and straight. She was very different from Dzovig.

"Dzovig told me that she had a sister, but she didn't tell me how beautiful you are," I said.

"Thank you."

"Go and make some tea," her father said. We were alone then. I expected him to ask me to leave at any moment. He was unshaven, a clear sign that he was probably out of work.

"I'm sorry to come here like this," I said. "I have just been wondering about Dzovig. I was——"

"Dzovig left two months after your son died," he said.

"Do you know where she went?"

"She left. I don't know where she went. She isn't coming back. That's all."

"She didn't… give you an address?"

"No."

Dzovig's sister brought out some tea and placed it on the table; it seemed ridiculous, given how hostile he was. But I wasn't prepared to leave yet, I needed something more. And because I didn't know what else to say I said, "My son loved her very much."

He seemed to abandon all pretense of politeness then and looked at me with his narrow eyes.

"Do you know what Dzovig did after your son killed himself? She prostituted herself on the street like a piece of garbage, that's how much he loved her!"

"Did she say anything——"

"Do you know what she said to me? What she said? She asked if my grandfather was shot in the head. She wanted to know if my grandfather was shot in the head!"

"I don't understand—"

"Please, don't come here ever again. I'm very sorry for you, for what happened to your son. I don't have a daughter."

He walked out of the room, slamming a door closed behind him, and I stood there, barely breathing. The young woman, Dzovig's sister, came to me.

"Would you like a sip of water?" She was standing in front of me, with a glass in her hand.

"Do you know?" I whispered.

She shook her head. "I know that she left the country. She said she couldn't stay here anymore. She took her papers.... I asked her to write but she hasn't yet. Maybe she will."

"Will you give her something, for me, if you hear from her? Will you let me know, please?" I scribbled my address and phone number on a piece of paper. I pulled out a little package from my bag, a set of pencils I had found in Tomas's room; Dzovig would understand what they meant, what they had meant. I also gave her a rolled up watercolour that I had painted years before, one of the pictures she had seen on my wall that first day when Tomas brought her home.

"I don't know your name," I said.

"Anahid."

"Anahid. Please tell your mother that I am sorry."

I opened the door but couldn't stop myself from asking one more question.

"Does Dzovig look like your mother?"

"No. I'm the one who looks like her," Anahid said. "We've never been able to decide who Dzovig looks like."

I left as quietly as I could and started down the stairs. I was halfway down the building when I heard the squeak of a door and a voice saying, almost in a whisper, "Wait! Please!"

I stopped. I waited, but there was no sound of footsteps coming down to join me. After a few moments I heard the tired hinges of a door again, and the click of its closing.

I paid a man to take me to the airport. Where else did I have to look? I had Dzovig's picture with me, a snapshot of her that I found in Tomas's room, folded in half and wrinkled as if it had been left too long in a pocket.

It was the middle of the afternoon and the airport was empty. The man who drove me said he would wait. I showed the photograph to the single person I found, a clerk sitting at a desk. She looked at me suspiciously.

"Who are you?" she said.

"I'm looking for this girl. She may have left the country. Can you help me please?"

The woman stared blankly at me. I passed her the photograph along with some folded money I had in my hand.

"Please."

She disappeared into an office and came back after a few minutes.

"No one remembers her," she said.

I sat on a chair against the wall, waiting. I knew there would be a flight at some point. I was used to waiting. We all are. Eventually they did come, men and women began forming a line at a counter, with giant piles of suitcases clustered around them. I joined the line, looking awkward with only my purse. The line didn't move. We all stood there with flies buzzing around us and the men sweating in their shirts. Finally, three workers appeared behind the counter and it was suddenly pandemonium, with names being called out and people cursing and pushing ahead of each other. I waited.

At the counter I held the photograph in front of them, flattening it with my two hands.

"Please, have you seen this girl, my daughter—"

"Do you know how many people come through here? Where is your ticket? Step aside."

I ran into the bathroom and sat on a toilet, sobbing. It had been months, I'd waited too long.

Do you know what it means to look for someone, Vecihe?

"Can I help you? Madam? Can I help you?"

A voice on the other side of the door. A woman with a bucket and a floor mop in her hands.

"You are looking for somebody," she said. "I saw you waiting, in the chair."

"Yes."

I showed her the photograph.

"It was maybe a year ago that she left," I said. "It's a long time, they don't remember."

She looked carefully at the picture, taking her time.

"She hid in here, in the bathroom. That's why I remember her. She fell asleep in here once. She hung around the airport for a couple of days before her flight. I know because I clean the bathrooms."

"Where was her flight to, do you know?" I was trembling like a leaf.

"There were young people on that flight. Students. The students always go to Moscow. Usually."

I gave her the rest of my money.

"Thank you," I said, "thank you very much."

❧

When I arrived home, I asked the driver to wait while I went in to get money. We always kept money in the house. I would have given her money, if she had come to me. She *did* come. I didn't help her.

Bedros was home. It was late, well after dinner time.

"Where have you been?"

"Just a minute."

I opened the drawer. The driver was waiting.

"What is it?" Bedros said. "Where have you been?"

I paid the driver and returned. "I was at the airport," I said.

"The airport? What for?"

"I was looking for Dzovig."

"At the airport?"

"She left the country after Tomas died. No one knows where she went."

"What has that got to do with us?" Bedros said.

"I want to know what has happened to her, Bedros, that's all!"

"That's what you are wasting money on?"

"Money? Is this about money?"

"I don't give a damn about the stupid money!"

"Then what are you shouting about?"

"I want to know why she is so important, a girl who meant nothing to us!"

"Nothing to *you!* To *you*, Bedros! Because I'll never know why Tomas did what he did and because I want to know! Because I loved her. Because my mother had a sister, a sister who was lost, who was taken in the middle of the desert and we never knew what happened to her, Bedros, we never knew and I want to know!"

"And what do you think it will change, exactly? Do you think you can just fit her into your life, that we could all go on happily as if nothing had happened?"

"Isn't that what we do, Bedros, isn't that what we've always been so good at?"

"You're right. And perhaps since we are on the subject you can tell me what I want to know!"

I looked at him. Some moments, some words you know are irreversible.

"Perhaps you can tell me," he said softly, "why you came back. I found the note you left, when you went away. I've had every single word of it imprinted on my skull, right here, all these years! I came home and found the note. But then, you came back."

"Bedros—"

"I never said anything to you, Vecihe. But I've known, all this time, that you tried to leave me."

"I didn't leave, I *couldn't*, Bedros."

"Why not? Was it out of pity for me, that you came back? Or because of Tomas?"

"No! No. Why didn't you ask me? Why didn't you tell me that you knew?"

"Because I didn't want to hear you say that you didn't love me, that's why."

"Maybe it would have been all the same to you, Bedros. I couldn't tell what you felt—"

"I've done things, I'm not a saint, Vecihe. But I never wanted to *leave*, it never occurred to me to even think it."

"Well, perhaps you had no reason to, Bedros. Perhaps you had everything you wanted, back then, everything."

What have I not told Bedros in the course of our marriage?

That I miscarried once, in those early years, clots of blood smeared on the towel even before I had given him the news that I was pregnant. I'd wanted to keep that pregnancy, my first, to myself for a while, a private secret.

That I found a wonderful pair of boots that Tomas had worn for two winters as a boy on a store shelf, behind a stack of canned food, and never paid for them.

That two of the women I worked with at the factory were lovers and that I kept watch on their behalf while they shut themselves in the washroom, in case the supervisor came.

That I found a yellow ribbon on the floor, beside our bed, a ribbon that wasn't mine, a kind of ribbon I would never wear because I don't wear ribbons in my hair, and that I stored it away in a box and have it still.

These have been some of my lies. And what do they matter, really, in the scheme of things? We all have our own secret lives. I forgave him the yellow ribbon. And when I came back and destroyed the note I had left on the bedroom dresser, thinking he had not seen it, I truly believed that if I kept silent, said nothing, it would pass. That in time this pain of ours would become like an old wound covered in new skin, a skin that held only the faint outline of our suffering.

And Bedros has had lies of his own.

But I've known. All this time. How much you can call into question with just these few words. How much has our silence cost us.

V

FRANCISCO

Through the window they can make out the shadows of people stopping at the door, noticing the *CLOSED* sign, and peering through the curtains with varying degrees of irritation or disappointment.

"That one will cry all the way home," Francisco says. "His mother isn't cooking tonight."

"He won't be the only one," Gordon says, though who he is referring to isn't quite clear. To himself, perhaps, or to one of the other two older figures sitting at the table, Francisco, whose tears are known to surface as suddenly as a child's, or Rosa, who bears her grief with a stoic resolve. Dzovig won't cry, Gordon knows, even though this is her farewell dinner, something they have been planning for a few weeks now, though they have known for three months that she would leave. Tomorrow, Dzovig will start working at the hotel in Cascais. *It's a better job*, Gordon has told her, *it will be better for you, really*, and Tito, almost no longer an outsider, is beaming with happiness.

Gordon has brought up two of his best bottles of wine from the cellar. Francisco has retrieved them. The stairs are steep. Years ago, when Gordon first bought the place, those stairs led to the only kitchen, a wall of open shelves with a few cabinets, a sink and a stove, and a slab of marble placed over a table in a room the size of a closet. Rosa cooked there for almost a year, with Gordon carrying food up the stairs to the dining room for men and women who, if they had known what the kitchen looked like, would not have minded. At the end of the night Gordon and Rosa would sit on two upturned wine barrels, the tiny table between them, eating their supper. He remembers those meals as the best meals of his life, and in his memory he can't separate the tastes in his mouth from the smells of wine barrels, of wood and clay, of the stone cellar walls whose colour was the white of fresh goat cheese, a cheese that Rosa still makes herself and serves to him on toast with marmalade on top. Among the many things Gordon is grateful to her for, and to Francisco now, is the pure joy of eating through all these years, and he is sorry that the slow wasting of his body has the appearance of a testament against this.

Tonight he has asked for an English meal, Beef Wellington, which Francisco has cooked to perfection, though of course it has a Portuguese flavour to it, something in the seasoning maybe that he can't quite put his finger on, but unmistakably Francisco's.

"*I'm* going to cry if I don't eat here again soon, this is so delicious," Tito says.

"Who is the cook at that hotel of yours?" Rosa asks.

"We have several; the kitchen is huge."

Rosa seems unsatisfied.

"None as good as you," Tito adds.

Rosa looks at Dzovig. "You make sure that you eat well, *filha*, you're so skinny."

"I've put on four and a half kilos since coming here!"

"Well, you needed them!"

"Ah," Francisco says, "the sea air will do her good," and Dzovig smiles.

Gordon raises his glass: "Dzovig, I don't know what brought you here, but you've been a wonderful help, a wonderful worker, and we're all going to miss you—"

"It was God who brought her here!" Rosa says, and though she sounds angry, her eyes are filling with tears.

"Don't get ridiculous," Francisco says.

"We have a little parting gift," Gordon continues, giving her a small parcel, wrapped in left-over Christmas paper and tied with string. "From Francisco and I."

Inside there are two beautifully bound leather books inscribed in gold with the name *Fernando Pessoa*, and Dzovig feels a rush of heat on her face at the sight of them.

"Tito said you've been reading Pessoa; now you have the works. Good to keep up with your reading anyway. And *this* is from Rosa," he says, handing her a large package. "She made it herself, been at it since you told us you were leaving. She hasn't slept in weeks."

"Stop it," Rosa says. "It's a simple pattern, there wasn't much time...." She is crying openly now, shrugging her shoulders like a little girl as Dzovig opens the parcel. It is a white lace bedspread.

Dzovig presses the gifts against her chest. "Thank you, thank you so much," she says, and she is kissing all of them, the others even kiss one another because there is an abundance of emotion around the table, and when Dzovig puts her arms around Rosa she remembers with a sudden clarity that her mother had made her a coat once, a winter coat that had the most remarkable buttons, buttons that glowed like opals. With the coat on she had felt her mother's arms around her and a kiss on the side of her neck, a place that felt strangely intimate. And Dzovig knows as she remembers this that she didn't say goodbye to Maro, her mother, that the coat was outgrown at the end of only one winter and perhaps Anahid wore it after that, though she can't recall.

It is getting late and Gordon is visibly tired.

"Well, Dzovig, I think I should be getting on.... Promise you'll come up and see us?"

"I guarantee it," Tito says.

Rosa puts on her cardigan. "I'll take him home and come back."

"No," Dzovig says, "I'll clean up with Francisco. Please, let us."

Rosa sighs. "En fim," she says. "É assim, filha."

Tito knows Dzovig well enough by now: he should also leave. He kisses her on the mouth. "See you tomorrow."

In the kitchen, Dzovig and Francisco work side by side. Francisco's new cat, Zé, has been joined by another, a poor soul whose name has not yet become apparent. One of them has curled up on a giant sack of potatoes.

"He's keeping the eggs warm," Francisco says.

Dzovig rolls her eyes. "If Rosa saw that...."

There isn't much to clean up; it doesn't take long. Dzovig wishes there were more. She wants to say something, she feels she owes it to him, though he's never asked anything of her. And for once, Francisco is quiet. He's not even whistling. He's drying his hands.

"Francisco?"

"Yes?"

"I don't know why I'm going."

Francisco stares at the floor for a moment and decides the occasion requires a glass of something. Two glasses. He pours out some cooking wine and they sit on stools at the counter.

"Tell me, I've always wondered, Dzovig, does your family know where you are?"

"I wrote to my sister, a little while ago. She knows."

"You ran away?"

"I don't ever want to go back to that country."

"But, you lost something, right?"

"Yes," she says. "Tomas. My boyfriend. He killed himself. He was twenty-five."

"Listen, Dzovig. I never wanted a cat. And then I met a cat and now I have two." Francisco rests his palms flat on his thighs. "You know, when Balthazar Rei died I was very sad. But then, after a time I realized that Mozart died too... *there's* a tragedy. And now I'm just happy to be alive." He takes one of Dzovig's hands and holds it on the counter between his own, playing with it as if it were an intriguing puzzle.

"When I was a boy," he says, "I had a little flute. My father gave it to me and I loved it, it sounded like a little bird, well, that's not surprising. *En fim.* I was sitting in this chair one day in my grandmother's house, with my flute. It was a huge chair for a boy, all these pillows and fabric, and I lost my flute in it. It disappeared in one of the folds of the chair and I never got it back. That chair swallowed it. I cried and cried. But I think now that, when I die, I'll find my flute again. All the things we've ever lost will be given back to us. I believe that."

He stands up and gives her hand a kiss.

"That Tito, he looks like he's in heaven already. You'll be fine."

"*Every beginning is unmeant*." This is one of the lines she has memorized, one of the few, because she didn't really like his poetry at first. It was a sort of habit for her, memorizing poetry, a Soviet habit, something she had done in school for years as a child. The line comes from the only book of poetry Pessoa managed to publish in his lifetime, *Message*, a series of poems glorifying some Portuguese kings—very patriotic, which is why Dzovig doesn't care for them. Dzovig has no patience for patriots. But the line gives her some comfort, if she can allow herself to believe it. She never meant to be here, working with Tito. This hasn't been her plan.

At the hotel, Dzovig has her own room. This was one of the conditions of her employment, one that even Tito's father, Henrique, insisted on. It is the most beautiful room she has ever had, more beautiful than any room she could have dreamed up in her former life, though she never dreamt of rooms, back then. Now she dreams up entire houses, sees them in their minutest details and wakes up startled but pleased, as one who wakes from an erotic dream. In this room, she can forfeit the memory of her walks around Lisbon; she has other comforts, other sounds.

Her balcony faces the sea, a privilege not granted to the other employees, many of whom don't even stay at the hotel. At first Dzovig had laid Rosa's lace bedspread on the bed, though she has since removed it, wrapped it in tissue paper and placed it at the bottom of a drawer. In Dzovig's bathroom there is a deep bathtub with a hand-held shower, a bidet and a marble ledge behind the sink. Dzovig cleans the white porcelain daily, rubs it until it gleams.

She keeps the two books, Pessoa's books, on her night table. When she goes downstairs to work at the front desk she takes one and places it in front of her, like that, so she can see it, sitting there, the way one would keep a family photograph on a shelf. She doesn't read on the job. She's efficient and the guests like her. She has bought some clothes at a boutique in Cascais. ("Remember, you are part of the whole presentation," Henrique had said, waving his arms), and she wears a gold name tag pinned to her shirt.

She has all this, her room, her name tag, her books. Even Tito, whose happiness spreads like a contagion. Who walks around with a permanent erection. She hardly thinks of Tomas's love-making anymore, except in dreams, dreams in which Tomas no longer has a face, only a body. She can tell it is him by his rhythm, by her own feeling of desperate wanting. Dzovig looks at Tito now and sees herself as she used to be, remembers being the one who was always asking. She doesn't know what Tito sees. When she sits on him and brings herself to orgasm there's no shame in it for her, no apology.

But more than all this, Dzovig has the sea. After work, at the end of the day, she and Tito go to the beach. She pulls him into the water, which has begun to grow colder now, with the end of the summer. People stare at them, at Tito, more specifically. They wonder. Sometimes Tito yells back, "She's my nurse!" and kisses Dzovig on the mouth and the people laugh or, more often, look away. Dzovig doesn't care. Her skin is darker, golden.

The sea is in the poems too, a character almost, a mirror of sky, one that sucks up lovers and sons. A sea of glory, an unending sea. A sea like a woman. Pessoa believes that, without the sea, the Portuguese are nothing.

But Dzovig knows how futile it is to reclaim what was lost, what a waste of energy it is. Pessoa knows this too, deep down. He blames it on God, which disappoints her. Better to be like the king, isn't it, Pessoa, the king who *was not anyone.*

"*I was not anyone.*"

Dzovig hears the sea, at night, beneath her window. But it is not the sea: she can never hear it now as anything less than this, "*the voice of the land yearning for the sea.*" A muffled scream breaking through the waves.

VI

VECIHE

On the day that I left Bedros, I woke very early. I was sitting in the kitchen, making tea, when he got up. Tomas would sleep until the very last minute, until I opened his door and called out the time to him as I did every morning, like a threat. He never ate before leaving for school; he never had enough time. Bedros coughed. He did this every morning, I had ceased to notice it ages ago, but I noticed it then. I thought, *tomorrow, I won't hear that sound anymore.*

We ate our breakfast: bread and cheese and tea. I had cut some fruit and placed it on a tray. In retrospect, so many details of that morning seem different: the rectangle of light creeping across the kitchen floor, the fruits on the tray, the wall clock ticking loudly and the silence of the house reverberating around it. I looked at a bunch of flowers that I had left too long in a jar. Should I throw them out? What would Tomas and Bedros think, seeing them, after I'd gone? Would they have the satisfaction of throwing them out themselves?

I decided to leave them.

I cleared the table as Bedros dressed for work. I washed the dishes, dried them and put them away, wiped the table and counter meticulously. Every move I made seemed prolonged, invested with waiting, with fear.

Tomas came into the kitchen, looking for a notebook. I helped him. I was always the one who could find things: a set of keys under a newspaper, a comb sticking out of a pocket. Bedros could be utterly blind. Whatever he searched for became invisible the moment he stood in front of it, and Tomas was the same. It must be genetic, I used to tell them. But on that morning I couldn't find Tomas's notebook either, and as he left, already late, I said pathetically, "I'll keep looking, darling."

He was sixteen. Did I think I was leaving my son? No. There was no finality to what I was about to do. I hadn't made any plans. My decision to leave had come to me as a sudden revelation, an act of courage or defiance that was unexpected but inevitable, as if all the failures of my life, my boredom, my helplessness, my unimportance, had been leading me towards it.

I was selfish enough to not blame myself entirely. Tomas's petulant tantrums, Bedros's numbness: I would save myself from these as from a slow asphyxiation. Yet there was a vagueness to it all as well, the sense that, if I left, what difference would it make, after all? My son was immersed in his friends, in his own passionate, adolescent world. He no longer needed me. My husband, whose personality had seemed to wash away into an even lack of interest in everything, functioned like an automaton on a treadmill. Except for her. He had his own reasons to be alive. I was no longer one of them.

I'd found the yellow ribbon on the floor of our bedroom when I was changing the sheets. It must have fallen. It was on his side of the bed. It was silky and yellow, a kind of thing I never wore. I smelled it. And then I put it away in the box.

I didn't tell Bedros. One day I pretended to leave for work, and instead called the factory to say that I was sick. I spent the morning walking in the vicinity of his office building. It was at lunch time that I saw her, crossing Khandjian Street and waiting on the corner until Bedros joined her. They didn't kiss. He placed his hand on the centre of her back, a gesture so simple and intimate. The protectiveness of love. She wasn't young. She wasn't even especially pretty. She was fatter than I am, a woman with round, welcoming breasts.

Perhaps, if I had been angry enough, the thought of leaving would not have occurred to me. I would have known at least that I was alive. Instead, I stood there and watched them the way old people stare at young lovers kissing in the street, with a mixture of curiosity and nostalgia and the complete acceptance of that kind of love as something no longer graspable, as something now foreign to me.

And I thought, *no one is as separate as we are, Bedros.*

It was as I got home that the horror of my own indifference came rushing at me. And with it, a craving. A desperate desire to leave.

I don't know when I decided that I would return to Odzun. In the months preceding the day that I left Bedros, I thought about Odzun constantly. I thought about it at work, at home. What had happened to Mida? To her children? Where was Hrach living? What of the house, the *kolkhoz*, even Mrs. Hagopian: I had never learned what had happened to her after her husband's death. I had not thought of these people in years. With the exception of my mother, I had considered them inessential. Not of me. Not mine. But now their faces haunted me, what I didn't know, the ends of stories, the span of years that had gone on without me and that I wanted now to reclaim.

And I wanted to see my mother's grave. Her grave, which I had never seen, called out to me like a beacon. It became my obsession. Obsession is a substitute for misery. I would kneel on the rocks at my mother's grave, bringing with me all my regret. I wondered what my dead mother would say to me then.

I waited until they had left the house. I made the beds, washed and dressed. It took only a few moments to pack the bag. I was ready very quickly. I had picked up a train schedule a few days earlier and looked at it briefly before hiding it in the inside pocket of my purse. I would take a bus to the station. I had money. They would miss me at work. Our phone would ring. The supervisor would be cursing, pressing her thin lips together in that way she had. I smiled as I imagined this.

I sat at the kitchen table to write the note. I had a pad of lined paper. My heart was beating in my throat. I looked at my hands. Nothing I wrote would be enough, I knew that. *Bedros, my hands are dry*—I wrote the note only once. And I folded it once, and placed it on top of our dresser, in our bedroom.

Outside, the streets were blatant with sunlight.

A woman was beside me on the bus. She was carrying several bags of groceries. She must have stood in line for hours, that morning. A box of eggs kept wanting to tumble out of one bag. My own bag sat on my knees. The bus was full, people were standing. The air filled with the odors of their bodies, perspiration, breath, bad perfume. I sat next to a window that wouldn't open. I looked out at the passing buildings, this city I had come to so many years before. What had I brought with me? My youth, my stupidity, my will. Now I sat on the bus with veins showing in my hands.

I remembered my first years in Yerevan. How weightless I had felt then, heady with excitement. I was eighteen when we arrived. I could hardly eat. Bedros used to say that I was disappearing, that he would soon be clutching at air in the dark. Yet I was inhabiting my body for the first time, just as he was. I came to understand that I had a kind of power over him even though my body was the penetrated one. When I sensed that Bedros was about to pull out, not wanting to make me pregnant, I could force his coming with a sudden shift of my hips. And when we collapsed against each other, sated, I felt such tenderness for him, for what our lovemaking had admitted, which was the vulnerability of desire.

I never told Bedros, during those early years, what my mother had told me the autumn that we left Odzun. I have not told him since. I sat on the bus that day, with a small suitcase on my lap, and I remembered my mother cracking open in front of me, all her life tumbling out at my feet. *My God, my God, Vecihe, do you think I would ever forget that face?*

I remember that she slept, afterwards. I sat on my bed, watching her with an inexplicable anger. I couldn't fit her story into the circumference of my life. She looked suddenly foreign to me, as if she had only pretended to be my mother, and I could no longer recognize her. I stared at the window, waiting for signs of daylight. I didn't sleep. In the morning I ran to the farm where Bedros worked.

I said, "Will you take me with you, when you leave? Will you marry me?"

And he said, as if he wasn't surprised at all, "Yes, Vecihe." *There were wells. You don't know about the wells.*

I did not say goodbye to my mother when Bedros and I left for Yerevan. I never said goodbye to Hrach or Mida. I told

Mr. Hagopian that I was leaving, that I would be married, and he gave me some money.

"Your mother, Vecihe, this is her home," he said. "I hope he is a good man, your Bedros."

I thanked him. I took my paint set with me, and some clothes. Someone had left a set of embroidered sheets, ironed and folded, on my bed. I looked at my room, the room in which I had lived with my mother, in Mr. Hagopian's house, and I saw Aghavnee's old sack sitting in a corner. I picked it up and took it with me.

I was on the train with Bedros. He kept looking at me— a worried look. Aghavnee's sack was at my feet. I checked from time to time to make sure that it wasn't sliding away from me, under the seat. And finally I picked it up and looked inside.

There were some rags, a hair comb, a tiny car, a child's forgotten toy, and few pieces of paper. I unfolded one of them, brittle as a leaf, and found my first painting, red blotches on a pale brown stem, with a hole in the centre where the branch had pierced it.

I unfolded picture after picture, remembering Aghavnee, her cackle and her black eyes and my mother's hands folding her flesh back into place. I remembered my mother, singing at the wedding, and the dress she wore on the day she gave me my paint set. And I remembered the grove, suddenly, and realized with a tinge of regret that I hadn't gone there one last time, in farewell.

Bedros had fallen asleep beside me. And as the train moved on I heard again the words Mida had said on the day following Aghavnee's death, after my mother had wrapped her body in white linen.

"You've kissed the dead," she'd said, "you will have news of a distant place."

I never told Bedros. My mother had given me what I had asked for. There was no end to what one could carry, that much I had been witness to. Well, I could do it too. I would.

It was the carton of eggs, in the end. It was as stupid and simple as that. The bus jerked to a stop and the eggs flew out, crashing to the floor. Some of them rolled towards the front of the bus before cracking next to a post, or to someone's foot. It could have been hilarious. But the poor woman was heartbroken. She stood up, trying desperately to retrieve her eggs. She was a large woman and the bus was crowded. The driver cursed. And she began to cry, holding her hands together around the few eggs she had managed to collect.

I tried to help her. How old was she? Perhaps five, six years older than me. I managed to get her back to our seat and I held some of the grocery bags for her. Someone behind us asked what part of town she lived in, suggesting the names of shops that might not have long waits.

That was when I lost it, my pathetic resolve. The woman cried beside me like a girl, and I thought of Bedros. I saw his mouth, the lines about his eyes. I thought of his frailty, and of my own, and I got off the bus.

I walked back, leaving my suitcase on a street corner along the way. I arrived home towards dinner time. Bedros was in the kitchen, reading a newspaper.

"Hello," he said.

I went into the bedroom. There it was, my note, still folded, exactly where I had left it. He hadn't seen it. He'd said,

"Hello." I crumpled it in my fist and hid it in my purse, then washed my face and went into the kitchen to make dinner. I was sure he hadn't seen it.

VII

TITO

"You were wrong about him," Dzovig says. "He wasn't an accountant. That was Bernardo Soares, one of his heteronyms. A semi-heteronym. The real Pessoa wasn't a bookkeeper. He worked as a translator, free-lance, so that he would have time to write."

"A semi-what?" Tito says.

"Heteronym. Like Álvaro De Campos, Ricardo Reis and Alberto Caeiro, the three poets he created. Did you know that he gave them entire biographies, horoscopes, he even studied the influences they had on each other? But the poems themselves, he wrote them almost in one sitting. He said they just appeared in him."

"Coo coo."

"Are you listening, Tito?"

"Of course. I'm fascinated."

"Well, Soares was the author of *The Book of Disquiet*, and Pessoa called him a semi-heteronym because Soares resembled him the most. He said Soares's personality was a mutilated version of his own. And it was Soares who worked in an office as a book-keeper and wrote alone, at night, in a little room, not Pessoa."

"I thought you said he was just a character, an invention."

"Yes. That's what I said."

"So it wasn't Soares who wrote, it was Pessoa."

"No, it was Soares *through* Pessoa."

"I don't see how that's different from a pseudonym."

"It's completely different. These writers *existed*. They were more real to him than he was to himself. Haven't you ever experienced something like that—"

"Schizophrenia?"

He's being funny, Dzovig, but he may be right. I always thought of myself as a hysteric, it was a tendency that was present in me since childhood…

"Sorry. I'm kidding," Tito says. "Come on."

"I mean a character in a book, someone who affected you to such a degree that you thought of them afterwards, constantly, like you would think of a real person."

"No, I've never experienced that."

"I can see how it could happen."

"Has it ever happened to you, Dzovig?"

"He said that they were sincere, his heteronyms, sincere in the way that King Lear is sincere. It's true, when you think about it. King Lear is as important as Shakespeare."

"That's clever, but I don't buy it. And I don't think Pessoa does either. Anyway, you'd have to be a tremendous egotist to say that your creations 'exist'."

"Or extremely self-effacing, depending on how you look at it."

"I'd believe that if he hadn't ever written a poem and signed it Fernando Pessoa, which he did, right?"

Of course I did. But as a man of genius I knew how insufficient a single self can be.

"His favourite book was *Pickwick Papers*, by Dickens. Have you read it?"

"Dzovig, why would I have read it?"

"He took it everywhere with him."

"Right, and perhaps those characters were more real to him than his own mother! That's something to pity, Dzovig."

"Soares didn't have a mother. She died when he was very young and he never knew her. He said that accounted for his indifference, his inability to feel."

"Soares is a character, Dzovig! I thought we were talking about Pessoa!"

He's right, Dzovig, I'm a fraud...

"I know, I know. Never mind."

"Put that book away, Dzovig. I'm aching, I'm dying here. Come to bed." With Dzovig's body next to him, Tito relaxes. His voice softens. "I'm glad you didn't get those books any earlier, or I might never have had a chance to seduce you. You know, there are some things you can't do with a book, well, with most books, I mean."

"And some things you can't do with a body," she says. Dzovig kisses him then, because the cruelty of what she has just said strikes her only seconds after she's finished saying it.

Tito pulls back, and because he knows that she owes him something now, he asks the question.

"Tomas. Was he a writer?"

"No. He was a student. We met during some demonstrations in Yerevan."

"What was he studying?"

"Architecture. He was in love with old churches. Armenian churches."

"Why did he kill himself?"

"I don't know."

"You must have an idea. You never talk about him, Dzovig, about anything that went on. One day you will have to."

"Why? Is it a prerequisite?"

"No, no. It's for you, for your—"

"I'm perfectly happy."

"Was he perfectly happy too?"

"No. But everyone is unhappy in Armenia. It doesn't stand out."

"So you didn't notice that he was unhappy, or are you just trying to avoid the question? Please—"

"I'm really tired, Tito."

"What was he depressed about?"

"I don't know. He wasn't depressed. Can we stop now?"

"What did his parents say?"

Dzovig gets up, starts putting on her clothes.

"There isn't an explanation Tito, don't you get it? We didn't *know*."

"No. There *is* an explanation. You just have to want to face it."

"Face it, face it for who? For you? Like I'll have to face the day when you can't walk anymore?"

"Wow. You flatter me."

Dzovig is shaking with anger. "Look, I told you, don't expect anything—"

"My God," Tito says, "she's alive after all."

"Fuck off."

Her father had stayed up once, sitting in the dark. Dzovig had been out that night, standing on street corners. When she came in, he was sitting at the table in the cramped living room, smoking a cigarette. Pinned onto the wall above him were a calendar and the framed picture of Mount Ararat, though she couldn't make these out in the darkness, she only knew they were there because they had always been there, on the wall. All she could see at first was her father's vague shape and the tip of his cigarette, a moving orange dot. The air in the apartment was stale, smelling of smoke and of the food her mother had cooked that evening, and of her father's old sweat. There hadn't been any light in the stairs either; she had groped her way up to the fourth floor. She had had sex with three men that night and she had money in her pocket.

"What have you been doing?" her father asked.

"Nothing."

"You'll kill yourself," he said, "and it isn't worth it."

"I can stay at Rebecca's if you like."

"What difference would that make?"

"None, to me," she said.

"What have you been doing, Dzovig?"

"I've been out dancing, Papa."

Her father seemed slightly deflated at that, at the blatant lie, the provocation of it, but he didn't move. Dzovig lit a cigarette. Waited.

"He was a very troubled young man, Dzovig, anyone could see it."

"Right."

"I should have stopped you right at the beginning. The two of you, going off like that—"

"Why? Because we were fucking?"

Dzovig could see the muscles on her father's jaw, twitching. His lips barely moved.

"Just watch it, or you will end up like him."

"I never liked that fucking lake, Papa, I never liked it. Don't think that I've ever forgotten."

Arzas stood up and moved towards his bedroom door but Dzovig stopped him with a question.

"Which village were your parents from?"

He turned. "What?"

"Where were they from? Tomas's grandmother was from somewhere near Erzurum. Her name was Zivart. Her family died in the marches. She almost died. We got the whole story from a woman who knew her, when we went to Odzun. We had a great history lesson, did you know that? Not just a church, those fucking churches.... So what I want to know is, where were your parents from and was your grandfather shot in the head, like all the other men, the men they rounded up in the villages?"

"What is the matter with you?" Arzas said.

"Your parents, they would have been children in 1915, like Zivart. They could have been walking right alongside her, in the desert. I just want to know. Vecihe never talked about it, but Tomas knew, after Odzun. He knew, he understood, all those deaths—"

"Shut up!"

"Just explain it, Papa, why you keep that picture up there, a little souvenir in case you forget who you are!"

Arzas put his hands on his head, rubbed his own face. When he looked at Dzovig his eyes were clearer than she had ever seen them and also more frail, as if one could damage his whole being by taking a stick to those eyes, to the thin eyelids with their straight lashes, wet and looking as if someone had cropped them.

"You can *never* explain it," he said. "You can never explain what they did to us because there are no words for it in any language. And if you want to understand it, if you want to *understand* it, you're just a piece of shit. You're no better than they are."

When Dzovig and Tito get into Lisbon, Dzovig feels like a traveller again, feels the momentary exhilaration of arriving for the first time in a new place, the disorientation and freedom of it. This trip is her idea. She wants to go drinking without a tourist around her. I know a place, you'll like it, she has told Tito. Dzovig is bouncy, almost joyous, even though the territory grows familiar as they walk from the train station to the Alfama, and she realizes, gradually, that she has kept herself away too long.

Tito made the suggestion some time ago, more than once. We should go up to Lisbon and visit those guys, we haven't seen them in ages. But Dzovig had refused. Apart from two short conversations on the phone, with Gordon, she hasn't spoken to anyone from the Alcobaça. And since their fight about Tomas, Tito has stopped making suggestions. In part he is keeping the promise he made to her the following morning, when he came to the front desk with eyes bloodshot from lack of sleep and said, "I promise I'll never try to be your shrink again for as long as I live." Also, he is keeping a balance, walking a sort of tightrope with her, knowing that they could tumble off at any moment.

Dzovig has been surprisingly calm throughout the autumn, working at the front desk, reading incessantly, though not in Tito's presence, and walking for miles on the beach, dragging Tito with her along the sand. Her favourite work shift is the one that ends at midnight because she likes to go swimming afterwards: the indoor pool is officially closed by then but Tito has the key. (Don't let anyone see you, his father said.) It's just the two of them, naked in the water. At those moments he knows she is happiest, swimming in the half light, in silence. When he makes love to her in the water, pressing her against the walls of the pool, he feels better, as if his body were the way it was meant to be, stronger than hers. He holds her arms raised up, over the edge. *You're not doing anything*, he tells her, *you're not allowed to move*. He thinks then that she must love him, that he has something to give her. But it costs him to be there: he works regular office hours, and in the mornings he is exhausted. He keeps his painkillers at the bottom of a drawer, where Dzovig won't see them.

In Lisbon now it is already dark, the pavements are wet from an earlier rain. There's a faint smell of gasoline in the air. Dzovig and Tito are holding hands.

"Where is this place, anyway?" Tito asks.

"Rua do Paraíso," she says. She keeps turning her head as they walk, as if she were looking for someone.

"You're sure you don't want to stop? They will still be open you know. We don't have to stay long."

"Maybe later," she says.

Later the Alcobaça will be closed. They both know this.

When they open the door to the *Taverna*, a wave of smells washes over them, odors of different foods and wine, cigarettes and grass.

"Isn't it great?" she says.

"Why do you keep doing that?"

"What?"

"You keep turning your head. Are you looking for someone?"

"No. I know the owner of this place," she says. "Let's order some drinks."

"You didn't tell me."

"Oh. I wanted to surprise you. Anyway, I don't think he's here."

"We could just sit here and get stoned. We wouldn't even have to smoke anything," Tito says.

"Only if we want to," Dzovig smiles.

Tito notices that she looks disappointed. Her earlier mood seems to have evaporated. A waiter approaches their table and Tito orders some beers and a plate of clams, *amêijoas à bul-hao pato.*

"Oh, and is the owner here?" he asks. "We're friends of his."

"I can check for you," the waiter says.

"You didn't have to ask for him, Tito, I don't know him that well."

"Sorry, I thought you—"

"It doesn't matter."

"These *amêijoas* are great," Tito says. He has olive oil on his chin. "Are you glad?"

Dzovig doesn't answer.

"Dzovig, I said are you glad we came?"

"Yes." She smiles. "I feel like I'm in another country."

"Me too. A third-world country."

Tito orders two more beers. If she is thinking about Pessoa, she won't say so. She and Tito have given up talking about him. She's too obsessed, Tito says. When the beers come a man in dread locks brings them. He seems bewildered. "Dzovig?"

Tito stretches out his hand. "You must be the owner. My name's Tito."

"Miguel. I'm very pleased to meet you, Tito. Welcome."

Dzovig still hasn't said anything and the man, Miguel, seems awkward, as if he doesn't quite know if he should give her the familiar greeting of one kiss on each cheek. He pulls up a chair and sits with them, finally.

"The *amêijoas* were wonderful," Dzovig says.

"We'll have to have more then," Miguel says.

"So, how do you two know each other?"

Miguel laughs softly. "Oh, we go way back," he says. He has a languid way of speaking and a smile that puts Tito off, despite its friendliness.

"We met when I was working at the restaurant. I used to shop at the Feira. Miguel has a stall there."

"And where are you now, Dzovig? I haven't seen you much."

"I live in Cascais now. I work in a hotel."

Tito doesn't add anything. He wants to see how much Dzovig will say, whether she will officially include him.

"Well, it's sunnier in Cascais," Miguel says.

Wine gets brought to the table and they go on talking. At first the conversation meanders between the three of them, as if they were all skirting one another. But after a while, because of the wine perhaps, Tito feels less irritated. The man, Miguel, has an easy way about him. Dzovig's eyes are sparkling. He talks to them about the characters who enter his bar, the people he sells to at the market.

"Maybe I should expand my business, open one of those little boutiques in Cascais, what do you think?"

"There is a market for everything," Tito says.

"In Moscow," Dzovig says, "people are obsessed with buying. Buying and sex."

"I think you have the wrong country—"

"No, it's true. Seriously."

The man, Miguel, puts his hand on top of Dzovig's for a moment. It's a quick gesture, harmless, with a hint of familiarity in it.

Tito says, "I think I've drunk enough. We should be thinking about the last train, Dzovig, you know I'm even slower when I'm drunk."

"Don't worry, there's plenty of room upstairs. You're always welcome."

The faint trace of a smile curls about Miguel's lips, and Dzovig lowers her eyes.

"I don't think so," Tito says.

"I'll get us one last bottle, then."

"At least he knows when to make his exit," Tito says.

"What do you mean?"

"Do you want to tell me what's going on, or is this some kind of practical joke?"

"We're just having a good time." She looks sideways again, at nothing.

"So, how many times have you two fucked?"

"Oh, hundreds, is that what you would like me to say?"

Tito gets up. "Enjoy yourself, Dzovig. You've never looked more radiant."

Francisco has just closed the Alcobaça, it is two a.m. He is walking the few blocks towards home, whistling in the quiet street.

When he sees Dzovig, he recognizes her immediately. He wants to call out, but can't bring himself to make a sound. There is something strange about her, something that frightens him. He blinks.

She is walking alone. She is talking to someone, her head is turned to the empty space beside her. He even hears her laugh at one point, a laugh that echoes in the street.

There are no trains at this hour.

VIII

VECIHE

Tomas would have loved this. This cold. The dark. It would have suited him. He could have ranted about it, been stoic. Or perhaps he wouldn't even be here, but somewhere along the border, in the war. There would have been a different kind of agony then, not this muffled silence.

The electricity returns for a few hours every evening. The heaters crackle at first, they groan with effort. There is not enough time to create a lingering heat. This cold sticks to us like an invisible film. We've closed off most of the rooms in the house. Too cold. We sleep in the kitchen, where the wood stove is. We are very lucky to have it. We burn whatever is available: wood, our books, paper. Yes, I have even burned some of my paintings when Bedros wasn't looking. I kept a few, and all of Tomas's notebooks. The walls of the kitchen have gone grey. Around the stove pipe is a black circle of soot, growing daily like an exploded star.

It is our second winter without power. How incredulous we were, at first. It won't last, we thought, how can it? Our new government stumbles along. Our own backwardness stares us in the face, finally. Every birth comes at a price. And we would go on, like this, if we needed to, we would go on indefinitely. Waiting always for the next spring. Last spring, I planted potatoes behind the house.

Bedros hasn't worked for a year. All but the fewest government buildings have been closed. He asked me if I wanted to go to Moscow, they would arrange it for us, he said. But I can't bring myself to leave, now that I should. He hasn't asked again. We lie against each other at night, layers of blankets heavy as stone holding us in place.

During the day we each go out on our own, looking for food to buy, candles, wood. Money is practically worthless. The city is treeless. And oddly, very clean. Not a speck of garbage left on the streets, anything that burns. It feels good to have only this to do, to look for heat, light, food. If we do not find these things, we will simply be colder, hungrier. When I walk the streets, my body stiffens in the cold, like an old woman's, and I observe myself with some degree of fascination. I do this only because my son is dead. If Tomas were here all of it would be different. We would be more desperate. To keep our children warm: isn't this one of the first instincts of the living? We would be fighting, and we would be angrier.

When I became a mother all my fears multiplied. I remember crossing the street one day, hurrying back from work to collect Tomas at school. I wasn't looking. I heard the screech of tires before I saw the car. Someone shouted, "You stupid lady, you could have been killed!" I just stood there, too terrified to move, because I had realized for the first time that I was afraid to die, I was afraid because I had a son who was waiting for me at school.

I'm walking now, back to the house where I live with my husband. It is dusk. I have been walking all day, I can't feel my toes. The electricity hasn't come on yet. I don't know if Bedros is in the house. I'm tired and cold. There is a grey mist around the house, you could lick the wetness in the air. The kind of mist that would look beautiful with the light passing through it. There is no light. I'm at the door, stomping my boots against the mat. I could step inside, start a fire, wait for the drone of the electricity returning, but the effort I need to do this seems infinite, I can't summon it. I rest my back against the door, looking out onto the quiet street.

I smile because the thought occurs to me that one day, this will all end. One day I will not have to be alive anymore.

Some of the paper I have kept I use for letters. I have written to a number of embassies in Moscow, to a number of offices. Thank God for the Soviet plethora of bureaus. When Bedros asked me if I wanted to leave Yerevan for Moscow, my immediate thought was of Dzovig. I would be closer there, I could ask in person. But I know with utter certainty that she is gone. She isn't in Moscow.

Bedros and I don't speak of her. We sleep and eat and sit with our unanswered questions hanging about us in the corners of the ceiling, near the tiny patch of green paint with some gold in it that used to remind me of Odzun. The patch I wouldn't let him paint over. We speak of other things.

A market has sprung up near Lenin Square. Around town they are calling it the *Vernissage*. An artists' market.

"You should go there," Bedros says, "you could sell some of your work."

"People are selling art at a time like this?"

"Other things as well," he says, "but I saw some paintings there."

"And they were selling?"

"They weren't as good as yours, Vecihe."

Sweet man. "I'll go this Saturday," I tell him. Of course I'll go.

"It costs nothing," he says.

I walk towards the market at midday. I know where it is. Along Abovian Street little shops have sprung up, the beginnings of privatization; they are half empty. I have never seen a soul enter one of them. It is March, the weather is getting warmer. The square is full when I arrive. Stalls and tables lined up as far as I can see. Near where I stand men are selling old watches and parts of motors, kitchen utensils. One man has a table of books. (You haven't burned them? I'm tempted to ask.) I move between rows of tables. There are many men and women here. Armenians. Are they all vendors? Or simply curious, like me?

I see some art work up ahead, canvases with flowers on them. A man selling miniature *khachkars*. And hundreds of Russian dolls lined up in rows, each a perfect replica of the other, the smallest to the largest. The vendors look at me with a mixture of curiosity and boredom. They know I'm one of them. They are not friendly but not unfriendly, just in case. Under the Soviets we had no need for politeness. When I reach the end of the market I turn back, walking along the other side. Here there are mostly women selling linens and carpets. Tablecloths hang from lines strung between poles. Some of it is beautiful work, I can tell even without looking closely. But who would buy them? I avoid looking directly at the women, keeping my eyes on the squares of white cloth. Everything meticulously ironed.

Then a detail catches my eye, an embroidered vine with insects and birds fluttering around it, flowers with petals in the shape of leaves. I stop. I've seen it before, this cloth, I've run my fingers along these vines, I know the hands that made them. She isn't looking at me. Still, I know by the bend in her neck, the shape of her shoulders, that it *is* her, unmistakably.

"Mida?"

The dark eyes lift up and, instantly, she knows me too.

"Vecihe? It's Vecihe! It's you!"

It has been thirty-six years.

It takes very little time to tell one's life story, in the end. Her husband is ill, but still farming in Odzun. She has two sons and a daughter, all three have left the country. Hrach has been in Moscow for years, working for immigration. He has helped each of her children out of Armenia. All the young people of the village have left, even some of the old, like her. She is selling her mother's linens, making whatever money she can.

"What use are these to me now," she says, "what use were they ever? I might as well do my part, see what I can get."

"They are so beautiful," I tell her. "They're still beautiful."

"Yes. No one does that kind of work anymore. I saved the best pieces for my daughter, Sara."

We sit on the edge of an old fountain, empty now, of course. A map of cracks in the concrete.

"I still have the set you left on my bed the day I left," I tell her.

She holds my hand. "It wasn't me, Vecihe. Did you not know? It was my mother who put it there. She chose it. And after you left she told your mother that she had given you linens and that your marriage would be blessed."

"I didn't know."

"Well, those two women hated each other much less than we all thought," she says with a faint smile. She hesitates, as if she is holding something back. "Things were different then, people adapted."

"Your father was very good to me. I never forgot it."

"And why shouldn't he have been? You were like a daughter to him. You could have been his daughter."

I look into her eyes. Why am I surprised, at fifty-five, to find that I am not the only one who knows, who understands?

I tell her about my house, the factory, the painting. And I tell her about my son, Tomas, I recount the single event that has marked my life, that has changed everything. But I don't have to explain it.

"When he came to Odzun," she says, "I knew him right away. Eyes like his father's. I would know you anywhere, I told him. And that beautiful girl with him."

"Dzovig."

"Yes."

What I feel as we weep together is a complete lack of shame.

"What will you do now, Vecihe?"

"Come here and sell my paintings," I tell her. "Bedros would prefer to leave. But what do we have, if not this? He's staying because of me."

"Anywhere you would want to go, Vecihe, Hrach could arrange it. I'm telling you."

"Perhaps in another ten years this country will be great," I say.

We both ponder this. And then we burst out laughing.

"I'll be dead!" she says. "Seriously, Vecihe, if my husband wasn't ill, I would leave too. I wouldn't hesitate. I would join my children."

Join my children.

We return to the stand, where another woman has been watching the linens on Mida's behalf.

"Mida, I stole a napkin from your mother's cabinet. With a cherry on it! I tied it to a tree. My God, I just remembered that!"

She laughs. "In the grove?" she asks.

"You knew about it?"

"I didn't then. Hrach took me there once, after you left. He said you painted there." She looks at me again, with an understanding I never expected. "You know, I think of all of us, he missed you the most."

The shadows are lengthening. Our days are still short. Around the market people are beginning to pack their wares. Mida hasn't sold a piece. I help her fold the linens. She is staying with cousins, won't hear of staying with Bedros and me.

"We have many bodies," she says, "we keep warm. And I help with the children."

She agrees to let me walk her home. We pull a grocery cart between us, with the folded linens stacked inside it. We travel in silence for a while, a mild relief, because I am exhausted from talking. But I am with Mida and some things never change; our silence doesn't last long.

She says, "When you left, I was angry. I didn't understand it. I suppose I was a little bit jealous. I kept wondering what it was that made you leave so suddenly like that, without saying goodbye, as if you were running away."

She nods to herself. "Sometimes," she says, "it takes years to figure things out."

And then the question that has held at the bottom of my

throat from the moment I set eyes on her explodes into my mouth:

"Tell me what happened to my mother, Mida."

I run home. Bedros is in the kitchen, reading. The lights are on. I can hardly breathe. I feel a kind of elation. Not happiness, but a lightness, something.

"What is it?" Bedros asks.

"You will never believe who I met at the market, Bedros. Mida! Mida from Odzun! She was selling her linens. I was just walking and I recognized them and she was sitting there, in a chair!"

"Have you eaten something?"

"Bedros, don't you want to hear about this?"

"Yes, of course. I just thought you might want to eat something. There's another forty minutes left—"

"I don't care about the forty minutes or the damn food, Bedros. I'm trying to tell you something!"

I fall into a chair, a wave of fatigue comes crashing over me again, my face is in my hands.

"I'm sorry," he says softly. "I'm sorry, Vecihe. Look, you still have your coat on." He pulls at my hands. "Tell me. Come on. I'm listening to you."

I tell him about Mida's family, about Hrach, her children. About how she found Tomas and Dzovig beside the church, and took them home. And I tell him what I have learned about Zivart, my mother, how Tomas had learned the story I was unwilling to tell him myself.

"After we left, my mother just kept on as before; she hardly spoke. She didn't even say anything when they told her that I had left. It was only after Mida's first child was born, a daughter, Sara, that she began to recover. She loved that baby. She started to sing to her, those songs again, songs she had learned in the orphanage. And she would tell her bits of stories, of what had happened to her in the desert. Stories about her life as a girl, her brother and sister, her grandmother. That's how Mida came to know everything, bit by bit. The baby didn't understand a word of it, but it didn't matter. It all came out again, what she had told me before I left. I never told you what my mother had said to me Bedros, before we left. I couldn't—"

"I know," he says.

He listens to all of it, to all of it that I can remember, the wells, the dead, the orphanage. The marches. Vecihe, my mother's savior, and Aghavnee. He listens to all of it.

"After a time, she became more like her old self again, caring for the house, for Mida's children. She read all my letters to them, did you know that? Mida said she read them to everyone.

"When Mr. Hagopian got sick, she looked after him night and day. She wouldn't leave his side. She slept on the floor of his room. He didn't last long, Mida said. When he died, my mother disappeared for three days. Everybody knew where she was. Tsiranavor. That small ruined church, do you remember it? They could hear her wailing. But they left her alone. After three days, Mida's mother went to get her. 'Zivart,' she said, 'you are coming home with me now. Your grandchildren need you.' And she took her home.

"After that it was Mrs. Hagopian who looked after her. They were like sisters, Mida said, always bickering and ordering each other around. Can you imagine? People called them the two hens. The old house was falling apart, by then, so they went to live with Mida and her family. And they just grew old.

"When my mother died, Mrs. Hagopian arranged the funeral. Mida wanted to bury her next to Aghavnee, that's what Zivart would have wanted, she said, but Mrs. Hagopian refused. She buried my mother right next to her own husband. And then she died a few months later.

"All those years, Bedros, I thought of her as if she was already dead.... Maybe I thought that there was no point, for her, after what had happened, how could she continue?"

"She had a daughter," he says, "she had you."

"I was so stupid."

He puts his arms around me. "Now you know," he says.

The lights have gone off again. I have no sense of what time it is. We have lit two candles and put wood on the fire. We have tea and bread. I see his features clearly in the candlelight, the blue of his eyes, his wide forehead.

"Vecihe. I can't stay here anymore. In this house. I can't live like this. Neither can you."

"I suppose we've just been waiting. We've both known."

"Even if I can't sell the house——"

"Bedros, it wasn't *you*. It wasn't even that woman, I don't know her name. It had nothing to do with you. I was dead. I felt empty, completely empty. I wanted to go back to Odzun, to go back home. I didn't know what I wanted. But I couldn't do it. When I came into the house, you were so normal. I thought you hadn't seen my note. I was terrified. I thought it better if you didn't know. I'm sorry."

"She never meant anything to me."

"Bedros, it wasn't about that, really."

"When I heard you come through the door——I never felt like that in my life——I was so angry, and relieved and afraid, all these things at once. Maybe, if I had said something, things would have been different. Worse or better, I don't know. Maybe it was better, in the end, to shut up."

"Soon after that, I left my job at the factory, do you remember? I started painting again."

"I remember that morning."

"Bedros, look at me. Do you believe me? Do you understand it now?"

We undress in the cold. His body covers me, the smell of our bodies which have gone unwashed for days, of his mouth, of his hands. I pull him into me, deep, into the centre where I can give him all of my heat.

IX

PESSOA

I used to love it too, this time of day, the freedom I felt when I closed the office for the night. Going to my room, having nothing to do but write, having to speak to no one. Just as you love coming here, to this pool.

Yes.

Just think, a few hours ago this pool was full of people and noise, smells. It's so quiet now, I can hear the sound of drops hitting a hard surface in one of the washrooms, a leaking faucet perhaps, can you hear them?

No.

You're a very good swimmer. I was never very athletic myself. I suppose I found it tedious.

Swimming?

Moving the body, just as any repeated action becomes tedious, even the daily actions of waking, eating, walking down the street. The one thing that saved me from monotony was writing.

"Far better to write than dare to live."

I see you are still in the habit of quoting me.

Perhaps it was simply a defence mechanism, your writing.

Of course.

So you admit it, that you were essentially terrified of living, to the point of paralysis. To the point where you couldn't even buy a bunch of bananas in the street, for example.

Ah, but you are wrong. I could have bought them, but I was ashamed to.

Why?

Because those bananas and the boy who sells them are part of something larger, something that will go on existing long after I have stood in front of them with my petty anxieties.

Your neuroses—

Exactly. You know, shame might actually be the only true emotion.

I don't understand.

What do you think of all these people who come to you at the front desk of this hotel, the women wearing fat gold bracelets on their fat arms, the business man who wants to know if his mistress has arrived, the one who wants an extra pillow, or a cancellation, what do you think of them?

I don't know. I don't think of them.

For example, that young woman who came to you this morning, wanting to use the phone.

She wanted to change her plane ticket, extend her stay.

And she wasn't even staying at the hotel?

No.

You had a little conversation with her.

Yes. She was very elegant.

You liked her.

I had seen her before. She had seen us, at the beach.

You and Tito?

I changed her ticket.

And did she strike you as ordinary?

No.

And after you helped her change a plane ticket, did you think that you would see her again, that she would play any kind of role in your life?

I haven't thought about it. No, I don't think so.

*But you don't know. It's possible that she might be as impor-
tant as your best friend, as a relative who dies, or she could be utterly
insignificant.*

It's possible.

*You see, when I look with distaste at the shabbiness of the city,
at the woman selling fruit at the tiny grocer's who hasn't changed her
dress in three days, I am filled with shame because I know, simultaneously,
that the woman, or the barber who cuts my hair, or the waiter who brings
me my wine, are as important as Dante, as any great poet.*

*You are really thinking only of yourself, aren't you? In your book
you wrote about the boy who ran an errand for you, or the barber who
told you stories or the waiter who said he hoped that you would feel better because you had only drunk half a bottle of wine.*

*There you have it, my shame. I am incapable of thinking of any-
one if not in relation to myself.*

*What about the man, the one with the ordinary back who was
walking ahead of you on the street?*

Yes, I felt a kind of tenderness for him—

You felt sorry for him, for "the somnambulist lives people lead."

*Did you feel sorry for the young woman who wanted to change
her ticket, what was her name?*

Fiona.

Yes. Did she seem awake?

I didn't feel sorry for her.

*My boss, Senhor Vasques, is the most ordinary of men and yet I
feel that he is extremely important, that in my other life, he meant more
to me than—*

Your other life?

Like that friend of yours, your boss at the restaurant—

Gordon?

Yes.

He was kind to me.

And you haven't spoken to him, visited him in months, in spite of the fact that you know he is dying.

I didn't know that.

Perhaps you did, Dzovig. Never mind. I was never one for visiting sick friends either. But perhaps, in another life, he was a father to you.

I don't believe in other lives.

Ah, my dear, but you do. You've had several already.

I've changed my life, if that's what you mean.

That's not what I mean. Nevertheless, I like this room of yours. I've always had an affinity for certain types of rooms.

I like the balcony.

It's a little bit too cold to keep the door open like that, after a swim, don't you think?

I hear the sea this way.

And smell it. I understand. I was an insomniac myself.

"By day I am nothing, by night I am myself."

Will you please stop quoting me?

I can't help it, I was brought up in the Soviet system; we learned everything by repetition. Anyway, I was trying to clarify what you meant by, as you call it, my other life.

Yes, by which I don't mean the one in which you lie here, with the window open on a winter night and your hair still wet from a swim, or the one in which you scrub the bathtub until it gleams, nor even the one in which you have sex with that young man of yours who is at this moment sleeping in another room, thinking about you, though all of these are lives. No, what I am talking about is that other life, the one that goes on in your head, Dzovig, the one that pollutes

all your thoughts, your dreams, like a virus, even as you eat your break-
fast, as you change a plane ticket, you know what I am talking about,
don't you?

> *Tomas.*
>
> *Yes.*
>
> *I used to love falling asleep.*
>
> *There's no anguish in dreams, Dzovig, only in waking.*
>
> *That's a lie.*
>
> *"To dream is to forget." I wrote that.*
>
> *Yes, in the dreams he was still alive but, even in the dreams—*
>
> *I think you are tired, Dzovig.*
>
> *Yes, I'm very tired.*
>
> *Good night, then.*
>
> *Good night.*

Tito is not quite himself lately.

> *No. He's still angry.*

Well, you can't blame him, can you, after that little stunt you
pulled at the Taverna, a very distasteful place, by the way.

> *It wasn't deliberate.*
>
> *Everything is deliberate, Dzovig.*
>
> *I just wanted a change.*
>
> *From what, exactly? From Tito?*
>
> *From his...need of me. I wanted him to know that he doesn't own*
> *me, I suppose. (This man at the counter is adding every single item on his*
> *bill in his head, I can tell.)*

He's a suspicious sort. Perhaps he has been wounded in matters
of love.

> *Very funny.*
>
> *Are you ashamed of Tito's love for you?*

He doesn't love me. He only thinks that he loves me. Doesn't that explanation suit you?

Do you believe that?

I believe that whatever it is, it is enough to hurt him.

You're stating the obvious, my dear. But he's quite perceptive, this Tito of yours. As I recall he was the one who noticed that even you are not immune.

I don't know what you mean.

'My God, she's alive.' Does that refresh your memory?

I was angry, that's what he was talking about.

Anger and anguish are actually much the same, Dzovig, we only pretend that they are different. It is only by avoiding feeling altogether that one can truly rest. The state of unfeeling is the one thing I have longed for all my life. I'm afraid I've failed.

To exist, as your poet would say.

My poet?

"The fields, when all is said, are not as green for those who are loved / As for those who are not."

Ah, Caeiro. Yes, I do admire him. You understand what I'm getting at. It's really a kind of trick, you see.

To avoid feeling anything?

Yes. Sometimes one has to will it and then, if one is lucky, it can happen very naturally. You are quite adept at it, you know.

No, I'm not.

Why, Dzovig, you're practically an expert. You started quite young. The wonderful thing is the stillness of it, the silence, it's like being under water, do you remember?

No.

Come now. Think back a little.

I'm going to supper now. Tito is waiting for me.

We never finished our conversation.

    Oh?

    I was reminding you of your father, of a day in your childhood, and you stormed off.

    There were many days in my childhood.

    Did you have a good dinner?

    Yes, thank you.

    Will you go swimming again, tonight, Dzovig?

    Yes, with Tito.

    He's been good to you, in matters of the body.

    You mean sex?

    One mustn't underestimate the senses.

    I'm having lunch with that woman, Fiona, tomorrow.

    You will eat sardines on the beach, how lovely. Do you think of Tomas when you are having sex with Tito?

    I think of him when I'm alone. I used to——

    Why do you say that with regret? It is enough to think of him. If you think of him then you are with him.

    And it should satisfy me, just as I could travel the world without ever setting foot out of Cascais?

    I've always preferred Lisbon myself, but, for the sake of argument, yes. You create what you imagine.

    I don't imagine Tomas. I remember him.

    You may think you do. But the memories you have are in fact not of him but of thoughts you had.

    I believe you are wrong.

    Perhaps what you remember about Tomas is that you were unable to save him. You are laughing.

That's what Tito said to me, the other night. That he was afraid that he couldn't save me. He said I was drowning. I said no, I'm floating!

No. No one could have saved Tomas. He was so wrapped up in his own dreams, in Armenia. The Armenia he lived in didn't exist, even in the past it didn't exist. But he wouldn't admit it—

He killed himself.

When I met him, during the marches, I thought he was extraordinary. I thought he would achieve so much, a mind like his, his eyes when he spoke. The days we spent in the square, we were drunk on air, with thousands of people around us. He could make me believe in anything. And then the weeks passed and it all started to crumble. We heard about the massacre in Sumgait and it was as if a switch got turned off. He dropped everything. Just the churches... All along I kept thinking he was obsessed with buildings. It wasn't the buildings. After Odzun, I knew... Never mind. It was for nothing. He never achieved anything.

Yes, but he had a dream.

Sure. "Some people have a great dream in life which they fail to fulfil. Others have no dream at all and fail to fulfil even that."

Now you are being sarcastic. I'm a great believer in dreams, Dzovig.

Why? Because in dreams you don't have to account for anything? Because you can enjoy your little life without having to face the realities of human cruelty, without thinking of children—

You sound angry, my dear. Do you really believe we are capable of empathy? The sad truth is that we are incapable of it, that no one ever assumes responsibility for another. It's what makes genocides possible.

Yes, I remember, you believe that it causes more grief to see a child slapped in the street than to think of a massacre in China—

Your memory is impressive, but think: From the point of view of the world's armies, war is a success. If we had any real sensitivity,

Dzovig, how could we live with ourselves? We would all be shooting guns into our mouths.

Tomas was a hero, then. I loved a hero.

Heroism is impractical, unless it leads to action.

You're getting on my nerves.

Forgive me. What's that you are looking at?

A letter. It's nothing.

From whom?

My shift will be over soon.

Tell me, Dzovig, do you think that the pigeon came back?

No.

You're wrong. They always come back. All they can remember is the point of return.

You are a fascinating man, Pessoa, but you know nothing about birds.

Who is the letter from?

I have to go. I'll look at it later.

By the way, Dzovig, you are mistaken. My name is Bernardo Soares, not Pessoa. I have met the fellow you speak of though, at a restaurant in the Chiado—

X

ANAHID

September 4th, 1993
Dear Dzovig,

    You would not believe how happy I was when your letter came. I almost couldn't believe it. It arrived in June, which is a miracle, the way things have been going on here. And I have wanted to write to you ever since, but there is so much to say, I don't know where to start.

    I don't know how much you have heard, if you get any news of us in Portugal. You wouldn't recognize Yerevan now, if you saw it. We have shops, there is even a Benetton shop, they all look kind of ridiculous. Dark and half empty. I don't know who has the money to buy anything. This is the good news.

    I have thought so many times of you in these past years. I often think how lucky it was that you left when you did. It has been a nightmare here with the war dragging on and electricity shortages for the past two years. Because of the blockade from Azerbaijan we have had very little food or supplies. Last winter we had one hour of electricity per day, sometimes less, if you can imagine that. We froze all winter. Now that we have been through the summer again I don't want to think about it, about how dark it was, I just want to sit by the window with the sun on my face. Papa says that we will have to board up the windows soon to keep the heat in, but I am dreading it, being shut up again.

We are lucky, last winter we managed to find a wood-burning stove and we drilled a hole into the wall to vent it. Mrs. Bogratyan from the fourth floor lived with us all winter; she is alone. All the trees have been cut down in the city, for firewood. People have been beaten for their wood, had it stolen from them as if it were gold. There are very few candles to be found anywhere.

The rubber factory closed down six months after you left and Papa has been out of work ever since. The whole country is. Seventy per cent unemployment, something like that. This past summer he has left the house every day, I don't know where he goes. He looks thin, much older. Mama has been surprisingly stoic. She and I have crossed the city on foot a number of times, looking for food to buy. There isn't much. People are selling everything, but not food. We are getting our own currency this year, did you know? The dram.

Papa says that if things do not improve we will leave. He says this but I know that we never will. Thousands have, to Moscow mostly, some to America. Wherever there is heat. Throughout the winter all the schools were closed down.

It was very difficult after you left. Mama cried for weeks. It was as if you had died. Papa never said anything. I tried to tell them that you would be all right, that we would hear from you soon. After a while it was as if they had decided not to speak of you anymore. When your letter came, I didn't know if I should show it to them, but I did. I showed them your letter and Mama cried and cried. Papa only said, you will sell those earrings. I put them on and I shouted no! He would have to cut off my ears before I would sell them and even Mama was shouting at him. I was still shaking when he left the house. I have worn them ever since. Thank you.

It is funny that you are working at a restaurant because, if you can believe it, I am too. A restaurant opened here recently, near the square. It is called Pizza Nova, it is an American-style restaurant. I was looking in the window one day at a large brick oven they have in the wall and a man was standing by the door, smoking. He asked me what I thought of it and I said it looked like a miniature chapel and he laughed. And then he asked me, just like that, if I wanted to work there. So I started. I work sixteen hours in a row for three days and then I get one day off. At first I thought I would die of exhaustion but now I am used to it. (This winter it will be warm there. I don't know where they get their power from, but the hotel also has power.) The restaurant is open twenty-four hours a day and there are eight of us waitressing. The others look at me strangely, they probably think I am not pretty enough, but I don't care. We all wear black pants and a red t-shirt as a uniform. They gave us these clothes. The money I make is good, it's incredible really, for now. I give all of it to Papa. He doesn't thank me but I know that he is relieved. We already have some wood stacked up in our old room for the coming winter. Maybe he is too ashamed to thank me. I only eat at the restaurant now.

Levon Ter Petrosyan has been our new president since 1990. Our first non-communist president. He keeps saying that things will improve but nobody believes him. Do you remember how people wanted the Medzamor power station to be closed before you left? They did close it, after the earthquake. They couldn't afford a nuclear disaster on top of everything. Now people are screaming to have it reopen. That's how it has been here, everything upside down. I don't know how long it will take for this letter to reach you, if it will reach you at all. I don't want you to think that I am telling you all this in order to make you come back.

Tomas's mother, Vecihe, came looking for you a long time ago. It was after you left. Papa spoke to her, he wasn't very helpful. He was angry at her for coming, for reminding him. When he left the room she gave me something. She asked me to keep it for you. It is a picture, and a set of pencils. I think they belonged to Tomas. She asked me to let her know if I got news of you, and I promised her that I would, but when I went to the address she gave me, I could never find anyone at home. There was no one living in the house, although it wasn't empty. I went back twice during the summer. None of the neighbours could help me. Perhaps his parents have left the country, like everyone else.

Sahag is in Moscow, sending money home. I haven't heard from Rebecca.

I hope, more than anything, that you are well and happy and that this letter reaches you, Dzovig. I won't send the picture yet, I'm afraid it will get lost or burned.... I will keep it for you. It's funny, in spite of everything, I feel better. I'm working, at least. I'm not unhappy. Until recently I never thought about happiness. I think that in a way it was good for me that you left, it opened my eyes a bit. I look at Papa now, he's just as helpless as the rest of us, maybe he always was. I just couldn't see it before, I was too scared of him. He looks so much smaller now.

You were right when you wrote that the country is all fucked up. Now that everything has changed it's as if people don't know what to do with themselves, now that they have what they thought they wanted. Maybe they don't have it yet. Like beaten dogs who are suddenly let free. At least I know now that I am not the only one.

If you get this, please write to me again. I'm sending you a paper napkin from the restaurant. I'm kissing it, and you, Dzovig. I send you my love.

Anahid

Dzovig puts the letter in a drawer, along with the paper napkin. She has read it once. She will not tell Tito about it; she will not reread it. She has put it in the top drawer of her dresser but after a few days she changes her mind and puts it in the bottom drawer instead, carefully hidden in a fold of the lace bedspread that Rosa made for her, which has remained out of sight for almost a year. There is less danger of Tito finding it this way. (He would be so full of questions.) Someone from the Alcobaça must have forwarded it, the inner envelope has the restaurant's address on it in Anahid's handwriting. Gordon, Dzovig thinks. Most probably.

She will not reply to the letter. From the sound of things a reply might not arrive for months, and who knows where she could be by then? She has put the letter away. Spring is approaching, and soon the sand will turn to gold beneath her feet.

XI

VECIHE

What I see as I look at Hrach's face is the face of his father. It still strikes me with surprise even though we have met twice before. The first time was last year, a few months after I ran into Mida, and then again in December. It has taken a full year to get our papers in order, Bedros's and mine. Hrach has arranged it all through his office in Moscow and with the help of a colleague, here in Yerevan.

Last summer, shortly after we met, Hrach offered us the use of his house near Artash Avan, just outside the city, and we gladly accepted, spending four months there. He bought the place years ago as a country house but has very little use for it now. For us it was a blessing, it made the wait more bearable, to be in the mountains again, to drink water out of the ground, with our hands. His neighbours kept courting Bedros, they all had houses to sell, they said, more beautiful than this one.

Hrach has been married and divorced; he has no children. Having left Odzun, like me, he never returned to stay, only to visit.

"It took my father a long time to forgive me for that," he says. "He just assumed that life would go on there the way it always had, that children would simply step into their parents' place."

He has lived in Moscow for more than half his life now, he has a good job, the opportunity to travel.

"Aren't you tempted to leave yourself?" I ask him.

"Every day," he says. "But first I have to get everyone I know out of Armenia."

His left eye winks imperceptibly and he smiles with an expression that is so familiar to me, a kind of irony he has inherited from his father.

"Life in Moscow is not as hard as it is here, right now, but give it time," he says. "Not to say that it won't be interesting."

We are sitting at a small table in a restaurant that has just recently opened. It serves a kind of American food, pizza, circular crusts of bread baked in a large brick oven with tomatoes and cheese, olives and sausage. It tastes surprisingly good.

"Next winter people will be moving in here for that oven," I tell him.

"Not you," he says.

Not me. Not Bedros. We will both be gone, by then, out of Armenia.

We have not yet sold the house, the house that belonged to Bedros's father, and to which I came as an eighteen-year-old girl. The house in which my son was raised and to which he did not return. I have loved and hated it the way we love our homes when we are happy and detest them when we are miserable. But in my mind it will never be as telling as the house I lived in with my mother, which stood at the end of a road in the village of Odzun, with fields and orchards and the tips of mountains all around it.

We have found a family who will be moving in after we leave. They have many children, which pleases me. A house should have children. They will pay a small rent which will be collected for us by Bedros's friend Hovsep. As in the countryside, everyone suddenly has a house to sell, with prices equal to what the desperate will accept. We have enough money to leave without selling and I prefer it this way, knowing it will still be here, in Bedros's name. (In this as in so many things I am still a coward.)

Bedros and I have each packed a trunk with what we will take. We are leaving to different places. We both know that we have come to an end, that whatever we start now we must start alone. We aren't angry. And in the year it has taken to prepare for this, my fear has lessened slightly. This last year, which has been the most tender one of our marriage. Our trunks sit in the dining room of the house. Like a couple of students, we take very little with us, very little for a lifetime's accumulation. Of things, that is.

Bedros will be going to France, to Lyons. He has several friends there, or friends of men with whom he has worked over the years. He has officially retired and will receive a pension of some kind. There are two hundred and fifty thousand Armenians in France. Somewhere, there will be some work for him to do. And there will be bread and wine and light.

I am going to Canada. I didn't want Europe. I wanted someplace new, a place that was young and large. Toronto is one of the cities that Hrach had suggested. As a landed immigrant I will have health benefits. An Armenian family has sponsored me as a caretaker for their children. This is the official line. Another favour from Hrach. Once I am settled, I can do anything I want.

"You could teach painting, for example," Hrach says.

He hands me two bundles of papers, each tied with an elastic band.

"You'll need hours at the airport. Be prepared. They'll try to get some money out of you, better have some handy, just in case."

I nod. I place my hands in his. There are no words for what I feel.

"You will be fine," he says.

"I know. I haven't been sleeping much. And Bedros...."

"Yes, it's very difficult. But you don't know. It might just be a holiday for you both. Life is very long."

"A holiday." I laugh. "Hrach, when I think about my life, I can't believe it. I think it is someone else who is living this life, not me."

"I have news for you," he says.

The young woman who is serving us brings the bill. She is wearing black pants and a red t-shirt, all the waitresses are. Hrach is returning to Moscow and this time I will say goodbye, as I already have to Mida.

"I have something for you, Hrach."

I pull a rolled up canvas out of my bag. What I have had to offer, throughout my life, has never changed. I unfold it carefully. I haven't done many oils, but this one is my favourite.

"I wish I could have had it framed," I tell him.

"Never mind, I like it better like this. As if you had painted it in that little place of yours, the trees, remember?"

"I remember. I never forgave you for finding me out."

"I never forgave you for not marrying me," he says, "but this is a consolation."

"Hrach, Hrach, thank you—"

We are embracing there, in the middle of the crowded restaurant, when a voice says my name.

"Mrs. Abajian?"

What I notice first about her are the jewels hanging from her ears, red stones surrounded by marcasites. Then I take in the face and I remember.

Bedros and I are in the house for the last time. It is four in the morning, not yet dawn. Bedros's plane leaves in five hours, mine, late this afternoon. Our trunks have gone on ahead of us and will arrive later; we have put our faith in this. We each have a suitcase as well. We haven't slept all night.

I will not go to the airport with him. Better to do it here, now, with the walls of the house around us. We see the lights of Hovsep's car from the window when it arrives. Bedros goes to the door. *Just one minute*, he signals.

I cannot speak. I've held onto him through the night. We kiss.

"What I think," he says, "is that I don't want to be alone before I die. I want you with me. Will you promise me that?"

"Wherever you are, that's where I'll be. I'll be there next week if you need me."

"Goodbye."

I have several hours ahead of me. The house is clean, waiting. We placed flowers at the cemetery yesterday, the two of us.

I've hired a driver. This seems like an extravagance, but I didn't want a friend with me. I didn't want to have to speak. He is taking me to Ptghni, and then to the airport.

I've never been here before, though I've seen it a million times. A ruined church, ancient, beautiful, all of it. Children and dogs from the surrounding village. Shade beneath the walls. Here is where my son died. Stones burning in the sun. For centuries, people have been praying here. Why did he come? Perhaps he believed he would be reborn. Perhaps he bought into the great myth, Ararat after the flood.

This church is my son's true grave.

How would I explain it to him now, if I could?

I would tell him that I don't understand. That what I wanted for him, and for myself, was happiness, and ease. That I can't face another deluge.

I would tell him that Zivart, his grandmother, and Aghavnee had this at least, a grave, unlike the thousands who rotted in the desert.

All these churches are graves.

I step into a small corner chapel where people have been lighting candles. It is more sheltered here but still open to the sky. I've brought some candles of my own. I light them, one for each of my dead: Tomas, Zivart, Aghavnee.

But not for Dzovig, not for Dzovig. Because Dzovig, I know, is among the living.

XII

TOMAS

It is April and Dzovig and Tito set out on a long walk. There is nothing unusual in this, they have been walking together from the beginning. They walk the way some couples play tennis, or cards. And the exercise is important for Tito. She doesn't want him to rust. She pushes him to the point of irritability, sometimes, but apart from this Tito seems content. Dzovig manages to keep quiet around him, saving Pessoa for the times when she is alone, like an illicit lover. She keeps him in a drawer, like her sister's letter, until she needs or wants him, which is often. She is a good dissimulator.

The morning is clear and bright. By noon the air will have turned pale yellow, a yellow she thinks of as Portuguese, except near the water where the light always seems thinner, studded with diamonds. In that zone she is lighter too, almost airborne, or else liquid. They take the road that follows the coast, their destination the Praia do Guincho, a wide beach that stretches like the back of a giant between the edge of the Continent to the west and the forest of Sintra to the east. The beach is only ten kilometres away, and there is a bus on the road if Tito gets tired. She doesn't think he will. Oddly, they have never been to Guincho, though she remembers now how Tito had suggested it the first time she came to Cascais to meet him. *Tito, you can't swim in big waves*, she had said then. *No, but I could watch you.*

The road isn't busy. Just outside of Cascais they pass the Boca do Inferno, where the sea's crashing has carved a hole into the cliffs.

"I came here with Fiona," Dzovig says.

"That Canadian girl?"

Dzovig rolls her eyes. "She wasn't a girl."

"Sorry. Wasn't she divorced?"

"Yes. She had two daughters. She brought her camera. She took dozens of shots of this."

"Is she coming back?"

"Where?"

"Here. I thought you had kept in touch with her."

"I told her what a great lover you were, right here on this rock."

"Maybe I should give her a call," Tito says, smiling.

Further on, along the shore, the ground is covered in huge, flat rocks. This is a place for fishing. The boulders are uneven, tilting in every direction; Tito stumbles more than once. Near the edge of the water men are standing in rubber boots with their lines cast out to sea.

"I'm not getting any closer," Tito says.

The fishermen have buckets filled with sea water, some already swarming with fish. Their eyes follow Dzovig as she passes.

"Bom dia," they say.

One man is fishing with his son, a boy of six or seven whose skin is dark brown from the sun. Only the man wears a hat. The boy is pulling out fish from one bucket and dropping them into another, his feet are splattered with water. Dzovig sees that the boy's hands are covered in blisters and tiny red cuts. The boy's father is looking at the sea. He has gold in his teeth.

The boy has a job to do but he is only a boy. He forgets. He wants to play. The father's yellow eyes are turned to the water and the boy thinks to himself that he can avoid their glare for a little bit of time. He leaves some fish in each bucket and he starts to skip, jumping over cracks between the rocks. The boy has a mother who is sitting, with a shawl on her head, a black shawl and she is shelling nuts and putting them into her mouth. She doesn't see the boy, her son, when he falls in the crevice. Dzovig is screaming at her, running to the place where the boy has disappeared, letting herself fall in, *just wait, I'll get you out!*

"Dzovig! Dzovig! What are you doing!"
      "What?"
      "Are you out of your mind? Who are you yelling at?"
      "I don't need your hand, Tito."
      Dzovig climbs out of the crevice, a triangle of space between two boulders, a few metres deep. There is blood on her elbow.
      "I thought I heard something."
      "But you were yelling at *someone*, Dzovig."
      One of the fishermen looks at them. "É maluca," he says, pointing a finger to his own forehead.
      There is a boy holding a line, standing next to a man.
      "I thought I heard a sound."
      "A sound?"
      "Never mind."
      "Dzovig, will you please tell me what's going on with you?"
      Yes, tell him, Dzovig.
      "Let's go," she says, "let's get back on the road. I can't stand the smell of fish."

Since when, my dear?

"Look at your arm."

When they finally arrive at the beach in Guincho, the strangeness of the moment on the rocks seems to have dissipated, or they pretend that it has. Tito is still preoccupied, Dzovig knows this because the crease in his forehead is still there. It gives him a comical look, she thinks. The beach is very wide and the sand is warm and incredibly white, finer than in Cascais.

"Like walking on flour," Tito says.

"Tito, it's beautiful."

To one side of them, across the road, are huge sand dunes.

"I used to run on those when I was a kid," Tito says. "And roll down. It was wild. It's illegal now. Pretty soon they'll be fining you for even looking at them."

"We'll do it later," Dzovig says.

Her eyes are on the sea. The waves are huge, crashing with an exuberant roar. There are surfers in the water, slim bodies in black suits standing on boards or clutching at little sails.

"Look at those idiots. If you came here in January you would see them."

Dzovig smiles. "I'm going for a swim," she says, "are you coming?"

"Very funny."

"OK. I'll go."

"Dzovig, you can't."

"Why not?"

Tito loses his patience. "Because the water is fucking freezing, that's why not!"

"*They're* doing it."

"They have those suits! There is a huge undertow here, especially at this time of year! People get pulled out all the time! Do you know how many—"

She's taking off her pants.

"Dzovig, you're not going!"

She knows he can't run after her. She dives head first into the belly of a wave. He hears her scream, and then for a few moments he can't see her at all. Tito runs to the edge of the water, calling for her, but the waves crash in front of him like an exploding wall. Then he sees her, her round head, her cropped hair, and a hand goes up. She is waving.

An elderly couple walk up to him.

"It's very dangerous," they say, "you should call her back."

Tito is crying with frustrated rage. "I can't," he says.

Another man approaches, wearing tennis shoes and a polo shirt.

"She'll freeze," he says.

Dzovig's head has become a little black dot. Tito can't see her arms anymore, can't even tell whether or not she is struggling. The elderly woman offers to go and find a telephone, call for help.

"What good would that do?" her husband says.

"If she doesn't fight it, the current will bring her back," the man in the polo shirt says.

"In a month or two," the old man says.

"Look, get that guy over there. Eh pà!"

A surfer is about to get in the water.

"Can you get to her?" The man asks. "Get her to come back?"

Tito can barely stand. "Please," he says.

"Jesus," the surfer says. He runs into the water and hoists himself flat onto his board.

The elderly lady comes back.

"The restaurant was closed," she says.

"You see, I told you," her husband says.

"Look, he's already there."

They all see them now, two tiny shapes scrambling onto something, bobbing in the waves like someone's lost toy. They seem infinitely far away.

The elderly woman pats Tito's arm. "Graças a Deus, filho," she says.

Tito's feet are in the water. He can no longer feel his toes. When Dzovig and the surfer finally pull themselves onto the beach, the little gathering applauds in unison, but Tito doesn't move.

"I have a towel," the lady says.

But the old man, her husband, is no longer smiling.

"Are you daft or simply trying to be, young lady? You should be grateful for this young man, if it hadn't been for him—"

Dzovig looks perplexed.

"I was swimming back...," she offers.

"Sure you were."

"Thank you, I'm fine. The sun will dry me off."

The old lady looks crestfallen. She turns to her husband now, looking for allegiance.

"Let's go, Maria."

Tito is also walking away. He picks up his shoes from where he had dropped them earlier.

"Hey!" Dzovig says.

Tito stops.

"Look, I'm really glad that you're alive, Dzovig. Now fuck off."

He keeps walking.

"Come on, Tito, we haven't even gone to the dunes yet."

She runs up in front of him, skipping and laughing, as if this is some kind of game they are playing. He pushes her away and it is when she falls backwards, in front of him, that she notices.

"What happened to your pants?"

"I had a fucking wet dream watching you out there, it was really sexy, you know that? What do you think happened? I pissed in them because I was out of my mind with worry for you! And guess what? It's happened before! It happens all the time! It's a new symptom, fresh out of the medical encyclopedia and right on track, in case you want to look it up. I have MS, remember? And I can't climb any fucking sand dunes, I can't do it, all right?"

"Oh, I see, it's the cripple talking."

Tito's hands are hanging by his side. His voice cracks.

"No, Dzovig. It's you, you're the one. You're not *here*, for God's sake——-"

"Noah's bird came back three times," she says.

"What?"

"He flew out three times before he came back with a branch. Olive, I think, it was an olive tree."

Tito shakes his head in desperation.

"I don't know what you are talking about, Dzovig, can't you hear me?"

"The water was so delicious."

"Dzovig, I'm leaving now."

Her eyes seem to focus then. She looks straight at him.

"Tito, I'm not in any pain. I'm happy. I'm happy with you."

"That's it," he says through his tears. "That's the whole problem, right there."

It's a strange feeling, walking on the dunes. It's like the feeling she had when she came out of the sea, as if she were tied to an invisible cable, pulling her back. The dune pulls her down, her feet sink into the sand, the ground shifts, *quicksand*, it burns her feet.

Well?

This is lovely.

It occurs to me that places of exile are always extreme landscapes. Siberia, for instance.

Or the Syrian desert.

You read my mind. One could say this is quite fitting for you, Dzovig. A miniature desert. Ironic, isn't it?

If it were true, which it isn't. In five minutes I could be back there, on the road, on the beach.

That would be unwise.

When Noah landed on Mount Ararat, he planted a vineyard. The exiled often survive.

Which might be unfortunate, depending on how you look at it.

He isn't coming back, Dzovig. Neither Tomas nor Tito.

We went to a church once, Tomas and I, Ptghni. You should have seen it. Wine cups everywhere, grapes on all the walls...

The cups of salvation, yes, but the roof was missing, wasn't it?

What does it mean, "Anyway, I was the only Nature poet"?

That was written by Alberto Caeiro.

I don't care what name you signed the poem with, Pessoa.

A true nature poet could never exist, I'm afraid. He would have to have never opened a book, or had a single memory.

Nice idea though.

Yes. Have you been to the circus?

I don't know.

You must have. Think.

I don't remember.

There's a clown riding a bike, not a usual kind of clown because he isn't wearing any funny pants, not even a wig. His face and body are all in white, and he rides that bicycle round and round in a circle, and the things he does on that moving object are more extraordinary than anything you have ever seen... And his face is a human face but it is more than human, with the slightest curl of his lip you see an entire story, and you see the clown in that instant but also in all the other instants that came before, and after. The clown doesn't make a sound. His eyes are huge. He's the Nature poet. He's the essence of childhood.

Well, for your information, Pessoa, there was no garden in my childhood. There was a wall and I banged a ball against it, a ball at the end of a stocking.

And what you are today is your having done that, is your having walked past the wall hundreds of times afterwards, is your having left—

No—

"To eat the past as a hungry man eats bread"—

No! Stop, stop—

It was at Ptghni. Those were the words that got her to the church. She had repeated them over and over to herself like someone demented as she made her way across the city, on foot because anything else would have been too slow, because Tomas was waiting for her, at Ptghni. Tomas was dead, Sahag had told her, *It was at Ptghni*, he'd said, *yesterday. Dzovig, wait, they've already gone to get him!* Sahag had also said this, but Dzovig was already running through the streets, through the morning. The sky was the colour of tin.

It was at Ptghni. She had been there once before. There was a road hugging a hill, and a village, there was always a village, and there were wine cups carved on the walls. Tomas would be waiting for her. Wouldn't he wait? She thought for a moment of Vecihe but stopped herself; there was no room for anyone else's pain inside her body, inside her throat. There was only room for Tomas, for the words that were said to her, *It was at Ptghni, he had a gun, Dzovig*, and her legs carrying her there. In the streets of Yerevan objects crashed at her feet like the debris of exploded comets, but she kept on running.

It was at Ptghni. She didn't stop at the village, there was no one to ask. There was nothing to ask. Have you seen my dead lover? It was raining by then, the blouse she was wearing was stuck to her skin and her sandals felt slippery on her feet. In the rain there would be no old men sitting against the church wall as they had seen them that day, the wall against which Sahag had stood, smoking, the day in which Tomas had said *Look, they've piled up the rubble in the shape of a cross.* He had loved that church, its ruined walls and collapsed roof, the single perfect arch reaching from one wall to another, a line traced through the sky like a tribute to perfection, to survival. Tomas had skipped across the stones piled on the floor like a boy skipping stones on the edge of a river.

It was to Ptghni that she came. It took her hours to get there. Ptghni, because Tomas had killed himself there, pointed a gun into the roof of his mouth and pulled the trigger. Had he thought of her at that moment? Had he smiled? She came to the roofless church in the rain wanting to claim his body, wanting something of him, anything.

It occurred to her how quickly one accommodated one's self, that if Tomas had been hit by a car she would have been happy to have him in a wheelchair, that she would have cared for him and been grateful, that if he had shot himself and somehow lived she would have gladly become his body, she would have fed him and spoken for him and she would have been grateful for simply having him exist. And now she thought that she wanted only to have his body, to touch him, to have his blood on her hands, that this, now, was all she needed.

It was a beautiful church, a ruined one, and perhaps Tomas had loved it because it was damaged, pierced with holes. And perhaps she had loved him for the same reason, loved what was wounded in him, what was angry. In the rain the stones had turned black. *I'm here, I'm here—Where are you, Tomas—*

There is no sound in the church. She is on her knees, crawling, looking for him. A corner chapel behind the altar where people still come to pray, where they leave pictures of themselves among strands of melted wax, where the severed heads of chickens are left on the threshold and feathers on the rocks. This is the place. The rain comes down in sheets. Where is he? She runs her hands along the cracks in the floor, rivulets of water run over her fingers and she is calling out his name, screaming for him, for a tiny trace of his blood.

PART THREE

You're many years late
How happy I am to see you.
Anna Akhmatova

I

DZOVIG

The room in which Dzovig stays is unlike any other room she has been in before. It is a room of strange sounds, the brush of metal against metal, of wheels rolling across the floor, of curtains being pulled. The door has a piece of glass in it, near the top, through which Dzovig sees a head before whoever it is enters. A nurse or a doctor, or a person wheeling a lunch tray.

These heads, which she sees through the square of glass in the door, are some of the few things she is able to focus on, though she sees them, as everything else, through a kind of haze. Her hearing is also affected, as if every sound were delayed a half-second, the way it is on some bad phone connections. She isn't tired, though she rarely sleeps. She feels no impetus to move, although she is now eating with her mouth and walking the few steps to the toilet. She has been doing both these things for some time and she is aware that the doing of them pleases the heads she sees through the door, the people to whom the heads belong. She hasn't tried to leave or question what is going on. She just stays. There's a stillness, a serenity of sorts in the room, which is what they are after.

One morning, the head in the glass is followed by two other people, people she knows.

"You have some visitors today, Dzovig."

They are Francisco and Rosa. Rosa comes straight to the bed and takes hold of one of Dzovig's hands.

"*Filha*, what has happened to you?"

Francisco stands away from the bed a little, hesitating. He is slightly afraid.

"Hey, Dzovig?" he says.

Dzovig opens her mouth, not to say anything. What she is trying to do, with infinite effort, is smile, and she doesn't quite know whether or not she is succeeding.

"Nossa Senhora," Rosa says.

Francisco approaches the bed and says, "Dzovig, I think it's time for you to come home."

"Yes," Rosa says, "we're taking you home."

There is some arguing then, an exchange of words between the doctor and the others that she can't quite make out. Rosa is very agitated. Dzovig feels herself sinking as she tries to listen, sinking farther and farther until she grabs the side of the bed and pulls herself up, sits up and then stands on her feet. She pulls at the bow which is holding the back of her gown closed.

There's silence from the others at this. And then the doctor's voice, addressing Rosa and Francisco.

"I think she's made her decision. I will need one of you to come and sign some papers."

"Let's get you dressed," Rosa says.

It has all come back to her now. It has all come rushing back since the day Francisco and Rosa brought her from the hospital to an apartment in the Alfama. It is Rosa's apartment, two blocks from the restaurant, four rooms on the second floor of an ancient

house. On that day, Rosa had unpacked Dzovig's things and
tossed three bottles of pills into the garbage.

"I won't have you doped up like a zombie," Rosa said.
"You are here now and you can say anything you want. You can
scream all day long if you have to, *filha*."

Still, it took more than a week before she could formu-
late a thought, before she could dream again. And longer still
before she began eating the plates of food that Rosa and
Francisco set out three times daily as if these were the only truly
required medicine. There was usually one of them around, they
were almost interchangeable. Francisco whistled more than she
remembered, though it may have been that he was nervous or
that she was no longer used to him.

She remembers everything now, all the moments and
faces leading up to the day in Guincho when she swam in the
sea and climbed the dunes. What she remembers is crawling up
the sand dunes, a barrage of words coming at her like hammers beating the inside of her skull, how a man, a policeman,
had stopped her, yelling, though she couldn't hear his yelling
through the hammers, she could only answer the other man,
Pessoa, and her hands and knees burned in the sand. The
policeman had pulled her down the mountain and put her in a
car, and from there she had gone to the room in the hospital
with a square of glass in the door. In that room, her memory
had stopped.

Dzovig wonders how she got here, how Francisco and
Rosa managed to find her; there's something miraculous about
it, though it isn't miraculous at all. Tito. She knows it has something to do with him although she hasn't asked. Speaking terri-
fies her. She hasn't seen Tito since that day, she thinks she hasn't,

anyway. And she hasn't seen Gordon. She hasn't seen him and she hasn't asked.

What Dzovig does all day is watch television and sleep. From time to time Rosa asks her for help with making the bed or clearing the table, tasks she could only perform at first with incredible effort but which are slowly getting easier. On some days Rosa seems satisfied with the progress Dzovig is making.

"You have a better face," she says.

When Francisco comes he brings a book of puzzles that is called *Spot the Differences*. There are no words in the book, only pairs of pictures that look identical but in fact contain tiny variations, a cloud in a different piece of sky, an empty button-hole. Francisco loves this book, the comedy of it. A poor sod fishing a boot out of a pond, a dog peeing on the suitcase of a man who has stopped for ice-cream.

"Take a look at this one," Francisco says.

At first Francisco brings a pencil to cross out the differences; now he places both the pencil and the book on the kitchen table when he goes, leaving them there for her, like homework. One day, when Dzovig is alone for a few hours, she leafs through the pages and sees a drawing of a man with a hat. And with the pencil she writes above the man's head the name *Pessoa*. Then she folds the book closed.

A few weeks have passed when she reaches the same page again, this time with Francisco sitting beside her. He sees the name there, *Pessoa*, and it stops him. He's quiet, thinking what to say, and Dzovig is afraid suddenly that she's hurt him, somehow, that she hasn't kept up her end of the game.

"I'm sorry," she says.

"For what, Dzovig? There isn't anything to be sorry for."

"I couldn't stop thinking——" Her heart is racing; it has taken her six months to say these words.

"You know, Dzovig, when they found you on the beach in Guincho it was because you were breaking a law, or something, otherwise they wouldn't have stopped you. But when they found you they knew that you were not well. They took you to the hotel but you were too sick, they had to take you to the hospital. Tito called us right away. He was crazy with worry but he was afraid too. He was afraid to go and see you. He didn't want to make you worse. He called all the time. He arranged for your private room, paid for everything. He still calls, at the restaurant, always asking how you are. I'm not a doctor or an expert, what I can do is cook, but I know that this sort of thing takes time. It's just a matter of time, Dzovig."

"I don't know," she says, "I don't know."

Francisco says, "I think you should come back to work, I really do. You'll be growing a beard if you stick around here any longer. Work is good, it keeps your head in place. And we could use your help, Dzovig, you know that."

She *does* know. She has sensed through the fog and routine of these last months in Rosa's apartment that something has changed at the Alcobaça. And Francisco, the diviner, answers her without having to hear the question.

"He's not there, *Querida*. He's been gone since last February, back to England. I think they have better treatments there, and he has his family.... When he calls he keeps teasing us that he's coming back, that we'd better be in shape. Rosa went to see him last June. I couldn't go, I'm a piece of shit when it comes to things like that, completely useless. Well, he's not coming back and that's the way it is. But you are. I think he'll be pleased to know it."

And so she returns. The restaurant feels utterly familiar to her with its smells, the noise from the dining room. There is a new cook, Ricardo Mendes, a young man who is pleasant and unobtrusive and doesn't question her sudden appearance on the scene. He has been there for almost a year but is nevertheless still an outsider because, unlike the other three, he hasn't known Gordon. He seems relieved at the end of the night when Dzovig sends him home so that she can clean up with Francisco.

Eventually, Dzovig takes her old room back, feeling at first that it is smaller than she remembered, like a kindergarten classroom you revisit as an adult, seeing everything in miniature. And the past she has in this room is also small, the only bit of her own history that she can draw comfort from, it's blank shelter, asking for nothing. A room without sea. On the bed is the lace bedspread Rosa made for her a little more than two years ago, with its creases still fresh from the drawer.

Dzovig works now as she did before, on her feet for hours at a time, awake until the early hours of the morning, and it is enough that she can do this. Many of the regulars still remember her, and they remember Gordon and speak of him freely, calling him Gordinho, and Rosa doesn't shut them up. At the end of each night Rosa stands behind the bar, sorting bills as Gordon used to, and she looks older now, her face has changed the way a woman's face suddenly ages when her mother dies, ages into a face where time has ceased to be elastic. A face that sees the end. And when Gordon does die they all know it instantly, reading Rosa's features like a telegraph, her head turning from the phone. On that day, Rosa leaves the restaurant with her apron still on and the day's money in a paper envelope, uncounted.

When Tito finally comes to see Dzovig, he calls in advance. It is Monday, a slow day for restaurants because nobody likes to spend money on a Monday. He calls in advance as much for himself as for her, hoping to spare them both from shock. And he comes early, towards noon, because he feels tougher at that hour, more resilient than at night.

She is the first thing he sees when he opens the door. She is holding a bowl of potatoes in one hand and a bowl of soup in the other. For a few seconds she doesn't move but then she has to put the plates down, the customers are waiting.

Tito smiles. "It looks good," he says.

"Would you like something to eat?"

"Yes, I would. But not here, if you don't mind."

"I'll get my jacket," she says, "we can go somewhere."

They start to walk, the space between them an invisible yardstick because that is always the problem with prolonged separations, the problem of not knowing who touches first, who is the more wounded one, who is braver or more forgiving. But this walking is like wine for Tito, within minutes his face is flushed, he's overflowing, reckless with emotion.

"Dzovig," he says, "I really need to sit down. I can't walk around like this. Let's just take a cab somewhere, we can go to the *Castelo* if you want, we can grab a sandwich."

"Are you all right?"

"Are you kidding?"

In the car she takes his hand, takes it and places it against her lips.

"You'll kill me," he says.

They don't eat. They sit on the observation terrace of the Castelo de São Jorge with Lisbon spread out in front of them.

"We've always had the best views," he says.

She still hasn't said anything but she is looking at him, straight at his beautiful face.

"I came here, my first day in Lisbon," she says.

"I've been thinking about this day for a long time," he says. "And now you're looking at me like that, I had all this stuff that I wanted say—"

"I know—"

"No, you don't. You don't know. All this time you've been away from me I kept thinking that you must be going through hell, but sometimes it made me happy to think that because that's where I was. That's where I've been, Dzovig.

"I wanted to tell you a million other things because all this time I've been racking my brain, trying to figure it out, and I was going to explain it to you because I wanted to save you, that was it, I wanted to save you even though we always thought that you were the one saving *me*...I always thought you were so fucking strong, Dzovig."

"I did too."

"You liar. You know, I kept your books when you were in the hospital, I read them from cover to cover and I still can't figure him out. But I've brought you something. You're going to think I'm crazy, that I have it in for you but I want you to read these, they're his love letters. Love letters that he wrote to a woman called Ophélia. They aren't even good love letters, you know? They are the stupidest love letters ever written. He liked to say that love was a distraction but he got completely derailed with this woman. Even him."

"I don't think he understood about love."

"Sure he did. He understood it like everything else. And he understood that he didn't have the guts for it. He was smart, his mind saved him. But he was always a visitor in his own life."

"It's not easy," she says.

"No, Dzovig. It's not that complicated. Look at dogs."

She laughs.

"I miss you," she says.

"You know what I miss the most?"

"Yes."

"That's almost the hardest part, isn't it?"

"Sometimes, yes."

"I'll never be sorry that I met you, and not only because I'm no longer a virgin but because what I feel about you is something that doesn't happen very often. We're both lucky that way, you've had it too and it doesn't matter that it wasn't with me. But look, I'm not going to stick around and let you watch me die, even if it takes me decades to do it."

"*I* could die tomorrow," she says.

"Yes, you could, but you won't, Dzovig. What will you do?"

"I'll stay where I am. I don't know what I did to deserve two people like Francisco and Rosa, even Gordon. It's been difficult since he died, but I think that it helps them to have me there, and it helps me. I feel like I'm learning how to breathe. I still don't know where to put everything."

"Maybe you should go home," Tito says.

"Only if I could take you with me."

Erika de Vasconcelos

"I don't think I would fit in your suitcase," Tito says. He is still holding the book of Pessoa's collected love letters. He hands it to her.

"Whatever happened to you, Dzovig, it wasn't about Pessoa. I know that. But I wanted you to read this anyway."

"I will," she says.

Dzovig stands in front of Pessoa's tomb with Francisco beside her. She feels rather formal.

The tomb is in the Mosterio dos Jerónimos, the stunning monastery facing the Tagus just outside the city. Francisco's head keeps turning from side to side in amazement; he hasn't been here since he was a boy. But Dzovig's eyes are fixed on the rectangular pillar in front of her, each side inscribed with a few lines of poetry by one of the heteronyms.

"It's a good monument, don't you think?" she asks.

"It's a little plain for my taste. But I suppose it suits him. Who he was. *Um Modernista*. It wasn't here before. He was buried in Prazeres at first, with his grandmother. I think this is quite recent."

Dzovig circles the pillar, reading the inscription on each side. She smiles with recognition. The first, or last side, the one on which his name and dates are, has a verse by Álvaro de Campos.

> *No, no I don't want anything,*
> *I already said that I don't want anything.*
> *Don't come to me with conclusions!*
> *The only conclusion is death.*

Francisco holds in one hand the hat he took off at the entrance to the church.

"He was the descendant of Conversos, did you know that?"

"Conversos?"

"Jews who left Spain during the Inquisition. The were allowed to settle here but they had to convert to Catholicism, which they did, but they still kept some of their own traditions, practising them in secret, behind the curtains."

"Francisco, how do you know a thing like that?"

"I just remembered it from some article, it was in the paper. I don't look these things up, you know. I just retain useless bits of information in a little drawer at the back of my brain, like everyone else."

Dzovig motions to the words etched the stone. "He's wrong, don't you think?

"Well, even if he was right, and it could be that he is, what good would it do to believe it? It seems to me he is talking about shape, the shape of things. But there's so much more than that, so much that we can't account for, like love, like grace. For example, when you leave Portugal, one day, what you take with you will be much more than a series of pictures and days."

"What makes you think that I will leave?"

"I don't know if you will. You may already be in the right place."

"I don't know what grace is, Francisco."

"You don't know? Poor girl. I'll tell you. Grace is a quiet wind on your face, coming off the sea. It's a wind that's been blowing forever, and it touches your cheek, just like that. That's what it is."

II

VECIHE

Toronto, December 10th, 1994
My Dearest Dzovig,

I have been waiting five years to write this letter. Since Tomas's death I have been looking for you and it is only now, now that I find myself on the other side of the world, that I am able to write to you. I have never stopped hoping, in all this time, that I would one day see you again and tell you what I couldn't say, that day, when you came. Even if it was only to beg your forgiveness. I am amazed at the chance of things: it was only a few days before I left Yerevan that I got your address. I met your sister by chance, in a restaurant, and she gave it to me. And what would have happened if I hadn't met her? I agonize over this sometimes, at night, I imagine that I could have left the restaurant ten minutes earlier or gone there on a different day, when Anahid wasn't there, or a dozen other occurrences that could have prevented that meeting and I would not be here, now, writing these words to you. This is a mother's lunacy. Years ago, when Tomas was still alive, I imagined all kinds of tragedies happening, one thought could send me off and an entire desperate scenario would be unfolding in my brain before I could stop myself. Perhaps I thought that in imagining it I could prevent it.

You see, I am already wandering when there is so much to tell you. Anahid. Your lovely sister. I met her a few years back when I went to your parents' home, looking for you. They had no news of you then. I never spoke with your mother but I left some things with Anahid, in case you came back. I didn't hear from her again after that, not until our meeting in the restaurant. She is working as a waitress, perhaps you know this, and as I was leaving that day she recognized me. I still have the piece of paper, an old bill, that she gave me, with your address scribbled on the back. She had it memorized. I held onto that piece of paper when I left Armenia, I had it in my hand as the plane took off. There are only two people in the world who could know how I felt at that moment: Bedros, and you.

Where do I start? I am living in Canada, in the city of Toronto. Bedros is in France. We both left this past fall after a year of waiting for our papers. Armenia is a mess, as you must know. People are suffering, thousands are dead in the war and the economy in shambles. We struggled along, a little better off than most. We could have stayed but there was nothing left for us, nothing holding us there but our common grief. In the years following Tomas's death Bedros and I forgot how to speak to each other. Maybe we had forgotten long before that, I don't know. Now that we are apart I receive letters from him, written in a voice that I never knew existed. I tell myself, this is my husband, the man I lived with for thirty-eight years: how can it be that I know so little of him in the end? We think we know our husbands and our children, we know their smell and the rhythm of their breathing and who they vote for, if there is voting. But we know so little of that other life, those layers of the mind where each of us live the life we would truly live if we could. In the end I think that Bedros and I saw a glimpse of this in each other, and we forgave each other too.

How I got here is extraordinary. You will remember a woman that you met in Odzun, Mida Assadourian, with whom I grew up. We found each other at an open market in Yerevan, another miracle, so many word-less years behind us. When she spoke it was like a giant carpet unfurling, a rolled-up carpet spilling across the ground with its hundreds of brilliant colours. She remembered you, and Tomas. And she returned to me the last years of my mother's life, as if they had been packed away in a box, waiting for nothing more than my coming to retrieve them.

Hrach, Mida's brother, works for immigration in Moscow. It was with his help that we arranged to leave. He was with me at the restaurant, that day, when Anahid found me.

I have been here since September. I am living with an Armenian family who sponsored my immigration to this country. Officially I am here to look after their children but the children are in school most of the day. These people are very kind and eager to help me. The wife's brother worked with Hrach for several years.

I have been taking English classes, improving on what I learned in Yerevan the year before I left. I have been painting and teaching the children to paint and this, more than anything, seems to please their parents. What I would like to do eventually is teach at a school of some kind, once my English is good enough. I realize now that I have been blessed, since childhood, with a set of wings, which is what painting, writing, singing are.

I am fifty-six years old, living in a new city, in a different country for the first time in my life. On a different continent. With a different alphabet. Sometimes I am simply enchanted, walking the streets. When I arrived the trees were dropping their leaves, the colours were beautiful and there are trees everywhere in this city. Now the weather has turned cold and grey but the houses are warm and the shops are like theatres, I could not believe my eyes when I came. You must have grown accustomed to it by now, the abundance of things, the efficiency. The food, grocery stores and restaurants. The space. Some days I am giddy with it and on others I am terrified, feeling utterly displaced.

The other day, as I was walking home from my English class, it began to snow. I thought Tomas should see this, not because he had not seen snow before but simply because it was lovely and I was happy, at that moment. Then I thought in a panic that because I was here he wouldn't be able to find me, he wouldn't know where to look for me when he came back…. *There are moments like this, they happen. I let them. There is a question I will never have an answer to, though I will spend years search-ing for it.*

I have written all this, Dzovig, but what I have too are questions about you. How you have been all this time. I know that you began in Moscow and are now living in Portugal, working in a restaurant. Beyond that I know nothing. And I would like to know everything.

You have been wondering about this check. It is for a plane ticket, for you, should you decide to come. I can't express what it would mean to me to see you again, Dzovig, to see your face. You will think me presumptuous, you may have created an entire new life for yourself, as you should have. I am not your mother. We knew each other for a very short time, in the scheme of things. For a very long time, in the scheme of things. Perhaps we are allowed more than one mother.

What I have come to realize through it all, through Tomas, Bedros and my own mother, is this: that our worst pain comes out of silence. And that it is unbearable to love this way.

So, come.

I kiss you,
Vecihe

III

DZOVIG

I land in daylight. From the air it looks white, incredibly flat. The people on the plane applauded when we landed, even the grandmother who was sitting beside me. Before we left she was crying like a baby. *Do your crying now, Avò, it will be less weight for the plane!* Only a Portuguese could come up with something like that.

I asked Vecihe not to come to the airport. Better this way, to get my bearings first. It's freezing outside, but sunny. Smoke is rising from the taxis. The highway is wider than any I have ever seen. I can't quite remember her face, I can't picture it.

"Is that north, off Winchester Street?" the driver asks. English.

"I've never been here before," I tell him. "I don't know."

The street, when we get there, is full of tall, narrow houses. I pay the driver and she is already outside, coming towards me, in shoes and an open coat. Grey hair to her shoulders. Jeans. And I remember.

She says, "Dzovig, how are you?"

"I'm fine," I tell her, "it was a good—"

"No," she says, looking at me. "How are you?"

That's when it comes. The gate opens. I'm crying, crying in her arms, crying for hours and she is saying my name, Dzovig, Dzovig, because she knows and she has room, for all this. For all this.

ACKNOWLEDGMENTS

I gratefully acknowledge the financial support of the Canada Council for the Arts.

Though I cannot list all the wonderful books I consulted during the course of my research, I would like to acknowledge the following. I could not have written this novel without them. They are: *The Book of Disquiet* by Fernando Pessoa, edited by Maria José de Lancastre and translated by Margaret Jull Costa; *A Centenary Pessoa*, edited by Eugénio Lisboa with L.C. Taylor; *Armenian Village Life before 1914* by Susie Hoogasian Villa and Mary Kilbourne Matossian; *Caravans to Oblivion: The Armenian Genocide, 1915* by G.S. Graber; *Survivors: An Oral History of the Armenian Genocide* by Donald E. Miller and Lorna Touryan Miller, and *'Gha-ra-bagh!' The Emergence of the National Democratic Movement in Armenia* by Mark Malkasian. I would also like to acknowledge the extensive Internet site of the Armenian National Institute, in particular for its collection of documents pertaining to the genocide.

My sincerest thanks go to Harach Kaspar for his great help in facilitating my trip to Armenia. Also, many thanks to Nubar Goudsouzian for his hospitality and kindness, and to our dear guide in Armenia and friend for life, Sahak Gizhlarian.

Thanks to Anne McDermid, my wonderful agent, and Sharon Klein, friend and publicist extraordinaire. I thank my parents, Maria-Helena and Aurélio de Vasconcelos, for their love and support. And I thank Louise Dennys, with all my heart, for her brilliance and dedication.

Most of all I thank Nino Ricci for his constant encouragement and praise, for all the things that I cannot say here, and for the missing flute.

The sentence "'When the living look after the dead,' she said, 'God looks after the living,'" on page 111, is a variation of a proverb found in *Armenian Village Life before 1914*, listed in the acknowledgments.

The following lines were quoted from Fernando Pessoa's works, by permission:

"Every beginning is unmeant." From the poem "THIRD/DOM HENRIQUE," in *Message*, translated by Jonathan Griffin, copyright © Menard Press and Anthony Rudolf, on behalf of the estate of the late Jonathan Griffin. (King's College, London: Menard Press, 1992).

"I was not anyone." From the poem "FOURTH/DOM JOAO, INFANTE OF PORTUGAL" in *Message*, as above.

"the voice of the land yearning for the sea". From the poem "SIXTH/DOM DINIZ," in *Message*, as above.

"Far better to write than to dare to live." From *The Book of Disquiet*, section 90 [54], edited by Maria José de Lancastre and translated by Margaret Jull Costa (London: Serpent's Tail, 1991).

"the somnambulist lives people lead". From *The Book of Disquiet*, section 40 [49], as above.

"By day I am nothing, by night I am myself." From *The Book of Disquiet*, section 23 [65], as above.

"to dream is to forget". From *The Book of Disquiet*, section 69 [132], as above.

"The fields, when all is said, are not as green for those who are loved / As for those who are not." From the poem "If I die young," in *A Centenary Pessoa*, edited by Eugénio Lisboa with L.C. Taylor, translated by Keith Bosley (Manchester: Carcanet Press, 1995).

"Some people have one great dream in life which they fail

to fulfil. Others have no dream at all and fail to fulfil even that." From *The Book of Disquiet*, section 78 [422], as above.

"Anyway, I was the only Nature poet." From the poem "If, after I die," in *A Centenary Pessoa*, as above.

"To eat the past as a hungry man eats bread." From the poem "Birthday" in *A Centenary Pessoa*, as above.

The four lines of poetry by Pessoa quoted on page 267 of the novel are the actual lines inscribed on the monument in the monastery of Jerónimos in Portugal, translated by me.